"*The Marcy Stories* begin quietly but ultimately consume the reader. Fran Zell unfolds Marcy Rosen's days in the Cleveland suburbs until her readers are as conflicted as Marcy about her parents, Jack and Leah, and as eager to find resolution for her life. What appears the day-to-day of family and family dysfunction becomes touching stories that can't be passed up and that, in their very ordinariness, reflect something from each of our journeys."
— Kate Dailey, Women's Studies, BGSU Firelands College

Bottom Dog Press

Bottom Dog Press
is an independent publisher and
a literary and cultural organization.
Contact us at:

Bottom Dog Press
c/o Firelands College
Huron, Ohio 44839
419-433-5560 / lsmithdog@aol.com
http://member.aol.com/lsmithdog/bottomdog

Also Distributed by
Small Press Distribution, Berkeley, CA

The Marcy Stories

Fran Zell

Midwest Writers Series
Bottom Dog Press
Huron, Ohio

© 2001 Fran Zell
Bottom Dog Press, Inc.
ISBN 0-933087-69-1

This is a work of fiction. All characters, events, and places are imaginary or used in an imaginary way.

Cover Art: Erin Johnson

Acknowledgements

These stories have been a long time in progress with many people to thank: Lore Segal, who first suggested that they could become a book; Valerie Miner, Bob Shacochis, Beth Franken Hepburn, Marc Niesen, Richard Ely, Pat Dyjak, Marianna Wright, Kelly Cherry, Jayne Marek, Ron Wallace, Jane Hamilton, John Ashley, Marion Stern, Lin Ryan-Thompson, Anna Smith, Phyllis DeGioia, Kate Dailey, Suzanne De Gaetano of Macs Backs Paperbacks in Cleveland Heights, Ohio, and the staff at Room of One's Own Bookstore in Madison, Wisconsin, for their support, suggestions, and encouragement.

I especially want to thank Holly Woodward, who has read many drafts of these stories and who let me rely on her during the last several years for her insightful comments and suggestions. Not to forget my sister, brother, and of course, Cousin Jonathan for their generous acceptance of a writer in the family; my publisher, Larry Smith for his wisdom and patience; and my uncle, the late Bernard Zell, for his love and belief in me.

I am very grateful to the Ragdale Foundation and the Anderson Center for Interdisciplinary Studies in the U.S., and Atélier Silex, and Quartier Ephemère in Canada for writing residencies during which portions of this book were written.

The following stories originally appeared as chapbooks published by Key Log Press: "Sunday School Blues," "Lady of Spain I Adore You," "An Adult Child's Christmas in Ohio," and "First Kiss." An earlier version of "An Adult Child's Christmas in Ohio" was published as "Christmas '93" in *Looking out the Window*, the literary contest anthology, (The Writers' Place, Madison, Wisconsin).

Contents

Daddy's Car — 5

Sunday School Blues — 17

Lady of Spain I Adore You — 29

Jane Majeski's Thirteenth Birthday — 43

Piano Lessons — 61

First Kiss — 75

In Loco Parentis — 89

Policeman's Wife — 111

Love Is My Drug of Choice — 137

An Adult Child's Christmas in Ohio — 163

Reinventing Leah — 177

Author's Biographical Sketch —206

For my nieces and nephews:
David, Dana, Aleta, Eric, and Michael,
who have moved the family forward in delightful ways.

Daddy's Car

    I once asked my mother why she stayed with my father and she said she knew that if anything ever happened to her he would take care of her and nobody else in the world would. It didn't turn out that way. She takes care of him now. She bathes him, changes his bandages, washes his behind when he doesn't get to the bathroom on time, nags him when he doesn't eat.

    "Jack, Jack, you have to eat something. I made you eggs, soft-boiled the way you like them. Taste them at least, Jack. You have to eat something."

    My father grimaces or groans, however the mood strikes him. His lips curl in around themselves, a baby's mouth, toothless. He has teeth, but he doesn't wear them, doesn't notice that they aren't in.

    "Jack…" She says it warningly.

    "I'm not hungry." My father pushes the plate away.

    My mother sucks in her cheeks and releases a long, pained sigh. A sigh of the ages, of a prisoner carving an "X" on a wall of endless "Xs." She goes over to the table, picks up the spoon that sits beside my father's plate. She stirs the eggs around a few times so that yellow and white run together into a warm, glutinous mass. She dips the spoon into the bowl, holds it to my father's mouth. His lips part. Grudgingly. He swallows.

    She spoons up more egg.

When my brother David and I were little, my mother invented a game to get us to eat our oatmeal, which we hated and which she made for us every morning, anyway. The name of the game was Daddy's Car.

"Daddy's car," she would say with our first swallow. "Mommy's car," with the second.

After that, you could make up your own driver. "Marcy's car... David's car... Uncle Eddie's car... Aunt Ida's car..." You had to go through all the relatives, all the kids on the block to get a bowl down. My brother was good at it. At pleasing her. I rarely got past "Marcy's car" without gagging.

"You have to eat *something*," she would shout at me through the bathroom door, while I stood over the toilet breathing deeply, fighting to keep three gulps of lumpy oatmeal in my stomach. "You can't go to school on an empty stomach."

"Daddy's car...Mommy's car," I think to myself now as my mother spoons egg.

"Please," my father says suddenly. It is a shout, a sharp command, punctuated by yellow and white drool from his mouth. "I'm not hungry," he says and tries to push her away.

She puts the spoon down and looks at me for help, affirmation, a sign that I am on her side. "He won't eat," she says with measured bitterness. "What does he want from me if he won't eat?"

My stomach churns. I have been in their house for exactly one hour. I had planned to stay three. One for him. One for her. One for me. Not necessarily in that order.

The second hand on the clock on the wall above the sink clucks steadily around the dial. Once, many years ago, my father sat David and me down at the kitchen table and pointed to that clock.

"Every time that second hand makes a circle around the clock, I will be paying your piano teacher another dime. I want you to pay attention to her," he said. "I want you to learn to play the piano."

Wow! A dime a minute! Who could imagine so much money? I paid attention. I practiced. I flunked oatmeal, but I mastered the piano.

The second hand begins another circle around the clock.

"It's hot in here," I say. "I need some fresh air. I'm going to take a walk."

"Your father isn't well," my mother says. "I have to keep the heat up. Do you think I don't want him to get better?"

"No," I say. "I don't think that."

My father doesn't say anything. He just sits there with egg on his chin, and an empty, bewildered look in his eyes, as if already he is trying to remember who I am.

"You're coming back, aren't you?" My mother calls from the kitchen as I stand in front of the hall closet, putting on my coat.

"Of course I'm coming back."

"Take the dog," she says. "She needs a walk. She hasn't been out all day."

Ginger, their Golden Retriever, jumps up from the living room rug as if on cue, romps over to the stairway, uses her teeth to grab the leash that hangs there.

"Okay, okay." I try to pull the leash from her mouth, but she pulls back. I stroke her silky head, pat her flank. She bounds around the room. A young dog at their age. How do they manage? But it's not "they" anymore, is it? My mother's the one with all the strength.

"Do you need any help?" my mother calls.

"No, no, it's okay. I've got it." I finally hook the leash onto Ginger's collar.

We go out the back door, through the garage. There's only one car there now. Mommy's car. Daddy's car is mangled, totaled. A twenty-three-year-old Ford Fairlane laid to rest, at last, as a battering ram.

"He's had six accidents in two months," David told me on the phone last fall. "But they're just bullshit fender benders because every time he was hardly moving."

The last time, though, he was moving. Across the center line on a snowy night, thirty miles from home, twenty-nine miles from the neighborhood grocery store he was trying to find.

"The amazing thing is," David said this time, "the amazing thing is the other driver walked away with barely a scratch." He paused a long time and I waited, listening to the hollow tunnel that crackled along the telephone wires between Chicago and Cleveland.

"They took Dad to the hospital," David said at last. "It was touch and go for a while. But he's going to make it."

Ginger is better trained than I'd expected. She takes an easy lead and we walk along, down the driveway and onto the sidewalk, past homes I think of as the McCarthy's house, the Williamson's house, the Page's house, even though I don't know any of the people who live in them now.

My parents looked at homes in the Jewish neighborhoods, but when they finally bought, they bought in the heart of St. Mary's parish. It is the least of the many things I hold against them, even though it meant growing up on a street where I never really felt I belonged.

"You mean you don't know what Purgatory is?" Brenda McCarthy gasped one day while we were playing tag in her backyard. "That means you're going to go to hell."

I got my revenge on Brenda McCarthy, and I wasn't even trying.

We were playing house in the magnificent tree house Brenda's father built. I was the mother, and I did what I thought all mothers did. I told Brenda she was bad, very bad, and she would have to go to bed without her supper. I said it over and over and over, but I never meant to make Brenda cry. Don't cry, Brenda. Don't cry. It's only a game.

But she did cry, and I couldn't console her.

Even now this street represents to me something unattainable. It is a beautiful street of solid English Tudors and Georgian homes on spacious, tree-lined lawns. Ours is the only frame house on the block, a pretty white colonial, but smaller than the others and years newer, built on a corner lot relinquished in an estate sale. I liked our house then, but I always liked the others better.

It's only a week after New Year's and most of the street still has Christmas decorations up. There's a large, round wreath on the McCarthy door, a Christmas tree glistens through the leaded picture window, a Santa Claus with reindeer skims the surface of the frozen front lawn. Mr. McCarthy used to string colored lights on all the shrubbery and around the shutters of every window. One year, my father, acting from some strange need to show the neighbors that Jews liked Christmas too, replaced our two clear porch lights with blinking red and green bulbs.

"How come you only have two lights on your house?" Brenda McCarthy demanded.

"I don't know," was all I said. But inside I was ashamed.

At the corner, I let Ginger make a right turn into Kensington Lane. They don't have lanes in Chicago. They have alleys. They don't have lanes like this one anywhere else, except maybe England, or so I used to imagine during countless rides through it alone on my bicycle, past the side doors of the big wonderful houses, bigger than the ones on our street, with their tangled yards and gardens, sometimes bordered by tall stone walls, so that all you really saw were gabled rooftops and upper branches. I seldom got a glimpse of the inhabitants of Kensington Lane, and I certainly never knew them. But they were happy—they had to be, I was sure of that—to live on such a picturesque, narrow road, right out of one of those English children's books I was always reading.

Amazingly, it hasn't changed, and even on this damp, gray day, I feel its magic. We walk as far as East Suffolks and turn right again to complete the circuit home. Ginger fusses here and there, sniffs the ground, paws dead leaves, makes a quick, apologetic tinkle. But she doesn't have any real business. I'm sure my mother had her out this morning. Did she really send her with me to ensure my return?

The thing about them, the thing I never get used to, I think as I round another corner and come into sight of the house again. The thing is they're so small. In my head they still loom as threatening giants, but when I see them for the first time after each absence, I am struck by their size, my mother a good two inches shorter than I, my father my height and shrinking. This time, if my brother hadn't sent the pictures, I might have thought I had the wrong people.

My mother hasn't changed that much. At seventy-two she still has her figure, a waistline at least, and the same wash and shake hairdo she wore to my wedding. It's silvery now instead of gray, and fluffier, a pouffe of white hair, framing a pale, rigid face with far fewer wrinkles than most women her age. It's her eyes, though, her eyes that give me pause. There's absolutely no light in them.

My father's the one who makes me weak in the knees. He's so thin, so emaciated. The whole texture of his face has changed. What are my father's glasses doing on this shrunken old man's head? What I search for in my father are signs of the man he used to be. The only clue to the past is his mouth, with its downward, resolute cast.

The pictures my brother sent were taken a month before the accident. My father looked terrible then.

"You can't tell him anything," my mother said, barely ten minutes into my visit. "He hasn't been taking care of himself, he hasn't been eating right. And since the accident it's been even worse."

"Yes," I agreed, shifting my weight from one foot to the other. I didn't know what else to say. I hadn't anticipated that the conversation would take this turn so soon. I thought that first she would ask me where I've been, why I stopped writing a few years back, why I didn't call. I was so afraid of this confrontation that I prepared a speech. But she didn't ask.

When Ginger and I return to the house there is another car in the driveway behind my Tercel. David's Saab. He checks on them often, calls several times a day. I wonder if he was surprised to see my car. I told him I might come, but I didn't say when.

My father is sitting on the living room couch, his hands lying awkwardly in his lap, as if he doesn't know what to do with them. My mother is nowhere around.

"Marcy!" My brother says, rising from a chair near the couch. Ginger shakes out her fur and trots ahead of me toward my brother, her leash dragging along soft carpet. "It's good to see you," David says.

We hug. My "little" brother is thirty-six years old and towers over me. My mother always said he got his height from her side of the family, which is where he got his looks. I never met any tall relatives on either side. Maybe it was the oatmeal.

"Dad and I were just talking about how good it is you're here," David says, sitting down again. Ginger licks his hand and plops down beside him. I go over to the closet to hang up my coat.

My brother and I have reached a tentative truce in the last couple of years. Which means, I suppose, that we accept one another's differences. I accept his world of country clubs and designer labels; he accepts my academic life and left wing causes. Anyway, we don't try to talk about these things anymore.

Every few months my brother comes to Chicago on business and takes me to dinner. After a few preliminaries about Rhoda, his wife, and their kids, about my latest boyfriend, we talk about our childhood, our parents, though even in this realm our area of agreement is small.

"Dad," David says as I pull up a chair. "Isn't it nice that Marcy came to visit?" My father's face has fallen towards his neck and his eyes are closed. I am sure he is asleep, but as soon as my name is spoken his head bobs up, his eyes open.

"Marcy?" he asks rhetorically and for a moment I'm almost sure I see a smile. "Yes, of course. It's good to see her. She should visit more often.

"Let's see, now." He looks at me, trying to focus. "You live in Chicago, isn't that right?"

"Yes, Dad, that's right."

"But what is it you do there? I can't seem to remember why you don't live here."

By *here*, I'm not sure if he means Cleveland or this house. I have an uneasy suspicion he means both.

"I'm in graduate school, Dad. Remember? I'm working on a Ph.D. in communications."

"Communications?"

David chuckles. "Don't worry, Dad. I don't understand what it is either."

I bristle reflexively, then smile too. "It has to do with the way people relate to each other." I turn toward David as I speak.

"Hey, don't look at me that way." David raises his hands in mock surrender. "I was just kidding."

My father is searching for something. His face turns quizzical, then a flash of light.

"What about Gregory?" my father asks. "Didn't he come with you?"

Gregory? David has told me these things about my father, that his mind wanders in time, that he has difficulty grasping the simplest concepts. But seeing it is something else. David, sensing my feelings, begins to speak for me. I lean forward and touch his hand. I want to handle this.

"Gregory and I were divorced, Dad. Almost ten years ago."

"Nooo...I didn't know that." My father puts a hand to his face.

"You knew, Dad. You've forgotten."

"I don't like Gregory," my father begins. "You had no business marrying him. But I didn't think you should get divorced."

"You should feel honored," David says to me with one of his mischievous little brother grins at this reference to my Catholic ex-husband. "He never asks about Rhoda, and she's Jewish."

"Rhoda?" My father is confused again. "Who's Rhoda?"

David laughs as if nothing unusual has transpired, and I suppose in a way it hasn't. My father never took much interest in David's life. He ignored his Little League games, missed the science fair the year David's project took first place. It would be unrealistic to assume David's marriage would change things.

"Rhoda, Shmoda," my father whispered to me co-conspiratorially at David's wedding. "You're the prettiest woman in this room."

It is no secret that I was our father's favorite. I once tried to assure David that under the circumstances he was the luckier one, but I don't think David was convinced. Still, in our more recent discussions, it's David who's tried to persuade me that love doesn't matter.

"So they're selfish," he has said. "And don't know how to love us. But they're our parents. You should at least let them into your life."

"Rhoda's your daughter-in-law," David is saying now. "My wife. Remember, she came to visit you at the hospital. She brought you flowers."

My father's memory is jogged again.

"I was in an accident," he announces, turning to me. "I don't remember it. I don't know how it could have happened." He is genuinely puzzled. "One car was going up a hill. Another car was coming down..."

There is a sad look in his eyes, a fearful plea. "Help me, Marcy," his eyes say. "How did I get to be this way?"

I squeeze my father's hand. I used to think I didn't love my father; now I wonder if I loved him too much. I have seen this look before. On my father. On Gregory. On other men I tried to love.

"The important thing is you made it through the crash, Dad," I say. "That's the important thing."

"Marcy..."

It's my mother, calling from upstairs. I never thought I'd be eager to see her alone, but I'm on my feet before she calls a second time.

"Marcy..."

She's in my bedroom, the sunny room facing south at the top of the stairs. They haven't changed it much. The single bed with the rose-colored bedspread and dust ruffle still sits against the wall near the window with matching curtains, the big oval rag rug on the maple floor beside it. There's a bookcase against one wall, full of old *Reader's Digests* now, and a junior World Book Encyclopedia they bought for me in grade school. There are some of my own books too, novels I read in high school English, a few textbooks from my freshman year in college. Every time I visited I would take books with me, but I could never bring myself to take them all.

This is the room where, when I was ten, my mother first told me that my father had gone too far, screamed too loud, been too mean; she was going to divorce him. And this is the room where I announced my own resolve to divorce my husband, and where she tried to persuade me not to. "Who are you going to meet that's any better?" she admonished me, forgetting all the things she had warned me against when I married Gregory. "Who are you going to meet?"

There's a wicker rocking chair near the bookcase, but my mother is sitting on the bed, a photo album open in her lap. I hesitate in the doorway, then sit down beside her.

"I've been going through all the photos," she says. "I've made up an album for you, and I'm making one for David." She hands the album to me.

"Those were good years for us. We were happy then."

I take the album and page through it. It begins with baby pictures. Mine. Then David's. Then David and me together. He's standing in his crib in diapers, his mouth open with drool. I'm next to the crib, my back to the camera, offering him a teddy bear.

I turn another page. There's my father's big black 1949 Buick. David and I are lined up in front of it, holding hands. I'm five, he's three. I'm wearing a cowgirl skirt and vest with fringes; my free hand hangs rigidly at my side. It was a joke in our family, my father's joke: "Marcy doesn't know what to do with her hands."

David's wearing a suit with a checkered vest and bow tie. The cuffs on both the pants and jacket are too long. He used to grow fast. My mother bought him clothes to grow into. In the picture his head is turned toward me, his lower lip pinched inward; he looks ready to cry. I stare straight ahead at the camera, at my father, my face obedient and scared.

My father used to take me out alone in that car. He used to tell me what to do with my hands. He said what I did made us partners.

And what *should* a father do when he takes his baby girl for a ride to the bank, the post office or the ice cream shop? He can't take her into the ladies' room. He can't take her into the men's room. He can't let her go in by herself.

Hold on to yourself. We're almost home now. Hold on to yourself, Marcy.

He said what I did for him made us partners.

There was a time when I didn't remember this part of my life. When all I remembered of much of my childhood was sketchy and vague, right up through adolescence. A few years ago, I started remembering.

I don't know what to say to my mother. So when I finally speak, I pretend to myself that I'm talking to the little girl in the pictures.

"You had a hard time of it," I say. "No wonder you were so frightened."

"Yes, it's been pretty terrible," my mother says. "The night your father had the accident I was scared out of my mind."

I look up from the album, relieved that we have found a way to proceed.

"He left the house at three o'clock," she says. "Three in the afternoon. Six hours later he still wasn't home. And he was only going to the mall."

"He shouldn't have been driving, Mom. It's lucky no one was killed."

"That's what I told him. He shouldn't have been driving. The way his memory's been. But he doesn't listen to me."

"Sometimes you rode with him..." I prompt tentatively.

"I had to ride with him, Marcy. I had no choice. He was driving."

I smile slightly. My mother's logic has its humorous side.

"Well, you know, Mom." I reach out and touch her shoulder, let my hand rest there a moment. I feel her body tense. We're not a family accustomed to touching each other in gentle ways. "You know, Mom, you don't have to keep him here, if he's too much trouble. David says there's a convalescent home..."

She doesn't let me finish. She's definitely angry now. "Your father's staying here," she says. "He's not going to a convalescent home. He's not going anywhere."

"Okay, Mom, it's up to you." I squeeze her shoulder softly, then remove my hand. "I only want you to know it's a possibility, an option."

"David has been through this with me already, Marcy. Many times. And what do you care anyway?" Oh, boy. I brace myself. Here it comes, after all. "Staying away all this time. Who are you to come here now and tell me how to handle things?"

It is probably time for my speech, but I can't for the life of me think how it begins. All I can think of, and the realization calms me, is this: In some way my father does take care of my mother. They don't need me to glue their relationship together.

"I stayed away because I was working through some things from the past," I say. "I didn't know if I could handle my feelings."

"Well, yes, your father always was hard for you to deal with." As usual, she assumes I mean just him. But she is instantly composed. She likes this. My vulnerability. Just as she likes it in my father.

I don't ask her why she didn't protect me from my father when I was young. She would say I was safe with him. She would say, it's no secret in *our* family that you were his favorite.

I don't tell her about my recent history either, that I was in the hospital for a few weeks, that on my way into the past I turned into a vegetable and lay in bed all day long, trying to think of a good way to die. I'm no longer sure the fact of my breakdown would upset her. But she would want to know why I didn't come home, why I didn't let *her* take care of me.

"Your activities must be agreeing with you," my mother is saying. "You seem happier now. Maybe we can have a better," she stops herself, pauses, "a more mature relationship now."

"Yes. Maybe." I am starting to squirm. I haven't thought of this visit in terms of other visits.

Before either of us can speak there is a commotion downstairs. Almost simultaneously my mother and I stand up.

"Jack," she calls. "What is it?"

"He's tired, Mom," my brother calls back. "He wants to sleep. I'm bringing him upstairs."

"I can walk," I hear my father say. My father can walk. But he can't climb stairs. The nurse must have been here this morning to bring him down. My mother and I watch as David makes a chair out of his arms and carries him up, sets him down on the landing.

"See," my father says, in the tone of a proud toddler. He tugs on the sash of his bathrobe and shuffles toward their bedroom, towards the bed he has shared with my mother for more than forty years. "I told you I can walk."

The three of us make a loose little circle around my father. My mother and my brother move with him now, trying to make sure he doesn't fall.

I step past them and head toward the stairs, looking back long enough to see the circle become a thin, wavering line. "I need you to move your car," I call to my brother as I go. But I am wondering how many times I have to leave this house before I really leave home.

How many times, I wonder, feeling in the pocket of my jeans for the hard, reassuring edge of my car key.

Sunday School Blues

When I was nine years old my mother decided David and I should go to Sunday school because we needed to know we were Jewish. I already knew. I don't remember when I found out, but I remember being six years old and pleading with my mother to buy a Christmas tree, knowing she would say no, we couldn't have a tree. We were Jewish.

We had Christmas, though. We had turkey and relatives and gaily-wrapped presents piled by the fireplace on Christmas morning because Santa traveled down chimneys, after all, and if there wasn't a tree to leave things under, well he just deposited everything on the hearth and whisked back up the chimney to the next house where there was one. I don't remember believing in Santa Claus. Not really. David and I had our pictures taken each year with a department store Santa, both of us smiling with proper wonder and respect. And I can remember, long after I was old enough to know better, staring out my bedroom window late on Christmas Eve, watching the sky for just the faintest sign of flying sleds.

But it was all just a game you were supposed to play, like hopscotch, Old Maid, pick-up sticks. "I Saw Mommy Kissing Santa Claus" was a hit when I was six, and David and I figured it out. We knew who Mommy should really kiss, even if we rarely saw her do it. We knew who brought the presents.

After all the relatives left on Christmas Day, after all the dishes were washed and put away and the carpet sweeper run to pick up Christmas crumbs, my parents bundled David and me into our winter coats and hats with ear flaps and took us to see the Christmas lights in Mapleton Hills. This nearby suburb was newer than ours, wealthier, and besides its great Christmas displays, famous for one important thing: If you were Jewish, or Negro, or even Catholic, you couldn't live there.

Home after big home glowed with twinkling lights of every color, floodlit Santas, elves, snowmen. Sometimes we came upon a manger scene complete with huge ceramic shepherds and sheep, even straw scattered on the snowy lawn, and if my father cranked down his window to flick cigarette ash, we might hear the recorded strains of "Away in the Manger," or "Little Town of Bethlehem," songs I never dared sing the words to when they taught us in school.

"Jack," my mother would nervously prod, when my father lingered too long in front of one of the manger-scene houses. "Jack."

"Wait a while," he would gruffly reply, if he replied, and continue staring out the window smoking, and I would wonder if my father felt the same horror I did, the same chilling fascination of our having come, undetected as Jews, so close to the forbidden heart of Christmas.

The Sunday school my mother picked for us was an Orthodox one. We weren't Orthodox, though I had an Orthodox grandfather who went to *shul* on Friday nights and prayed in Hebrew with the men, while the women sat upstairs in their section and prayed in Hebrew, too. We weren't Conservative or Reform Jews, either. We lit candles on Hanukkah, ate matzoh on Passover, stayed home from school on Yom Kippur and Rosh Hashanah, and on Sunday mornings we ate bagels and lox that my father went out early to get from the Jewish deli.

Except for the Sunday breakfast ritual, everything Jewish in our house was my mother's doing, even the Orthodox grandfather. My father didn't care about Jewish traditions. My father wasn't interested in being Jewish. In fact, the terrible truth was my father was a little like the people from Mapleton Hills. He didn't like Jews.

"They're noisy and pushy," he told my mother once when he thought I wasn't listening. "They have no one to blame for their troubles but themselves."

It was after David and I were supposed to be in bed. David, in fact, was in bed, sound asleep, his frayed little teddy bear cradled to his cheek. I was sitting at the top of the stairs on the second floor landing, my favorite spot for finding out what was really going on in our house.

"All the same, Jack," my mother responded in an excited, high-pitched voice. "The kids should at least go to Sunday school. They have to know they're Jewish."

"And where do you think you're going to get that kind of money, Leah?" my father asked. "From your father again?"

"I'll ask him if I have to." My mother's tone carried meaning I could barely begin to fathom. It was only because of my step-listening skills that I already knew we had my grandfather to thank for the house my parents owned, and my mother's new 1957 Plymouth.

"What do they need to know about being Jewish for?" my father countered with impatient urgency, ignoring my mother's last remark. "It's all an hypocrisy. The rabbis are only out for money. They're all hypocrites."

"Hitler would say they were Jewish," my mother announced with an angry finality that signaled the end of the discussion. "That's why they need to know."

I knew about Hitler. I knew about Hitler before I knew about Christmas trees. Hitler arrested Jews, separated parents from their children, stole everything they owned, then gassed them—parents and children. Hitler killed six million Jews. It wasn't something my parents only talked about privately. My parents were born in this country, had no relatives who were caught in Hitler's death camps. But they could never get over the horror of it. They talked about Hitler all the time. I don't remember ever not knowing about Hitler.

My mother picked the Orthodox Sunday school because it was the least expensive one she could find. All the other synagogues, she said, had initiation fees, membership dues, building funds you never stopped paying into. This synagogue didn't even have a building, she told my father, when he at last came up with the money for our Jewish education. It occupied a little house in the poorest, most Orthodox section of our suburb where a lot of the European refugees lived. The sanctuary had been carved out of the former living room, which was big enough to accommodate the small circle of pious Jews who showed up for services. On Sundays, they rented classrooms in a nearby public grade school.

From the very beginning I hated Sunday school. I hated having to get up early on Sunday mornings to get there. I hated sitting in a stifling classroom for two and a half hours listening to boring lessons about Jewish history and holidays that had nothing to do with my life, and about Jewish holocausts that I wanted nothing to do with.

The only good part of Sunday school was the opportunity it offered me to torment my mother.

"Mrs. Salzmann says Jews shouldn't eat hamburger," I informed my mother very early in my Sunday school career.

"Mrs. Salzmann is wrong," my mother said, in such a way that I knew she assumed the conversation was over. We were in the Plymouth, threading our way through the crush of traffic that lined up in front of Abraham Lincoln Elementary each Sunday at noon to pick up my classmates.

"She says it has pork in it," I continued, just to be arbitrary. We ate pork anyway. We ate bacon, sausage, ham, even pork chops, though I didn't like them because their smell reminded me of the pigs at the country fair we went to each summer. My mother once told me that the first time she ate pork chops she threw up.

"Well, it doesn't have pork in it," my mother said and leaned on the horn because somebody's father was blocking us.

"Mommy, don't beep," David squealed from the back seat, looking up from a coloring book open to the scene of Joseph being sold into slavery by his brothers. "That's Danny Greenberg's father."

"Shut up David," I swiveled around to glare at my brother. "The stupid Jew doesn't know how to drive."

"Marcy!" my mother yelled, screeching so close around Danny Greenberg's father's car that I thought we might collide. "I don't ever want to hear you talk that way again."

"Yeah, Marcy," my little brother echoed.

"Yeah, yourself," I taunted. If my father talked that way, why couldn't I? And turning back to my mother I said, "If you think I'm going back to that awful place you better not ever make me eat hamburger again or anything else with pork in it."

"You'll eat what I give you or you won't eat at all."

"I bet I'm not really Jewish," I said. "I bet I was adopted."

"No Marcy," my mother replied in her coldest, most sarcastic voice. "You are definitely ours."

I didn't say anything then. I sat in sulky silence for the rest of the ride home, and when she offered me lunch—johnny marzetti, made with hamburger, of course—I marched off to my room in triumphant refusal. The hunger pangs sawing through my belly were a small penalty for the knowledge that I had succeeded in making my mother miserable.

She sent my father to talk to me. My father of all people, who didn't believe in anything.

He entered my room without knocking, creaked across the floorboards with heavy purpose, then stood there, towering over me, the man I loved more than any man in the world, the man I most feared.

"Marcy," my father said finally, "your mother says you sassed her."

"I didn't sass her," I whispered. I huddled cross-legged on the floor, weaving a potholder on a loom I had been given one Christmas. I didn't particularly like making potholders. I didn't mind either. It was simple work really, baby stuff, but it was something to do. You just strung a bunch of different-colored loops across one end of the loom, and then one by one, threaded more loops in and out in the other direction. I had a green loop in hand now and was getting ready to weave it through.

"I can't hear you," my father was saying. I could tell from his voice that he meant business, that he was in one of his "moods." Something my mother told him had clicked in his head and been filed in the place where he kept things about us that were wrong and irredeemable.

"I said," I began, in an exasperated tone— I don't know where I ever got the nerve to talk to my father that way— "I said I didn't sass her."

"*Vonsen*," my father muttered under his breath. "That's what I have for children—*Vonsen*." *Vonsen* was a word my father had used before in reference to David and me. It was a Jewish word. It meant lice.

"I don't understand why we have to go to Sunday school." I looked up at my father from the floor. His head seemed to be getting further and further away. "I hate Sunday school."

"You go to Sunday school because your mother wants you to go to Sunday school." My father's voice grew louder, a harsh, gravelly voice that sounded like boots crunching across stones. "End of discussion, case closed. There's nothing else you need to know."

"I know some other things," I persisted.

"Oh yeah? Like what? What else do you know?" His voice boomed down on me like thunder, his face fiery red. His eyes seemed to bulge out of their sockets. I didn't know what to do, so I picked up another potholder loop, a white one this time, and started it on its journey across the loom. But my father wanted an answer.

"What else do you know, Marcy?" he roared. "What else?"

"Nothing," I gulped.

"That's right, Marcy. You think you're smart. But you don't know anything." Then he lifted one of his size ten, triple E shoes and stepped on my loom, narrowly missing my hand.

"If you like going without lunch," he said as he marched quickly away, "just wait and see how much you enjoy missing dinner."

My grandfather came over that night. I could hear them all talking in the kitchen. Exaggerated happy talk. For my benefit, no doubt. They seldom got along that well on their own. My father didn't like my grandfather. He labeled him cheap, unwilling to part with his money.

I wasn't crazy about my grandfather, either, but it had nothing to do with money. The trouble with my grandfather was he didn't like girls. Maybe a little bit he liked girls, but he liked my brother better. He took David places. To the barber shop for haircuts, to *shul* to show him off to the other old men; even, I learned much later from David, to the homes of his lady friends for tea. There was one way, however, in which my grandfather treated David and me equitably: If one of us was being punished he didn't interfere. He asked where I was that day, I could hear him from the stairs. But when the answer came, cold and muffled in my mother's voice, he didn't say anything. Nobody crossed my father when he meted out punishment. My grandfather was afraid of him, too.

I didn't let on to anyone at Sunday school about my double life. That I was Jewish on Sunday and the rest of the week, God knows what. I didn't talk to many kids, anyway. That way I could always be safe. If I didn't tell them about the things that went on in our house, how could they laugh at me, or screech out little sentences of horror?

Mrs. Salzmann was more difficult. She asked questions, all kinds of questions, as if she worked for the government or something, the FBI. So I got good at lying in Sunday school, because I feared what she would say if I told the truth. I told her my mother lit Sabbath candles, when really my mother only lit candles to singe pinfeathers out of chickens before she made soup. I told her we didn't drive anywhere on Saturdays, when of course we drove everywhere.

I also told Mrs. Salzmann, when she asked, that I got a lot of gifts for Hanukkah. "I got a doll that cries real tears and a bassinet for her to sleep in and a baking set with a little toy oven. And on the second night of Hanukkah I got..."

"Marcy," Mrs. Salzmann interrupted, "You got so many presents only on the first night?"

"Yes..." I hesitated, squirming, uncertain in which direction to move.

"That's not right," Mrs. Salzmann announced righteously. "You're only supposed to get one present each night."

"Well, my parents wanted me to have everything right away," I offered lamely. "They didn't want me to have to wait." Even as I said it I knew it was a mistake. I could feel all eyes turn on me in astonishment.

"They are spoiling you," Mrs. Salzmann said coolly, and she moved on to the next student.

Her reprimand took my breath away and made my heart pound so that I didn't hear what the other kids got, didn't listen to the story about the Macabbees and the miracle of the oil that burned in the temple for eight days and eight nights. I just sat there wishing it would be time to get out of that room and run to my mother's waiting car.

But at eleven forty-five the door opened and I was ushered into an even worse fate. I was wanted in the office, a messenger said. Right away I worried that something had happened at home. My parents had had a fight, maybe, and no one was coming for us. Or maybe the Plymouth had broken down, like the time my mother flooded the engine in the grocery store parking lot and called a tow truck that took more than two hours to arrive. Or maybe one of my parents was sick or had died. It was possible. It happened in the children's books I read.

But it was none of those things. It was David. I should have known. He was perched on a bench in the office with his biblical coloring book, his tongue curling pink out of his mouth as he crayoned in a picture of Judah Maccabee, slaying Hellenite soldiers. Above him on a wall otherwise jumbled with safety posters, PTA announcements, and other official-looking notices hung the pictures of three American presidents: George Washington, Abraham Lincoln, and Dwight D. Eisenhower.

"Hi, Marcy," he said as casually as if he sat in the back seat of my mother's car. David had no sense of things, no grasp of the trouble that tornadoed around him.

"What have you done, David?" I demanded, hands akimbo, my body tilted angrily towards him, the way my mother would stand. But before David could speak, I realized we were not alone. There was another presence in this room, a presence that went far beyond the ordinary self-righteous authority of one of the Sunday school teachers. This was a far more powerful force: Rabbi Kinski himself, head of the whole Sunday school, the whole *shul*. Rabbi Kinski stepped forward now, looking like God, like Moses coming down from the mountain. He wore only black. Black pants, black jacket, black *yarmulke* resting on a mountain of white hair that sprayed forth from his head in every direction and flowed from a gnarled, onion bulb nose into a long white beard.

I wondered if Rabbi Kinski was a hypocrite, like my father said rabbis were. I wasn't sure what the word meant, but I knew it must be something bad. The possibility that Rabbi Kinski was a hypocrite made me shudder.

"Are you Marcy Rosen?" Rabbi Kinski stepped toward me after what seemed like hours. I supposed the other children had all gone home by now, and that my mother waited alone in the Plymouth in front of a deserted school. "Are you Marcy Rosen?" the rabbi repeated. He had an accent, somewhat different from my grandfather's accent, which was Russian. Rabbi Kinski came from Poland.

"Yes," I said, my voice very small. Why was he asking? Would they have sent for some other little girl?

"And is this your brother?"

"Yes."

"Your brother told his teacher today," Rabbi Kinski began, then stopped, as if suddenly struck by the incredible weight of what he was about to say. "Your brother told his teacher that your family doesn't celebrate Hanukkah. Is this true?"

So that was it. The little jerk. I wheeled around and glared at David, who seemed not so oblivious now, parked on the public school bench, squeezing a stub of purple crayon between his forefinger and thumb.

"We celebrate Hanukkah," I told the rabbi, mustering the sort of courage I brought to conversations with my father. "We light the menorah. My mother makes *latkes*. Sometimes my grandfather gives us *gelt*." That was a lie, about the *gelt*. My grandfather never gave us money. But I thought it might appease the rabbi.

"Your brother told his teacher," Rabbi Kinski continued, unmoved by my little appeal. "Your brother told his teacher that your family celebrates Christmas."

There was no hope for my brother. This I now knew, so I didn't even bother to look at him.

"We have company on Christmas," I acknowledged. How could I lie to this man who knew everything anyway? "But we don't really celebrate it. We never have a Christmas tree."

"Yeah," David suddenly volunteered. My brother had absolutely no shame, no sense of self-preservation. "Santa leaves our presents by the chimney."

This was too much for Rabbi Kinski. He glowered at both of us, lowered his head and white beard, like a wild animal, about to charge. "Do you know," Rabbi Kinski suddenly wailed. "Do you know there are children in this synagogue whose parents survived the ovens?"

Wide-eyed, David and I shrunk towards each other in our need to escape the rabbi. No, we didn't know. And now that we did, what did it make us? Culpable? Co-conspirators? Guilty somehow for the death of our own people?

"Go home, Marcy Rosen, and ask your parents this." Rabbi Kinski waved an accusing finger in my face. "Ask them how they expect me to let you stay in this Sunday school, how they expect me to *bar mitzvah* this boy some day, when they raise you like *goys*?"

I sometimes wonder now why I didn't see Rabbi Kinski's threat as an opportunity. Here, after all, was an escape hatch from Sunday school. All I had to do was wriggle through. David wasn't going to be *bar mitzvahed*. My father had issued that edict long ago, and my mother acquiesced. She didn't need *bar mitzvahs*. She came from a family of girls. Just let them go to Sunday school, she had pleaded. I want them to know they're Jewish.

But I didn't challenge Rabbi Kinski to go ahead, throw us out of Sunday school, see if I cared. And I'm not sure why not. All I can figure now is that expulsion meant failure to me; my failure, my parents' failure. Maybe even death.

"You can't kick us out, Rabbi Kinski," I said. "You have to keep us even if our parents don't follow all the rules. We're still Jewish. Hitler would say we were Jewish. Hitler would throw us in the ovens, too."

Rabbi Kinski sucked in his breath so hard I could see his beard jump. He stepped back a couple of feet and I feared he might lunge. I took a protective step toward David, who sat very still, clutching his coloring book with one hand, his crayons scattering around him on the bench. One or two of them descended to the floor with mournful little pings.

But Rabbi Kinski was not, as it turned out, like our father. He would not lash out at us with all the fury of his own frustrated, anguished life. And he was not our grandfather, either, running away from contact and confrontation.

"Marcy Rosen," Rabbi Kinski drew another breath and danced toward me, but slowly, gently. *Adaggio.* "Marcy Rosen," he wondered quietly, "who told you this thing, this terrible thing about Hitler?"

I didn't answer. I couldn't. This awful fact I heard my parents discuss between themselves at night suddenly looked naked and ugly in front of Rabbi Kinski, like a dead, singed chicken.

"Marcy Rosen," he said. "You are not Jewish because of Hitler. You are Jewish because of God, the God that created you."

I held my breath, just waiting for David to spit out something stupid, to tell Rabbi Kinski that our father didn't believe in God. But my little brother just sat there, staring at Rabbi Kinski, strangely mesmerized.

"God is great," Rabbi Kinski said. "God is life. But for Hitler there was no God. Hitler killed six million Jews and he tried to kill God because there was no God inside him. But he couldn't kill God. And do you know why?"

David and I looked at each other, blankly, helplessly. I didn't know what Rabbi Kinski wanted from us.

"He couldn't kill God because God wasn't his to kill. No one can kill God. Did you know that?"

I wondered why God, if he was so great, had allowed Hitler to slaughter His "chosen" people, but I didn't ask Rabbi Kinski. I wanted him to be finished with us. I wanted to go home. I sat down on the bench next to David and concentrated hard on the Rabbi's generous, onion bulb nose, as if it could help me forget about all the bad things in the world.

"You should pray to God," Rabbi Kinski was saying in his strange Polish accent.

"You should pray to God and thank Him for giving you life. Do you know any prayers?"

I shook my head. I honestly couldn't think of any. Now we would really be kicked out of Sunday school, and I no longer cared.

"I know the prayer for the wine," David suddenly chirped. And forgetting his inhibitions again, perhaps because Rabbi Kinski reminded him of our grandfather, he began reciting, very pleased with himself: *"Baruch atau adonai elohanu."*

"Blessed art thou, oh lord our God, king of the universe," Rabbi Kinski interrupted before David could go any further, to the part about the wine. "That's what the words mean in English. Did you know that?"

He was still looking at me. "Yes," I nodded limply. I knew a prayer, after all. And I also knew the prayer for the bread, and the Sabbath candles. They all started out the same way. "Blessed art thou oh lord our God, king of the universe..." Was this all Rabbi Kinski wanted?

"You can go now." Rabbi Kinski said suddenly, as if he could read my mind. "But this is only a start. There are many more prayers for you to learn. Pay attention to your teachers."

With this he swept out of the room, beard first, nose next, then a blur of black cloth, heading down the hallway. When we were sure he was gone and wasn't coming back, David and I jumped up from the bench and ran out of the school.

We were among the last of the Sunday school students to leave that day. But our mother didn't notice. She got that way sometimes, lost in her own world. But she was in a good mood. She asked us what we wanted for lunch.

"Hamburgers," David and I shouted, almost in unison.

If anyone from the Sunday school ever spoke to our parents about their religious practices I never heard about it. Anyway, nothing changed in our house. Not my father's temper, nor my mother's need to have me agree with her. And we kept right on celebrating Christmas and ignoring most Jewish traditions.

Not until I was twenty-seven years old and brought my Catholic husband home for the first time, did my mother see any need to become more observant. Then she lit Sabbath candles and talked about her meat dishes and her dairy dishes, though from everything I could see she still had only one set of dishes. I was too much in love with Gregory at the time to be angry with her for flaunting practices she had never instilled in me. I just laughed and told her Gregory and I weren't planning to get bogged down in either of our religions.

David married, too, about five years later, and by that time I was already divorced. He took a Jewish bride at a Jewish wedding; they drank wine and smashed the glass under the *chuppah*. When their son was born a few years later, they had him circumcised with a rabbi presiding and relatives in attendance. My parents went, but only after much complaining. They said the *bris* ceremony was barbaric.

I don't think it was Sunday school that turned David into a Jew, but rather college in a small southern town rife with anti-Semitism. David had a roommate freshman year who hung a swastika on the wall just to bait him.

I dated a Jewish man for a while after my divorce. But it ended abruptly when I found out he'd been sleeping with someone else, and from then on I didn't worry about who was Jewish and who was not. I had trouble with relationships across the board: Jews, Catholics, Protestants. I figured I might as well broaden my chances. But no matter who I'm dating, or not dating, I light candles on Friday evenings when I'm home, using the pretty pewter candlesticks I bought the year after my divorce. I cover my face with my hands and say the prayer for *shabbat* and let the light from the candles shine into my house. *Shekinah,* I think to myself, and I concentrate until I see her dancing in all that warm, safe light: the sabbath queen. With my eyes still closed, I take her hands and dance a few steps with her, bidding away the heaviness of the week, the detritus. After that I bless the wine and the *challah. Baruch atau adonai elohanu*, I say, as I begin each prayer.

I think of Rabbi Kinski, long dead now, as I pray: Blessed *art thou oh lord our God, king of the universe*, I hear him say. And I wonder if it's really true that no one can kill God.

Lady of Spain I Adore You

My father didn't eat supper with us the night David almost died. It was the day after the teapot fight, and my parents weren't speaking. I helped my mother make a pie that afternoon with cherries from our backyard tree, a small tree that produced cherries so tart even the birds left them alone. I could, at eleven, reach the lower branches without standing on anything. David was nine, and he didn't want to pick cherries or make pies. He only cared about baseball.

It took about an hour to pit enough cherries to fill a pie shell, a job my mother gave to me because I hung around the house a lot that summer, looking for things to do. We had a little plunger tool that spit out pits in one quick stroke, but it was still a messy job that turned my hands sticky red. Every once in a while I'd forget how bad the uncooked cherries tasted and pop one in my mouth, and then I'd sputter around the kitchen madly looking for something sweet.

"No, Marcy!" My mother plopped her hand down hard on the sugar bowl, the fourth time I reached for it with a spoon. "You've had enough for one afternoon. You'll rot your teeth."

"But, Mommy…" I screwed up my mouth in exaggerated pain. "They're so sour."

"Well, don't eat them then." My mother concentrated on the pie dough she was rolling out between two sheets of waxed paper.

"They look so beautiful," I replied. "I keep forgetting how they taste."

"Go see if Daddy will be joining us for supper," she instructed. "Tell him we're having pie."

"I thought he had someone in there with him."

"Just knock on the door," she said, lifting the dough into a pan and beginning to crimp the edges. Say, 'Excuse me, Mr. Rosen. Mrs. Rosen would like to know if you'll be done with your client in time for supper.'"

"I can't talk like that," I protested.

"He has an office in this house, Marcy." My mother used the back of her floury hand to brush a shock of hair off her forehead. It was a hot day, very hot. She wore a sundress and had pinned her hair atop her head, but little damp tendrils kept escaping from the pile. "We have to set a professional tone," my mother said, and for a moment—a split second—I almost didn't recognize her, standing there with hair clinging to her face, telling me about a new way to be.

"Can you act like a professional?" I demanded of David when we gathered around the supper table that night. There were just the three of us; my father was still upstairs in his study with the client.

"You mean a professional ball player?" David took a long drink of milk and came up with a white mustache pasted to his lip.

"No, stupid, everything in the world doesn't revolve around baseball."

"You're stupid," David rebutted.

"Me?" I practically screamed. I hated it when anyone called me stupid, even if I'd called him stupid first. "You think *I'm* stupid?"

"Marcy. David," my mother said warningly, and turned back to her plate. We were having knockwurst and canned baked beans with applesauce and frozen broccoli. It was David's favorite meal, except for the broccoli. He loved hot dogs, even big fat ones like these, which my father bought from the kosher meat dealer near where he worked. He only had clients in his office as a sideline. My father's real job was as an accountant with a big Cleveland paint company.

"Yeah, Marcy," David wolfed down his knockwurst in rapid, out-sized bites. I ignored him. I was thinking about my father, and how he had been when I'd knocked on his office door that afternoon and called him Mr. Rosen.

"Just tell your mother," he had said, then paused, looking at me through his dark-framed, heavy glasses. My father was very nearsighted, something he'd passed along to me. I got my first pair of glasses back in 1954, when I was only six. "Tell your mother not to wait for me." The bulky frame of him nearly filled up his office doorway. "She can give me supper later."

"David has little league tonight," I volunteered because my mother and I wanted to go. And how could we, if she had to wait around to feed my father?

"Tell your mother not to wait for me," my father repeated, his face round and certain. He had a low, bassoon-like voice, but his tone was open, like in a dance. I drew a grateful breath. Calling my father Mr. Rosen must have been the right thing. I'd interrupted his meeting and mentioned David's game, but he wasn't mad. "I'll get my own supper, later," my father said, actually smiling, a broad jack-o-lantern smile, except his mouth was full of teeth.

"Okay." I smiled too, catching a glimpse of my father's client, the back of him anyway, in a chair pulled up close beside the desk. He had a crew cut and wore a rumpled linen suit. My father was in shirt-sleeves, rolled up above his wrists, but he wasn't sweating like my mother was downstairs. He'd installed an air conditioner in this room.

I felt triumphant, breathing in my father's placid mood along with the cool air in his study. I felt like Queen Esther in the Bible, whom every girl in Sunday school wanted to be when we celebrated Purim. Beautiful and brave Queen Esther. She visited the king when he hadn't sent for her. Queens were like children in biblical days, not supposed to do anything on their own. The king could have killed Queen Esther for coming uninvited. But Esther's uncle had told her she had to go to him in order to save the Jews.

"Marcy." My mother's sharp voice yanked me back to the supper table. "Stop daydreaming and eat your supper. And David, stop shoveling your food." She waved her hands at me, then David, like the crossing guard at school. "You'll be too sick to play if you eat like that. Take your time."

"I don't *have* a lot of time," David complained, dragging a piece of bread around his plate to soak up bean gravy. "The game starts pretty soon."

"It's only at Cumberland Park." My mother swiveled around in her chair to check the clock. "And it doesn't start for forty-five minutes. I'll drive you there. I just wish Daddy would finish up so I could give him supper first."

"He said not to wait for him." I repeated what I had told her when I came back downstairs from my father's office.

"I don't care what he said." My mother took a precise, methodical slice of knockwurst from the platter. "If I'm not here to give your father supper, there'll be hell to pay."

"He wasn't mad," I reminded my mother, wondering if *she* felt like Queen Esther when she approached him sometimes, not knowing if he would be cheerful or enraged.

"He was mad yesterday," David piped up, as if anyone had forgotten. "He sure was mad about that teapot."

"No, it was a TEApot," I instructed David, pronouncing the word the way my father had when the fight began. It wasn't a fight exactly, not in the way people fought on television anyway, with everybody knowing what was going on. My father had brought a teapot yesterday when he came home from work, and his face had turned red as rhubarb because my mother had asked him what she was supposed to do with it.

"It's a TEApot, goddamn it," he'd said, storming out of the room. "Make TEA." We were at the table then, too, eating cold meat loaf made with Lipton's onion soup mix. The meat loaf wasn't supposed to be cold, but my father was late getting home from work and my mother had held up supper.

"Teapot, shmeepot," David laughed now, imitating what she had said yesterday after our father had marched upstairs.

"David. Marcy." Mom switched into her crossing guard voice again. "Let's just get through supper, and I'll take David to the game."

But she didn't take David to the game. He rode his bicycle. Because my father showed his client out the front door just as my mother started cutting the cherry pie and when we heard him go back upstairs and start washing up, she said she'd better stay put and heat up the knockwurst and beans.

"Can I go?" I asked as David began tearing around the house, gathering up his baseball things.

"No. Stay here. I don't want both of you riding bicycles in all that traffic."

"But it's just as unsafe for him as for me."

"He's a boy," she said, as if that explained it.

"But I was planning to watch the game." I loved baseball. Sometimes my father got tickets from his job for the Cleveland Indians, and my mother would take us. We would scream our lungs out, then wait by the back entrance of the stadium afterward for autographs from Rocky Colavito, Minnie Minoso and our other favorite players.

David's little league was the next best thing to a real baseball game and my mother and I usually went. My father never attended. He was always working—at his job or in his study.

"You're *not* riding your bicycle to the game with me, Marcy." David was in the kitchen now, all geared up, right down to his baseball mitt, which he pounded meaningfully with his fist.

"Why not?"

"It's not safe." I knew he said it only because he'd overheard my mother.

"I'll walk then." Ever since he'd joined little league this summer, David wanted me around less and less. We used to do things together all the time—ride our bicycles, swim at Cumberland Park, play catch in the backyard.

"Okay, walk, I don't care. But don't embarrass me when you get there," David growled, heading for the back door.

"What is that supposed to mean, you little jerk?" I cried indignantly, but he was gone, the back door slamming solidly behind him. I could hear him banging into things in the garage to get at his bicycle.

"Don't call your brother names, Marcy," my mother chided, handing me a slice of pie, and cutting a wedge for herself. "We'll both drive over to the park as soon as I feed your father."

"Where's the little jerk?" My father asked, minutes later, taking his seat heavily at the table. I was still eating pie, rolling the individual cherries around in my mouth, marveling at their transformed sweetness.

"David has little league tonight," my mother replied, smiling guardedly at him. She didn't seem to notice that *he* had called my brother "little jerk." But of course my father often called him that. David didn't even have to say anything. I thought it had something to do with the way David looked, so unlike our father, who was round all over, like a snowman. David was a skinny boy with a long, oval face like my mother's, and a habit of pinching his lips together when my father was around, as if trying to figure out a way to make himself look more like him. He'd gotten glasses that year, too, had chosen dark frames like Dad's, but they only made his thin face look thinner.

"Marcy and I are going to the game in a little while," my mother said, dishing up my father's food from the stove. "Would you like to come?"

As far as I knew, it was their first conversation since the teapot fight, but my mother acted as if nothing had happened. She filled my father's plate and smiled pleasantly, more pleasantly than usual in fact. I didn't have anything better to do, so I sat there, savoring each bite of cherry pie and listening to my parents talk.

"I have work to do, Leah." My father pulled a handkerchief from his hip pocket and wiped sweat beads off his brow. The kitchen was even hotter than it had been that afternoon, before my mother turned the oven on for the pie.

"Maybe you'd like to take a break for a couple of hours, Jack." My mother delivered my father's plate to him and went back to the stove to pour herself coffee from the percolator. She hadn't yet touched the pie. All the while she had waited for my father to come down, she had just sat there staring at it, as if he wouldn't come if she ate any. "David's team is doing very well."

"They play him in the outfield, don't they?" my father asked, as if searching for a reason not to go.

"There's nothing wrong with the outfield, Jack."

"I've got work to do, Leah," my father repeated in a high-pitched voice, and pointed to a jar of mustard on the table, his way of asking for it. My mother passed it to him and my father took some and my mother sipped her coffee and filled her fork with pie. Then the phone rang.

They were gone, both of them moving in rapid tandem with uncommon grace. I stood in our living room picture window in the suddenly silent house, watching the car ease out of the driveway and disappear down Coventry Street, into a glint of fading light. My mother's shriek still vibrated through the house.

"Jack! There's been an accident. David's hurt!"

I stood in the window a very long time, looking out at the street. I counted cars. We lived on a corner, a busy corner on the

Coventry side, far quieter on Chelsea Way, the street our house faced. I counted cars heading north along Coventry, the direction I thought my parents would be coming from when they returned. It was a game David and I sometimes played to please Mom while we waited for our father to get home from work.

"I think the fiftieth car will be Daddy," my mother might say, and we were supposed to provide a counter guess. "Twenty." David would suggest. He always guessed low. He didn't have enough patience to stand there counting cars. He'd swivel away from the television long enough to count twenty cars, then return to the show we'd been watching. Or, if the news was on, he'd pull out some baseball cards from his pocket and lie face down on the rug, studying them. David knew every earned run and RBI average for almost every Cleveland Indian.

I always guessed high. I had the patience, the perseverance to stick to any task my mother set before us, though David usually tackled me by the ankles before I could finish this one.

"He's not going to be the one hundred thirty first car, Marcy. So stop counting," he would squawk into my face when he had me pinned to the gray, wall-to-wall carpet. "I can't think."

"You're not thinking anyway, David." I'd laugh, trying to wriggle out from under him. "You're memorizing baseball statistics."

"That's thinking."

"No it's not."

Then he would loosen his grip so I could roll out from under him and we would have a real wrestling match on the living room floor. David was younger than me, and smaller, but he was strong and could beat me right away if he wanted to. But he never did, because then he would have no one to wrestle with. It was the only thing he still wanted to do with me that summer. So we would roll around for awhile, laughing and screaming for each other to say, "uncle."

Whoever said uncle first—usually me—had to put the other in a half nelson, a come-from-behind neck brace of a tackle that David learned from television and taught to me. The loser should have been the one in a half nelson, but David liked when I did it to him, because then he could try to break out of it, which he usually did.

"Marcy and David stop fighting," my mother would eventually call from the kitchen where she'd be trying to keep our supper warm for when my father came home.

"We're not fighting," one of us would shriek, and we would roll all over each other again at the joke of it. "We're wrestling."

"How many cars did you count, Marcy?" my mother would ask, knowing what a sucker I was for counting cars.

"One hundred seventy-five!" I would shout out the first wild number that came to my mind.

"Well, pick another number then," she'd advise. "Maybe this time you'll win."

Nobody ever won. My father could outlast us all, and so my mother would usually sigh and call us in to eat, saying, "Daddy'll be home any minute now. A watched pot never boils, you know."

I stood in the picture window after my parents drove away, almost as if David was in the room with me, and I was waiting for him to grab me by the legs so I could stop counting cars. I couldn't remember ever being in the house all by myself. My parents hardly ever went anywhere at the same time, least of all together. If they did, they would have left David with me so I wouldn't be alone. The floors were shifting again as they often did in this house, as when my mother looked up from her pie and said, "Call your father Mr. Rosen." David had to be there with me, I thought, sinking to the floor. Without David clinging to me in a wrestler's hold, I felt dizzy.

Who showed up after the two hundred twenty fifth car was Aunt Ugly, my mother's older sister. As I watched her light blue Chrysler pull into our drive, I remembered that my mother had phoned her just before she and my father flew out the door, asking her to come over and stay with me.

She must have been giving herself some kind of beauty treatment when my mother called, because her face was more blotchy than usual. Her real name was Ida, but David and I called her Ugly to each other, partly because of the birthmark under one eye that looked like a map of Ohio and clashed with her tight whorl of peroxide-red hair. And partly because we didn't like her.

"Everything's going to be all right, Marcy," she announced walking in the door, my teenage cousin, Ina trailing heavily behind her. Aunt Ugly clanked loudly, as usual, because of all the bracelets she wore, including her famous charm bracelet, which must have weighed at least five pounds. It contained a little silver charm for every special moment in her life. Aunt Ida liked to begin each visit to our house by showing off the latest charm, and then reminiscing through all the others: the little heart she got when she fell in love with Uncle Eddie, the bootie after Ina was born, the tiny car for when she got her driver's license, the minuscule playing card for her skills at bridge, the fish to symbolize their first trip to Florida, etc., etc., etc.

Tonight, however, she had other things on her mind: first-off, cigarettes. She settled into one of the little gold-cushioned armchairs that flanked our living room couch and began searching frantically for them in her big straw handbag.

"Ina," she called out throatily to my cousin who had plopped down on the couch and was staring at the ceiling. Aunt Ida had a permanently throaty voice, as if she were forever gargling mouthwash. "You haven't seen my cigarettes, have you?"

"Of course not, Ma," Ina muttered, eyes still focusing upward. "You know I don't smoke."

Ina did smoke. I had seen her myself last Thanksgiving when our families got together at her house and Aunt Ida sent me to the basement for some cranberry sauce. Ina was sitting atop the washing machine, puffing away, fanning the smoke out a nearby window with her arm.

"If you tell anyone about this, I'll wring your little neck," she had said as I found the cranberry sauce on a nearby shelf.

"Who would I tell?" I asked, backing quickly out of the room.

Ina was five years older, and I barely knew her. Mostly, I knew her clothes, which ended up in my closet sooner or later, waiting for me to grow into them. Our mothers had a love-hate relationship that dated back to before I was born. But they were usually on speaking terms long enough each year for me to accumulate a new crop of hand-me downs.

"What a time to be without cigarettes." Aunt Ida still pawed through her purse, bracelets jangling on her thick, freckled arm. "I don't suppose your father has any around, does he, Marcy?" She looked up at me.

"I don't know," I said, knowing, of course, that my father bought cigarettes by the carton and kept them in the top drawer of his office file cabinet. But I didn't think my father would want anyone to have them, let alone Aunt Ida, whose noisy bracelets and forward manner drove him crazy.

"Never mind." Aunt Ugly heaved a giant sigh that made her shoulders practically touch her ears. She pulled a plump red wallet from her purse. "Ina can go get some, can't you, Ina?" She waved a five-dollar bill toward my cousin, who jumped up quickly and snatched it.

"What about the keys?" she complained, standing before her mother with one hand outstretched, the other cocked pointedly on her hip.

"What keys?" Aunt Ida wriggled her nose like she was pushing back a sneeze, the way my mother sometimes did, and looked blank.

"To the car, mother," Ina said impatiently. I thought I would never ever dare have the nerve to speak to my mother that way. Ina teased her hair and wore it ratted high atop her head with a little brown curl coming forward onto each cheek. She had on tight, *very tight* tan cotton pants and a short, white, sleeveless over-blouse, fitted around her breasts. I had never seen any teenagers besides Ina close up, and I couldn't help staring at her, as if she were a visitor from a strange country that I would one day have to live in.

"Oh, no, just walk there," Ida insisted. "There's a drugstore down the street."

"It's a half mile down the street," Ina replied, wrapping both arms tightly across her chest.

"There's already been one accident in the family tonight," Ida began.

"David was on a bicycle. He wasn't driving," Ina noted angrily. "I could get killed too, just crossing the street, you know."

"Shhh." Ida wagged her red head nervously toward me.

"Well, I could." Ina stamped an indignant foot.

"Here, just take them." Ida dug into her purse again and came up with a hefty key chain that matched her bracelets for noise. "But drive carefully."

Ina smiled happily and dashed out the door. When she was gone, Aunt Ida crossed and recrossed her legs and opened her purse again for another quick look, as if she thought maybe the cigarettes would materialize after all. "Ina got her license this summer," Aunt Ida said finally. "She likes to drive at every opportunity."

"Oh." I studied my bare leg, which festered with a mosquito bite I'd scratched too hard. The living room was hot, and I was itchy and sweaty in the blue cotton shorts outfit I'd been wearing all day. I could hear intermittent traffic noises outside, and just above that the muted song of birds and insects and a faint ringing sound I had never noticed before, and which I thought was coming from outside, but wasn't sure. The house had never been quiet enough for me to notice it before. It was a shrill, high-pitched sound, and it was driving me crazy.

Maybe it bothered Aunt Ida, too, because she put her pocketbook down finally, stood up, and wandered into the kitchen.

"Marcy," she shouted excitedly. "The dishes aren't done in here. Don't you think we ought to get things cleaned up for when your parents get back?"

"Isn't David coming back?" I asked, arriving in the kitchen in time to see Aunt Ugly cut herself a healthy wedge of cherry pie.

"We don't know yet about David." Her cheeks bulged with the sour cherries I had picked and pitted that afternoon and she blotted her lips several times with a balled up paper napkin. "I'd be lying if I told you otherwise, and I would never lie to anyone, least of all a child."

My parents didn't come home until morning, because David's leg was being operated on at Mount Sinai Hospital, and they wanted to be with him. Uncle Eddie picked Ina up on his way home from his shift at Republic Steel. Aunt Ida spent the night, camped in front of the television on our living room sofa with her cigarettes and the rest of the cherry pie. She didn't tuck me into bed as my mother always did, and I couldn't fall asleep for a long time.

It took me a while to get used to David being gone, but maybe it was hardest for my father. He came to supper on time the day after David's accident and looked around the table, at me first, then my mother, then the place where David always sat.

"Where's the little jerk?" my father asked gruffly, gesturing at David's empty chair, his face blank with amnesia.

He's in the hospital, I said, but not aloud, because my father slapped his hand over his mouth and then his eyes. He shifted in his chair a little in order to pull a rumpled handkerchief from his back pants pocket. He blew his nose loudly. I had never seen my father cry before and my stomach turned to jelly.

"We're having lamb chops, Jack," my mother said. "With mashed potatoes and corn on the cob and fresh pineapple for dessert."

"Fine," my father said, as if my mother always rattled off the menu before we ate, like a restaurant hostess. "Fine," he said, and blew his nose in the handkerchief some more.

After David was at Mount Sinai a week, the doctors decided to move him to Rainbow Hospital, for children in need of long-term, orthopedic care. It was my one and only chance to see him because they didn't let kids into hospital rooms in the 1950's, just sick kids, or those smashed to smithereens by a car, like David.

"There he is," my mother said.

"Where?" She and I walked down a long corridor near the rear entrance of Mount Sinai. Hospital staff fluttered all over the place in pale green or blue or snowy white uniforms. I spotted a little old man in a wheelchair sitting near a set of glass doors about thirty feet further down the hallway. But I didn't see David.

"Hi Marcy," the old man said, as we got a little closer.

"Hi, yourself," I said, realizing that the old man was David. "I didn't know you broke your arm, too."

"It's just sprained." David's left arm was in a sling, folded across his chest. His right leg was in a cast from toe to hip, and his face looked very white and thinner than ever. It seemed too small for his body. The cast on his leg was all white too, except for a place just above his knee, decorated with a little cartoon-like drawing of a bicycle and the words, "July 16, 1959, fractured right tibia, fibula and femur."

"Wow!" I said, pointing. "Who did that?"

"The doctor," David said proudly. "He's an artist."

"Does it hurt?" I asked, meaning his leg. It looked like it would be a long time before David and I could wrestle again.

"It itches." David indicated the cast and smiled at me shyly.

David was being taken to Rainbow Hospital in an ambulance, and the paramedics let me ride in the back, all alone with David. My mother followed us in the car.

"I rode to Mount Sinai in an ambulance, too," David told me as we started moving. He still sat in the wheelchair. The paramedics had rolled it up a ramp right into the ambulance. I sat next to him on a bench-like chair that seemed to be built into the bumpy metal floor.

"Was the siren on?" I asked David. The siren wasn't on now, and I thought it would have been real exciting if it were.

"I don't remember," David said.

"How could you not remember a siren?" I asked, flabbergasted.

"I don't know." David shrugged. "But I don't."

There was only one window in the back of the ambulance and it looked into the passenger side of the front seat. All I could see when I peered into it was the back of the paramedic's head and flashes of sky, road, and trees. I remembered our father at the supper table a few days ago, and how he had forgotten—for just a few moments—about David's accident. So I supposed it was possible that David could have forgotten the siren.

"Marcy," David exclaimed suddenly. "I learned a new song in the hospital. Do you want to hear it?"

"A song?" David wasn't usually interested in singing.

"Lady of Spain, I adore you," David suddenly cried out. "Pull down your pants, I'll explore you!"

I shrieked so loudly in shocked surprise that the paramedic on the passenger side turned his head and tapped on the window glass. I could tell from his alarmed expression, even before I read his urgent lips, that he was asking if everything was all right.

I nodded and waved back cheerfully, not wanting him to guess what was going on. I wasn't sure what this scandalous version of "Lady of Spain" *really* meant, but I knew it had something to do with sex, a subject nobody ever talked about at our house. The fact that David had ridden off on his bicycle and ended up in the hospital, learning a song like this—it made my heart beat a little faster. I felt dizzy, as if he had spun me in circles a few too many times and locked me in a secure half nelson.

"Lady of Spain, I adore you..." David began again, softly this time.

"David," I burst out before he could get to the explosive second line. "David, I saw Daddy cry."

"You did?" His eyes grew round with a combination of wonderment and disbelief, and I congratulated myself silently for having one-upped his song.

"Yes, I did," I assured him. "It was the day right after your accident. Daddy came to the supper table and he couldn't remember where you were. He said, 'Where's the little jerk?' and then he started crying."

David's already pale face blanched a little and his eyes grew large with a new kind of wonderment, and I thought maybe I shouldn't have told him everything our father had said.

But David's hospital-issue pallor soon returned, and I breathed easier. "Daddy's going to get me a radio with earphones," he announced grandly. "He says I can use it to listen to the Indians games after lights out at Rainbow Hospital."

"Oh," I said, pained by an unexpected twinge of jealousy. "That's nice."

"Daddy's good to us," David offered. "He's a good father, isn't he?"

"Yes," I agreed, cheered that he had included me under this fanciful umbrella of parental grandiosity. "He is."

We sat there for a while, not saying anything. I listened to the rushing sound the hot summer wind made against the outside of the ambulance. I heard the steady thud, thud, thud of heavy tires as we rolled closer and closer to Rainbow Hospital, where if David learned any more naughty songs, I never heard about it.

David never told me much of *anything* about his life when he finally came back to us nearly three months later. He turned more to his own activities than ever, his own friends. I was changing too by then, my body traveling at the speed of light toward that strange country where my cousin Ina lived, an overgrown jungle country, which I would understand even less when I arrived.

So we never did wrestle again. At least we never again wrestled *physically*.

"Lady of Spain I adore you...." David began anew, after the silence in the ambulance had begun to take the shape of an unwelcome presence. He whistled the rest of it under his breath this time, eyeing me slyly.

"Lady of Spain I adore you..." I chimed in, whistling too.

I didn't really want to sing that song. And I don't think David did either. But it seemed like the only thing to do. It was as if having finally managed to agree on something, neither one of us dared talk about it further...just in case we had agreed on the wrong thing.

Jane Majeski's Thirteenth Birthday

Funny how you don't think of people for years, then suddenly they're in your head and won't get out. That's the way it's been this winter with Jane Majeski. I last saw Jane spring break, 1970, as we both rode the bus into downtown Cleveland. It was the day of my fateful interview with Stouffer Foods. I remember this distinctly because I told Jane about it and she said how nice that I had chosen public relations.

"You always had a way with people," she said. "You made them feel included."

"I did?" Did she have me confused with someone else?

"Oh, yes." She smiled so ingenuously I couldn't confess that public relations hadn't been my idea at all. I'd majored in English, yearning to be an editor with a major New York house. But my mother had instilled me with a fear of living in that city.

Jane said she'd majored in microbiology at Ohio State and would start graduate work at the University of Michigan that fall. After that she didn't know, but said she would definitely not go back to Cleveland.

The other thing I remember: Jane looked good. She had her hair cut short, swept invitingly around her face. She still wore glasses, but they fit her now. She didn't have to keep pushing them up off her nose.

I told Jane I didn't want to stay in Cleveland, either, but that I'd agreed to this interview to please my mom. I figured she, of all people, would understand.

"Well, good luck." Jane flashed the same commiserative smile I'd seen on her in seventh grade when we both stood mortified before her mother. "However it turns out."

Thinking of Jane Majeski brings forth a slew of other names—Amy Baum, Susan Sutter, Maureen Dolan, Penny Schwartz, Ginny DeGenova. There were nearly forty girls in my class at Herbert Hoover Junior High, but I believed back then that only those five counted. They were thick, fast friends and everything went right for them. Amy won the district science prize *and* made gym cadettes. Susan and Maureen were majorettes, owned horses they rode in shows. Penny and Ginny edited the school paper and became class officers. The whole lot of them sang in girls' chorus.

They had good complexions, too, and clothes they got new, not from an older sister or cousin. They had straight, thick shiny hair that hung where they wanted it; or pretty curls that fluttered easily around their faces. Susan Sutter trained her hair into a tight jelly roll-flip she was forever squeezing. This habit irritated Amy Baum and probably planted the seeds for their eventual schism. But that didn't really happen until high school when Susan's grades dropped and she started sleeping around with boys.

During the period I'm talking about these girls were all close chums who'd raised a wall around their friendship. It wasn't so tall a wall you couldn't see in, observe their every smile and perfect movement, but a wall just the same. Other girls ignored this crowd. They had their own friends, their own activities, if not the most prestigious ones. They kept their distance.

Jane and I were hangers-on. But the more we strained to get inside the further from the wall we landed. In seventh grade we had no place to go; so we kept trying.

Jane, I think, suffered from unrequited love for Susan Sutter. Once upon a time in sixth grade, Jane and Susan were best friends. Then puberty struck and crushed Jane like a steamroller. Where she should have zigged she zagged. Where she should have zagged she zigged. Other girls experimented with makeup; huddled together in upstairs bedrooms listening to rock 'n roll, tittering over boys; played kissing games at boy-girl parties. Jane didn't do any of those things. She didn't keep giving tea parties for her dolls or running to her mother every time she knicked her knee. But in some deeper, more inexplicable way she clung to childhood.

Her body, however, kept moving. Dark hairs sprouted on her legs, underarms, and of course, around that hidden place from where menstrual blood now flowed. Once, in study hall, she bled right through her underpants, slip, and skirt and had to see the nurse for permission to go home. Her breasts swelled into little mounds. Her face grew oily around her nose and chin. Everything she did looked awkward. Her elbows caught on things. Her brassiere straps slipped down her arms. She screwed up in gym. She'd swing her legs at soccer balls and miss. Softball captains played her in the outfield. Girls like Amy Baum called her "dear" and tried to tilt her body in the right direction to swing a golf club.

All of these things might just as easily have happened to me as Jane. But I prefer to remember they didn't. That's the beauty of time and memory. Nearly thirty years go by and I can rearrange, reorder, subtract here and there. Now my adolescence is a doll-sized room full of miniatures I reassemble to suit my pride. Who gets hurt? Where's the loss if I say Jane Majeski, not I, couldn't/wouldn't jitterbug, was afraid to do the stroll?

The truth is, I don't have to remember how I was. I remember Jane.

Susan Sutter dropped Jane when she made majorettes, another thing Jane couldn't see. She followed Susan around the halls, loitered at her locker after school, because all through sixth grade and part of seventh, Susan and Jane walked home together. Now Susan spun her baton in Jane's dazed face and tossed her precious curls. "I have *practice,* Jane," she'd boast.

While Jane pursued Susan, I mooned over Amy. Amy fascinated me. She was Jewish, but you couldn't tell. She had blue eyes, dark blonde curls, and a perfect little snub nose, so unlike my bumpy one. Amy did things I didn't know Jewish people did. She took figure skating lessons, went camping with her family in Vermont, belonged to Girl Scouts. Amy drew the most attention in a crowd of gentile girls.

Back in sixth grade I had one good friend—Runa Rauthgrynich. Runa was my age, but a year behind me in school. Her family moved to Cleveland from somewhere in Hungary to escape a war. I found that terribly romantic and brave and reminiscent of my favorite book in sixth grade—*The Diary of Anne Frank*. I considered Anne Frank my other friend, or at least I thought she would have been my friend if we had grown up together. Sometimes I thought maybe I *was* Anne Frank—her reincarnation, I mean. She was so incredibly sensitive, and she'd suffered terribly. Not that I ever suffered anywhere near as much as Anne, but it made me feel better to think I might be her when the other girls laughed at me.

They laughed because I read all the time, even when the teacher left the room, the signal for everyone else to start talking and joking and throwing things around, like rabbit's feet and Cracker Jack charms. They laughed at me because of Runa, who was legally blind and used to place her hand on my arm when I walked her home from school. Actually Runa's mother paid me to walk her home. She paid me three dollars a week, which also included reading to Runa for an hour, two afternoons a week. Runa spoke limited English. She could say things like "please," "thank you," "ice cream," "hot dog" and "time you should go home now," but she never found words for a real conversation.

"Runa understand English perfect." Runa's mother had insisted when we first gathered in the threadbare Rauthgrynich living room to discuss the terms of our friendship. "She need help walking busy street; she need help read the words. Runa eyes bad, you know. Doctor very worry about her eyes."

"Marcy will be *delighted* to help out Runa," said my mother, who of course had come along, always trying to make plans for me. "Marcy has an eye problem too. See how thick her glasses are."

"Mmother," I stammered, shocked that she would call attention to my own nearsightedness, which I had lived with since age six without ever considering it a problem.

"Well, Marcy, this girl has a much worse case. Much worse." My mother leaned toward me on the faded flowered sofa, the only real place to sit in that room. Mrs. Rauthgrynich and Runa sat on painted green wooden chairs they'd dragged in from the dining room. "Just look at *her* glasses."

"Mother!" I gasped, but I did look, and that's when I knew that neither Runa nor her mother understood much English. How else could they have both sat there with slap happy smiles on their freckled faces, saying only "Tuesday, Tuesday," the day we had all agreed I would start reading to Runa.

My teacher had originally suggested that I befriend Runa. Mrs. Harrison had called my mother in for one of those parent-teacher conferences, and the next thing I knew there we were at Runa's house, on Lancashire Road, a few blocks from Coventry Elementary.

"Your teacher thinks you're too shy, Marcy," my mother said when she had returned from the conference and changed out of her good dress into something she could cook in. "She says you do very good work in school, but thinks you should socialize more with the other girls. She says there's another shy girl in another class, and she thinks the two of you ought to meet."

I would have been glad to read to Runa for free, if she really planned to be my friend. But my mother was a big one for not letting people take advantage. She said if Runa's mother didn't pay me, the friendship would be one-sided: me giving everything and getting nothing in return.

In fourth grade my mother discouraged me from joining a club for more or less the same reason.

"They're all going to want to meet at our house," she had said, tears actually rolling down her cheeks because she was in the kitchen at the time, chopping onions. "It wouldn't be fair to have me host all those girls every week."

"They're going to meet at different houses," I explained, hoping this would make things all right. "All the girls in the class are going to join. We'd only have to come here every tenth week."

"Marcy!" My mother waved her knife like a pointer. I took a step back, even though I already stood a good few feet from her chopping block. "Some of those girls have mothers who work, Marcy," my mother instructed. "I can't have you in a house with no adults around."

"We won't go to those houses," I promised, even though I didn't know how this would happen. Ceila's mother worked. So did Rachel's and Jill's. My mother shook her head and swiped a hand across her wet cheek. "If you don't go to those houses you'll have to come here, Marcy, don't you see? And then I'll have to give all those girls rides home, since their mothers work, don't you see? They'll be taking advantage of me."

"Oh," I said, feeling sorry for my mother. My mother had had a hard life. She'd been raised by two different stepmothers, each of whom had children of her own and worked my mother like Cinderella. Only no prince ever came along to rescue Leah Landau. Just my fussy father, Jack Rosen, who yelled at her a lot—for no reason as far as I could see.

"I could go to the first meeting and find out what it's like," I suggested, but my mother squinted at me like she might really cry.

"Marcy, you don't have much in common with those girls. They're not your type." I thought her very beautiful when I was nine. She wore her hair long then, piled high atop her head into a gallant swirl, and it shone dark and thick against her face, a longish face with a long, determined nose like mine, without the bump.

Almost all the other girls at school lived in shabby apartment buildings or run-down two flats on the other side of the district from us. We had moved away from such a neighborhood when I was six. We lived in a nice house—three rooms downstairs, four rooms up—and I thought my mother wanted me to play with girls who also lived in houses, though the girls who lived on our street went to Catholic school or private school so even though I played with them sometimes, my mother said they couldn't be my real friends.

Runa Rauthgrynich waited for me on the playground after school almost every day in sixth grade so I could walk her home. I tried to talk to her as we walked. I would ask Runa why she wore the same dress all week long. I thought maybe the other kids wouldn't laugh at me if Runa at least wore different clothes. I asked her if she washed her clothes out every night before she went to bed. Or did she have a secret way of keeping them looking fresh? She only owned three different outfits from what I could tell.

Runa never spoke to my questions. It always seemed like we were having two different conversations.

"Pretty dresses," she said once, pointing to my blue flowered jumper and smiling faintly.

"My mother shopping," she called out excitedly another time and I burst out laughing because I thought she'd said, "My mother *schlepping*." Runa looked at me suspiciously and said nothing more for the rest of the way home, even after I tried to explain myself.

One cold April day Runa didn't come to school, and when I went to her house she wasn't there. No one was there. I stood on the sagging porch and pressed my face against the glass of her living room window. It was dark inside, but I could tell it was empty. Emptier even than it had been all along. No flowered sofa, no green wooden chairs around the clunky dining room table where Runa and I used to sit while her mother filled the whole minuscule house with the smell of boiling cabbage.

Mrs. Rauthgrynich owed me for three weeks, but I never said anything to my mother. Runa didn't talk much, but she had a curious way of looking at me through her strange, cloudy eyes. She would tilt her chin in concentration as I read, and twirl a chunk of sandy brown hair around and around a forefinger. I didn't care if she had taken advantage of me. But I wondered if she had really been my friend.

Jane Majeski reminded me of Runa a little, the way she stared so owlishly and seldom spoke, concentrating on the other girls in the cafeteria at lunch. Jane had sandy hair too, but stringy. Wayward strands of it sometimes fell into her mashed potatoes and gravy when she leaned forward in her chair. Jane never noticed this, that was the sad part, the part that made the other girls exchange sideways glances, as they ate their own cafeteria food, or munched dainty white bread sandwiches they brought from home.

It wouldn't be totally accurate to say Jane and I ate lunch together. We ate with the girls we wanted to belong to—Amy Baum, Susan Sutter, Ginny DeGenova, Penny Schwartz, Maureen Dolan. I didn't talk much either. I plugged into *their* conversations.

"Did you see the way Mr. Collier and Miss Jensen were talking to each other in the hall?" Penny might giggle. She was a rosy-cheeked girl with a mass of bright red curls and she liked to giggle.

"Yeah," Maureen would crackle back like a veritable Rice Krispie, tossing her dark, sleek hair. "He touched her hand too!"

"Whoaaaa!" Susan whistled through her teeth and jerked her arms as if yanking horse's reins.

Everyone laughed heartily at Susan's little mime and then Amy threw a green pepper ring in the air and caught it with her teeth. "My big sister told me," she whispered so that everyone had to lean forward to hear. "My big sister told me that she saw Mr. Collier and Miss Jensen at a movie!"

I had looked forward to junior high as my clean slate, a chance to get away from the girls whose club I didn't join, girls who by sixth grade wore lip gloss and nylon stockings and no longer included me in their plans. All those girls went on to Eleanor Roosevelt Junior High. Yet at Herbert Hoover I encountered the same thing, with different names and faces.

"Are you going to the jam on Friday night?" someone would ask, maybe Ginny DeGenova, the wild-eyed jitterbug queen, looking right past me.

"My mom can drive this week," Amy Baum would volunteer. She always offered up her mom as driver, which caused me to stare especially hard at her, wishing I could *be* Amy Baum, if only for a day, and have a mother who didn't mind chauffeuring kids around.

"I'm going to wear my new blue poodle skirt and ask Eugene Richman to *dance,*" announced Susan Sutter, who had a *gigantic* and continually growing wardrobe.

"Ooohhweee! Eugene Richman!" Penny Schwartz whistled through her teeth, and turned to me. "I bet even Marcy wants to get her hooks in *him*!"

All the girls—the right girls—roared loudly then and I felt myself turn red.

"Isn't that right, Marcy?" Ginny's dark eyebrows rose vigorously up and down.

"No, *Jane* adores him!" Susan retorted, and the table shuddered with girlish glee. Jane laughed too, a good-natured, awkward laugh, her face totally crimson.

"I don't like boys," she said and the whole table screamed.

"Marcy," Jane leaned over the empty dishes on her cafeteria tray one wintry Thursday after the other girls had dashed off to jitterbug with each other in the first floor gym. "Saturday is my thirteenth birthday." Jane pushed her glasses up off her nose and released a long, slow breath. "My parents are taking me out to dinner."

"That's nice." I contemplated a hefty corned beef sandwich I couldn't seem to finish, wondering why Jane had shared this news with me.

"We're going to Alescio's," she said. "On Murray Hill. It's my favorite restaurant."

"It is?" I tried to look impressed. I knew Murray Hill was the neighborhood people called Little Italy, but I had never been there. And I had never heard of Alescio's. Our family went out to eat maybe once a year on my father's birthday. We went to Gruber's for prime rib with Yorkshire pudding. My father loved Yorkshire pudding, but my mother couldn't make it without smoke coming out of the oven. My mother cooked Jewish foods best, like brisket with farfel or chicken soup with noodle *kugel*. She made corned beef too, and packed it onto thick slices of Jewish rye for out-sized sandwiches like the one I struggled with now.

"I can bring one friend," Jane was saying, still talking about Alescio's.

"Oh," I said, beginning to picture the major snowdrift this was heading toward.

"Would you like to go?" she blurted, strands of long, wispy hair dusting the edges of her empty mashed potato bowl.

"Me?" I stared at Jane. This was not the invitation I'd been waiting for.

"I asked Susan Sutter," Jane murmured. "But she doesn't want to go." I could tell from the slope of her shoulders, the sad slant of her head, that she knew things about her standing with Susan that she had refused to see before.

"Well, just don't bring *anyone*," I suggested roughly, wondering what the other girls would say if they thought I went places with Jane Majeski.

"I *have* to bring someone." Her oval face ripened with fear and panic.

"Oh." I looked down at my bulging rye bread crusts to avoid Jane's gaze. I didn't want to go, but I didn't know how to just say so like Susan Sutter.

"I always get a lot of money for my birthday." Jane began talking rapidly. "I get a lot of money and it's really not that important to me because I have everything I want. I can give you some of it." Jane had this strange, desperate look on her face that for a moment made me wonder if maybe Jane, not me, was Anne Frank reincarnated.

"I have everything I want too," I lied to Jane. But what would I do with another friendship based on money? I still had all my Runa Rauthgrynich earnings, minus the last three weeks. My mother had made me put it in the bank for college.

"I have to bring *somebody*," Jane repeated, running her fingers along the edges of her cafeteria tray.

I tossed the rest of my sandwich back into the paper sack my mother had packed it in. I didn't want any more to eat. I didn't want any more to eat for as long as I lived, but Jane's desperation had caved in on me, and I felt trapped, like in a mine disaster.

"I've never been to Alescio's." I forced a smile. "So I guess this is my big chance."

Jane smiled too—a big, relieved smile that made her glasses slide back up her nose a little. Then she said that I'd have to go home with her after school so I could meet her mother.

"I'm not supposed to invite anyone out to dinner," she explained, "who my parents don't know."

Jane lived a few blocks from the school in a big white stone house, with actual pillars holding up the wide front porch. The roof sloped downward toward the second story windows, which were framed by blue-green shutters, the kind that actually worked.

"How long have you lived here?" I asked as we trooped up a front walk lined with dormant shrubbery.

"We've always lived here." Jane tossed out this information like an insignificant snowball, and I thought, she *couldn't* be Anne Frank, not living in a house like this *and* eating gooey Herbert Hoover mashed potatoes.

I followed Jane through the front door, into a foyer with a gleaming black and white tiled marble floor. In one corner stood a small black table with a coppery statue on it. The statue was of a woman, naked and extravagantly large on top.

"My mother made that," Jane whispered when she saw me staring.

"She made it?" I was incredulous. My mother made supper, she made beds, made me run the carpet sweeper and wash the bathroom floor. It would never, never occur to her to make statues.

"She's kind of an artist." Jane blushed.

"Ohhhh." I began to wish I hadn't agreed to come.

The foyer led to a long staircase with a wooden banister that curved into a spiral. Jane took off her winter coat and draped it over the newel. I unbuttoned my coat, preparing to follow suit.

"Is that you, Jane?" a woman's voice called from a nearby room.

"Yes, mother."

"I didn't hear you hang up your coat."

Jane pushed her glasses off her nose and slid her coat from the banister. "Just keep your coat on," she instructed me, and fumbled in a nearby closet to find a hanger for hers. "You won't have to stay long."

Jane's mother was in the living room, in a large armchair covered with purplish floral fabric, her nylon stockinged feet propped up on a matching stool. A bowl of walnuts rested in her lap, a half-filled brandy glass on the lamp table beside her.

"Mother," Jane sounded breathless as we approached the chair. "This is Marcy."

"How do you do, Marcy." She smiled without showing teeth. "I'm afraid you've caught me in the act of getting fat." She patted her stomach through her tan corduroy skirt, and made a sour face.

I smiled back politely. She wasn't fat. She wasn't even large on top like the statue. But she was pretty, with carefully-arched black eyebrows and a mass of thick, dark hair swept stiffly off her forehead into a flip. She didn't look at all like Jane.

"I don't believe Jane's mentioned you." Mrs. Majeski squinted past me toward the curved bay window. "What's your last name?"

"It's Rosen," I said.

Mrs. Majeski lifted up her brandy glass and took a slow sip.

"I invited Marcy to go out to dinner with us," Jane piped up. She was standing next to me on the soft white carpet, and everything about her—voice, face, ungainly arms and legs—seemed to be growing smaller.

Jane's mother took another look at me, then turned to Jane. "I thought we decided you would invite Susan Sutter," she said and something inside me snapped in two, like a breaking bone.

"Susan can't come," Jane protested softly. "She's doing something with her family."

"Well, then, you should have discussed this with your father and me." Jane's mother spoke as if she'd forgotten I was there, even though I hovered just a few feet from her face, sweating into my heavy winter coat.

"You said I could invite one friend." Jane sounded as miserable as she had in the cafeteria.

"Well, young lady." Mrs. Majeski took a deep, exasperated breath. "We have rules in this house and you have broken one of them. You have invited someone out to dinner who we don't know."

I remember the commiserative look Jane flashed me then, but not much more about being in her house. In my memory, Jane and I stand in front of Mrs. Majeski, like supplicants before a queen. Then the scene shifts suddenly. I'm at home two miles away, eating supper with my family. The telephone rings and my mother walks across the room to answer.

"Yes," I hear her say, tentatively. "Mmmmhmmmm. Yes. Oh, I see." Then I hear her listening.

"Jack," my mother addressed my father first when she finally got off the phone. "Marcy's been invited out to dinner on Saturday with a little girl from school. Isn't that nice? Her father's a lawyer and her mother graduated from the Chicago Institute for Art."

"Why did they invite Marcy?" My father frowned. He didn't like our meals being interrupted by the phone.

"Marcy." My mother ignored my father and turned to me, her face flushed with excitement. "Why didn't you tell me you'd been invited out?"

I looked at my mother, then at my plate, my appetite disappearing for the second time that day. "I didn't think it was definite," I said.

"Oh, it's definite, all right." My mother beamed. "They're going to Alescio's!"

A glass-encased candle flickered on every white-clothed table in the romantic little restaurant I went to that Saturday night with Jane and her parents. Colorful Italian lights hung at all the windows, casting a fairy tale glow over everything, including us, I suppose, as well as silent waiters in bow ties and tails, swimming somberly about the room like so many guppies in a tank. I couldn't get over the huge, beautiful mural that covered one entire wall and showed people being serenaded in little boats.

Mr. Majeski leaned towards me early on, and said the painting was of Venice, which he and Mrs. Majeski had visited twice. "It's even prettier in person," he said.

"They went there on their *honeymoon*," Jane gushed emphatically, stringy hair swishing dangerously toward her soup bowl as she swiveled in my direction.

"We've been there *three* times, Ross." Mrs. Majeski placed her right hand on her husband's left and suffered one of her tight-lip smiles. She was quite dressed up, in a textured gray wool suit she wore without a blouse so that a generous wedge of creamy skin glared out at us from beneath a strand of pearls.

"No, twice." Mr. Majeski reached for a crusty, horn-shaped roll and broke it firmly at the center. "Our honeymoon and our fifteenth anniversary trip last summer." He was studious-looking and fair-skinned, with thin brown hair, glasses, and a high forehead that furrowed when he spoke, suggesting just the faintest cloud of doubt. There was no question, looking at him, who Jane took after.

"*And* the alumni conference two years before that." Mrs. Majeski let go her husband's hand and plumbed her minestrone with a soup spoon.

"That was Rome, Carol." Mr. Majeski muttered between bites of roll, his crisp white shirt cuffs smiling stiffly from just below the edges of a dark gray jacket. It was a handsomer, more expensive-looking suit coat than any my father ever owned.

"The meeting was in Rome and we weekended in Venice." Mrs. Majeski's eyebrows narrowed into two prickly points as she soothed a spoonful of soup to her lips.

"Oh yes." Mr. Majeski squinted at the mural with pale blue eyes, the exact same shade as Jane's. "The St. Mark's Square Hotel. I loved that place."

Mrs. Majeski wagged her head, an especially lacquered head today, as if she'd lost it with a can of hair spray while dressing for this dinner. "We stayed at the *Hilton* that time. Remember? Their restaurant served the most exquisite risotto?"

"Oh yes, oh yes, that's right." Mr. Majeski mumbled into his soup. "*Risotto alla Milanese*. I've never had a finer version anywhere."

"Ross, for heaven's sake, it was the *con funghi secchi*, how could you forget those amazing mushrooms?"

Their conversation droned on and on, with a kind of black and white television blandness, as colorless as their clothes. Jane and I stood out like flowers, in bright satiny dresses leftover, in my case anyway, from sixth grade. We sat silent and transfixed, much as we did when we ate together at school. Only instead of standoffish girls, we faced Carol and Ross Majeski, debating the pleasures of their travels, right down to the Arborio rice. I was beginning to think they had forgotten about us, when Mrs. Majeski turned sharply to her left, soup spoon cradled toward her lips as if she planned to kiss it.

"Jane, dear," she began, eyebrows narrowing again into bits of barbed wire. "Jane, don't slurp your soup so. Take nice easy gulps." She bobbed her mouth into the spoon a few times, in a way that reminded me of a freight train coming around a bend. I couldn't help myself. I laughed, spraying soup that was in my mouth all over the tablecloth. Jane laughed too, soup sputtering from her mouth, even as she dabbed frantically with her napkin at the wet spots in front of us. It was the closest we'd come to really being friends. If her parents hadn't been sitting there, watching us like hawks, I might have hugged her.

"Teenagers!" Mr. Majeski chuckled at last, and winked in our direction. Jane's mother, however, released a wounded sigh, and I sat up tense and silent in my chair. Jane slumped into hers.

"We should send you to boarding school," Mrs. Majeski suggested, barely moving her lips, perhaps because a waiter hovered over us now, clearing away soup plates, his lips flapping senselessly. "You'd learn manners there." Mrs. Majeski's words seemed to come out of the waiter's upturned mouth, like in a ventriloquy act. "No one attends boarding school without learning manners."

"Yes, that would be fine," Jane said, looking at the waiter, and I realized he had said something to her, separate of her mother's words.

"And what about the other young lady?" he turned to me just as Mrs. Majeski started moaning all over again about the joys of boarding school. She was a harper, not unlike my own mother when she didn't have her way. Except *my* mother moved her lips.

"I don't think my parents would send me to boarding school," I blurted, confused in the crossfire between the waiter's stare and Mrs. Majeski's stifled anger.

"And why is that?" Mr. Majeski jumped in, like a bathtub plug trying to contain the conversation.

"Because," I began tentatively. Adults seldom solicited my opinion, and now it seemed as if both Mr. Majeski and the waiter were anxious for my answer. "Because..." I stopped myself. My parents wouldn't send me to boarding school, because even if they had the money, which they didn't, they would never let me out of their sight for that long a time. They practically monitored my every movement *now*. But I couldn't say this in front of the Majeskis, who obviously (a) *had* the money and (b) weren't troubled by the possibility of spending long periods of time away from Jane.

"Just tell him what kind of salad dressing you want," Jane stage-whispered in my ear and nodded toward the waiter.

"Salad dressing?" I wondered helplessly.

"*They* always get Italian." She rolled her pale blue eyes. "But the blue cheese is the absolute best." She sounded self-assured for once.

I'd never had blue cheese *anything*, but I ordered it in solidarity with Jane.

"Actually," Mr. Majeski cleared his throat shortly after the salads had arrived. "Actually," he looked at me. "We like the ethnic mix of public school. We think that's good for Jane."

"Oh," I said. He seemed to be speaking to me, but I didn't know what he was talking about. There were no Runa Rauthgrynichs at Herbert Hoover, fresh from war-torn lands. There was a cute Italian boy in our class named Michael Scullini who brought pizza to school sometimes from his father's store. I had the maddest crush on him. And there was one Black girl in the whole school, who I think went home for lunch. I never saw her in the cafeteria. But what did any of this have to do with Jane, who didn't mix with anyone?

"We have some Jewish friends." Mr. Majeski poked gingerly at his iceberg lettuce salad as if it harbored explosives.

"Oh." I pushed my salad aside. I didn't like Mr. Majeski dragging the conversation around to Jewish people. There was something terribly pungent about it, not unlike the blue cheese dressing, which I didn't plan to ever try again.

"Weren't the Greenbergs Jewish, Ross?" Mrs. Majeski directed a forkful of shiny lettuce toward her mouth.

"The Greenbergs?" Mr. Majeski regarded her, blank-faced, as if here was another trip to Europe he'd forgotten about, another perfect risotto he'd blanked out.

"The Greenbergs, Ross," Mrs. Majeski pouted. "From the bar association banquet last fall. They sat at our table."

"Ohhhh, yes." He broke another hard roll contemplatively. "I think *he* was."

"I liked her." Mrs. Majeski waved her emptied fork. "We ought to have them for dinner sometime."

"Yes," he began eating his salad more freely now, as if it'd been okayed by the bomb squad.

Mrs. Majeski started in all over again on Jane when the pasta arrived. Or actually pasta for Jane and me. The Majeskis had ordered risotto. "Jane, dear, hold the fork against a spoon as you twirl, and for goodness sake, don't suck the strands into your mouth."

"Is that the way they teach in boarding school?" Jane snapped. Quiet, timid Jane snapped at her mother and made a frightening face.

"Your mother's only trying to help, Jane," Mr. Majeski interjected, poking at his food. "Social graces you know." He laughed good-naturedly. "You can never have too many of them."

Maybe, I thought, maybe if Jane's parents could find a restaurant in Cleveland that cooked risotto as good as what they'd had in Italy, maybe they'd accept Jane for who she was and Jane would therefore be a different girl, a very popular girl, who wouldn't have needed to invite *me* to her thirteenth birthday celebration. But it appeared that this had not yet happened, and would not happen at Alescio's that night, the way Mrs. Majeski stared disconsolately at her plate, and her husband cleared and cleared his throat.

"You'll never send me to boarding school, Mother, so can you please just drop it." Jane sat upright in her chair, chin thrust forward in untypical defiance, stringy hair clinging to her face like a loyal friend. "You're afraid to turn me loose with all those girls," she said. "You're afraid I'm queer."

No one spoke at our table for what seemed a very long time. I stopped eating, feeling awkward trying to twirl forkfuls of spaghetti against a spoon in all that quiet.

"If you'd just agree to take dancing lessons after school like Susan Sutter," Mrs. Majeski managed at last, her face very pale against her dark, dark hair. "Everyone else takes dancing lessons in junior high. I'm sure Marcy does. You take dancing lessons, don't you Marcy?"

"Yes," I said, which wasn't a total lie. My mother had been rumbling lately about a ballroom class for teens at the Jewish Center, and I'd been rumbling against it. But I supposed that now I would let her sign me up. I wouldn't want people calling *me* queer, even though I wasn't sure—I mean really sure—what it meant.

"I have a cousin who went to boarding school and came out queer," Jane informed me, informed the whole table, though I assumed I was the only one who didn't already know. She put her hand on my arm as she spoke, as if for balance, the way Runa Rauthgrynich had done when I walked her home from school. Reflexively, to my own shocked horror, I moved my arm away.

The evening ended somehow. I went back to school on Monday, but I don't remember that Jane was there. In fact, for many years I remembered that Jane's parents *did* take her out of Herbert Hoover in favor of private school. But this winter my mother sent a scrapbook she'd found while cleaning bedroom closets and it contained the program from junior high school graduation. Jane's name was on the list along with all the others.

"Guess who I saw today?" I asked my mother that day so long ago when I returned from the Stouffer's interview.

"Bonnie Carroll?" my mother guessed. "I wonder if she ever got her comeuppance."

"No, not Bonnie, Mother. Jane Majeski."

"Jane Majeski? Wasn't she that funny looking girl who asked you to dinner once and then snubbed you? I always thought she was a little queer."

"Jane didn't snub me, mom. We went our separate ways," I said, afraid to ask my mother what she meant by "a little queer."

"Well, rich people." My mother sighed. "They come and go."

My mother and I had a huge fight that night, the biggest we'd ever had. It started when I announced I wouldn't take the job I'd interviewed for, even though they'd made an offer. I told her they had an opening at their Chicago office and that maybe I would apply for that.

"I didn't send you away to college to lose you," my mother screamed. "If I had known you wouldn't come back, I would never have let you go."

I barricaded myself in the downstairs bathroom, and cried silent, painful tears.

"Most daughters live at home until they marry." My mother shouted through the door. "Some daughters never leave. Where could you find a better place to live than in this house?"

I stayed in the bathroom until after the house grew quiet. Then I splashed cold water on my swollen face and crept upstairs, past my parents' bedroom, where my mother slept alone. Past the study where my father slept on a daybed, fully clothed, as if he'd only planned to rest a moment before getting back to work. Past my brother's bedroom, which was empty. David came and went that year. We hardly saw him.

Piano Lessons

My father wore a suit, his only suit, and actually finished getting ready before Mommy. Jack Rosen, you look wonderful, I thought from a lofty fourteen-year-old perspective, watching Daddy descend the stairs like a triumphant suitor. Overweight, yes. Nobody's father I knew carried as much poundage as Jack, but the dark suit sliced at least fifty pounds off him. He moved so gracefully, down the stairs, across gray living room carpet, toward the couch where I sat, butterflies cruising my own slender stomach in anticipation of the night's big event.

"I told you I wouldn't make you late, Marcy." Daddy stood before me, his round face calm as a silent sousaphone, and very smiley. "It's your mother we have to worry about now."

"Thanks, Daddy." I jumped up from the couch and eased around the marble-topped coffee table to hug him, inhaled a heady melange of tobacco and gingery aftershave. He felt solid and comforting, like an overstuffed pillow. He didn't exactly hug me back. Daddy didn't come from a demonstrative family, Mommy often reminded me. But he didn't push me away either. He kind of just started walking across the room toward the spinet piano.

"Now here's one you ought to do tonight." Daddy folded himself onto the mahogany bench and stretched his stubby fingers toward the keys. I recognized the song at first note.

"Down the old ox road," I sang as Daddy played. "Oh you'll never find out just where it is by looking at maps, but with a little investigation you'll discover perhaps, that it's not a place but just a proposition called the old ox road... Down the old ox road..." He started in again, right way from the top because it was a circular song that never really ended.

The miracle about my father was he'd never had lessons, couldn't even read music. The piano had arrived in our house one day when I was eight and my father had gathered Mommy and David and me around him and serenaded us with happy songs that I'd never dreamed he knew. He favored the black keys. I'd noticed that right off the bat before I knew about words like sharps and flats. The black notes gave his music a rich, lush sound, like heavy gravy—which my mother unfortunately seldom made—over mashed potatoes.

"Oh you'll never find out just where it is by looking at maps," my father crooned, turning his head away from the keys to wink at me as we both sang. The words meant a lot, but wouldn't mean anything if you tried to explain them, like for school or something. Ordinarily, my father did like to analyze things. He had massive viewpoints about everything from President John F. Kennedy on down to the particular brand of peat moss my mother selected for her garden each year. He saw all the angles, as my Grandfather Landau liked to say, and never saw the same angle as anyone else. You needed a lot of time once my father got talking. I liked it better when he played the piano.

"Oh you'll never find out just where it is by looking at maps." Newly arrived downstairs, my mother joined the chorus, off key as usual, but looking radiant in a fitted turquoise silk dress she had bought specifically for tonight's occasion. "So with a little investigation you'll discover perhaps..." Leah Rosen, nee Landau, actually did a little rumba around the living room, pumping her arms in a way that embarrassed me. A lot of things about my mother embarrassed me lately, in particular her new home permanent, an overcooked bird's nest of curls that shimmied with the rest of her. She, in turn, seemed more impatient with me these days and inexplicably teary. We were going through a rough period, as she herself proclaimed, and I had promised myself to be nice to her, particularly tonight.

"Jack, we'd better go." My mother broke into the music after a couple more choruses. "Marcy has to be there early."

But of course we didn't leave, because my father wanted to take a picture of the whole family outside on the front steps and suddenly no one knew the whereabouts of either the camera or David, who no longer took piano lessons or worried about recitals, but who had promised to come tonight and cheer me on.

"Let's take the picture when we get back," I suggested.

"It'll be dark then, Marcy." Mommy dashed around the house, simultaneously calling my little brother's name and helping Daddy find the camera. I grabbed my music book and ducked out the front door, breathing deeply into the gentle June evening, thinking Chopin and Haydn and waiting for my family to collect themselves.

"Marcy, where were you?" Mrs. Brummer paced outside the side entrance to St. Celeste Church, all nervous energy in a flame-colored gown licked with black bric-a-brac. "You were supposed to be here early." She clicked towards me in high-heel shoes that matched her dress, matched her lipstick too, which she'd applied around the outsides of her lips as well as on them. What with her usual whorl of spun sugar-red hair, and giant silver hoop earrings waving crazily at her neck, she looked like a movie star expecting an Oscar.

"We were taking photos," I exclaimed, still giddy with the excitement of it, the way my father had arranged my brother and me on either side of Mommy and snapped away, pausing only to tell us how great we all looked.

"Now there's a family I can be proud of," he had said, something he never noted when he viewed us head on, but with his face tilted into a camera lens for the first time in years, he saw us in a different light.

"Why don't you let me get one of you with the kids," Mommy had fussed, pushing a kinky shock of hair off her eyes. "We never have any with you in it."

"Relax, Leah," Daddy had replied. "This is for my desk at work, and everyone there knows what *I* look like. Besides, I'd break the camera."

David and I laughed uproariously at that and even Mommy grinned. Then she extended her arms, mother bird style, and pulled David and me close against her.

"Well, anyway, you're here now, and looking very well." Mrs. Brummer's silvery earrings glittered in the early evening sun as she inspected me more closely. I'd worn a straight dark blue skirt and a white fitted over-blouse, scooped just enough at the neck to make me feel grown-up. Mommy had hesitated when I'd picked it out, but I was using my own money from a birthday gift and, after all, I'd pointed out, people saw a lot more of me than that in a bathing suit.

"Let's go inside then, with the other recitalees." My piano teacher threw an arm around my shoulder as my mother had for the photo. "So's we can all reconnoiter."

"Marcy, Marcy," My father's basso profundo voice cartwheeled toward us, craggy and unmistakable in its need to be acknowledged. I turned, even as Mrs. Brummer pulled me toward the door. "Marcy," she stage-whispered into my ear, as Daddy loped up the walk. "It's less than fifteen minutes to curtain, we need to reconnoiter."

"Just a minute," I whispered back, because good mood, bad mood my father came first in our family. That he'd been in a good mood lately, especially about Mrs. Brummer's advanced students' piano recital—it had actually gotten a write-up in the community paper—took precedence over everything.

"Marcy," Daddy hovered over me, a small white florist's box in one eager hand. "Marcy." He whispered too, for some odd reason. "Marcy, I didn't want to make your mother jealous, giving you this in front of her, but…" He fumbled in the box, produced an actual orchid corsage secured in see-through wrap. "Marcy." He tore the wrapping off. "Marcy…" he began again, then stopped, as if he'd snagged himself on something. "Congratulations, Marcy." He beamed at me, brushed his hand against my breasts in his haste to pin the flowers to me. Reflexively I stepped back, away from my father.

"Here, let me do it, Mr. Rosen." Mrs. Brummer trounced toward us, her face pinched with concern for the ticking clock.

"No, no, I'm her father, I'll do it." Daddy insisted, his gray eyes watery behind thick, dark glasses, his breath hot with the scent of a freshly smoked cigarette. He wrestled with the corsage a few moments longer before securing it to my blouse.

"Thanks, Daddy." I hugged him for the second time that day, but only lightly, so as not to crush the flowers.

"You're still my little girl," my father announced and just stood there like a parked truck as Mrs. Brummer steered me away, towards her pre-concert encampment.

I had never wanted piano lessons. I had certainly never asked for recitals. They had both come to me, like *latkes* on Hanukkah, shiny in my parents' enthusiasm, but not nearly as delicious. Mrs. Brummer had come to me, too, when I was eight years old, replete with bright red "excellent" stickers splashed with G clefs, and clever little sayings to help you learn to read the notes. Every Good Boy Does Fine for the lines on the musical staff (EGBDF) and FACE for the spaces, "as plain as the nose on your face."

We had been through many recitals together, Mrs. Brummer and I. If you could memorize "Go Tell Aunt Rhoady," she considered you ready for the stage. "Go tell Aunt Rhoady, Go tell Aunt Rhooooady. Go tell Aunt Rhoady, her old gray goose is dead."

In less than two minutes the song was over, the goose was dead, and you could walk away from the piano, back to your seat under your mother's beatific gaze. Fathers didn't come to piano recitals when you played the baby songs. At least my father didn't. He'd bided his time, waited six years until I graduated from the nursery songs, progressed through the simple rondos and sonatinas.

My father had always wanted piano lessons as a kid, but never got them, growing up in a poor family where it was first come first served at the supper table, first served at the piano as well. His oldest sister Lottie got the music lessons, practiced on a rented old upright they had to return when their father lost his job. His father lost his job stirring vats of molten liquid at a tannery, and his mother lost her head; she put an end to music in that household. My father harbored the notes in his brain like a subversive politico all those years until he found himself a wife who bore him a daughter to whom he could bequeath his great love for the keyboard. Jack Rosen would work long hours as an accountant at a Cleveland paint factory, and long hours with clients on the side, before he finally bought the piano of his dreams. He would tickle those ivories with every senseless old vaudeville ditty he'd ever adored, but I, his daughter Marcy, would study with Mrs. Brummer and learn to caress them.

"Make it nice and schmaltzy, Marcy," Mrs. Brummer would instruct, seated so close to me at the old upright piano in her cement basement studio that I could smell her Colgate toothpaste breath. Sometimes I pretended hers was the same upright piano my aunt had practiced on long ago, and which had to be returned to the dealer after the grandfather I would never know lost his job. Pianos sometimes circulated from one household to another. And Mrs. Brummer wasn't rich. Maybe she'd latched onto that same old piano at an estate sale. I never knew the aunt who'd been the pianist in the family—she and my father shared more than musical differences—so why couldn't I at least know the piano?

"Okay, now," Mrs. Brummer would reiterate, as if she'd known I'd been daydreaming during the lesson. "Schmaltz it up in that particular part, Marcy. Schmaltz it up. That's right, that's good, that's the ticket."

I knew what schmaltz meant relative to chicken soup and rendered chicken fat, the secret ingredient in my mother's recipe box —the power behind the noodle *kugel* that made my father use words like "thank you," "please," and "Leah, you're beautiful." But I didn't understand the term in relation to music. I tried to play the way the notes spoke to me, glomming on to the sad, melancholic parts with particular ease, growing up in a household where longing bloomed like perennial flowers on a thickening vine. My mother longed for her mother, dead before Leah had turned eight. My father longed for his father, gone with the piano from Jack's boyhood home. My grandmother had booted her husband out when he lost his job, which was just an excuse to get rid of him, my father always complained, just a terrible, inexcusable excuse. Nevertheless, you never caught my father sloughing off. He worked long hours at the paint company, long hours afterward at home. Just let my mother get any wise ideas about kicking *him* out.

I had no real musical ability, not like my father who plucked chords and whole tunes from the air. Not like my brother either, who shrugged off piano lessons at age ten in favor of baseball and Elvis hits he learned by himself. It had never occurred to me that I too could quit lessons. Who would translate my parents' sadness into a *valse triste*? Who would there be to turn their thwarted dreams into a sonata?

"Okay, now Marcy, why don't you sit over there and I'll bring you some beverage." Mrs. Brummer broke through my reverie when we reached the little reception room in which I'd been scheduled to arrive at least thirty minutes earlier. She directed me toward a row of empty folding chairs set up near a wall, and I plopped down on one of them, wondering through a descending curtain of jitters, what had happened to Mrs. Brummer's other advanced students. The only other person in the room was Mr. Brummer, fussing over trays of cookies on the table where the punch bowl waited. He was a tall, unathletic looking man, who taught trigonometry at the high school and did the wash sometimes on the other side of the flowered curtain from where Mrs. Brummer gave lessons.

"Hi, Mr. Brummer," I said. He and I had a little friendship going that revolved around laundry questions, such as which colors to mix with what and when to add the bleach. It fascinated me to see a man do the wash, even though my mother said it meant Mrs. Brummer wore the pants in that family.

"Hi Marcy, good luck, today." Mr. Brummer looked up from his cookie arrangements as his wife high-heeled toward me with a red paper cup.

"I want you to drink this and breathe deeply for awhile." Mrs. Brummer urged the cup into my hand. "You need to relax."

"I *am* relaxed," I insisted, then laughed, because obviously I wasn't; my hand actually quaked as I tried to sip the punch. But neither was Mrs. Brummer the picture of calm, tossing around words like "recitalees" and "reconnoiter," and painting lipstick on her face.

"You're going to shine, Marcy." Mrs. Brummer settled into the folding chair next to me.

I set my cup on the floor and hugged Mrs. Brummer lightly so as not to crush my corsage. She looked like she needed a reassuring embrace. Mrs. Brummer was the nervous type like my mother, and like I evidently was becoming. Though I shouldn't have been sooo nervous tonight. I knew the Chopin waltz inside and out and the Haydn sonata was for two pianos. Mrs. Brummer and I were going to play it together, though we had never practiced it that way. I had never heard Mrs. Brummer's part and so I would use my music book in order to follow her. How could I be nervous when I didn't even have to worry about forgetting the notes?

"You're going to shine, Marcy," Mrs. Brummer repeated. "I know your father makes you nervous, but I'm positive you're going to play wonderfully tonight."

My father? My father didn't make me nervous. My father was my father. He made other people nervous, teachers in particular, I had noticed, a few months ago when my mother dragged him to the senior class open house at Herbert Hoover Junior High. My father bent Miss Silbaugh's science teacher ears, asking about chemical theories she hadn't taught us. He quizzed Mr. Van Roy on Cleveland Browns stats, even though it wasn't part of Mr. Van Roy's job as football coach to know them.

My father made my mother nervous sometimes, cannonballing unpredictably from one mood to the other. But that was between them, she assured me, and even if she ever did divorce him, which she sometimes threatened—not to *his* face, but mine—he would still be my father. *So you ought to love him for his good points*, Marcy, my mother always said. *And believe me,* she'd add, *he has plenty of them.*

"My father doesn't make me nervous," I told Mrs. Brummer, wrapping both hands around my punch cup to steady them. Maybe she was jealous, as my father said my mother would be if she saw him give me flowers. "I love my father."

"Well, then." Mrs. Brummer smiled more like a friend than teacher and patted my knee. "Nerves are all part of the game when you perform. So why don't you take a couple more deep breaths and come join the other students in the recital hall when you're ready, and we'll get started."

She got up, crossed the room elegantly, looking like the good witch in *The Wizard of Oz*. Mr. Brummer gave the last tray of cookies an affectionate glance, flashed a V-sign in my direction, and vanished with her.

"One one/thousand, two one/thousand." I counted slowly to ten, the way my mother had taught me to measure the distance between lightning and thunder in an approaching storm. I counted to ten until my belly inflated like a leaky beach ball with calm.

Afterward, everyone said it was the best I'd ever played, in public or private. I floated through the Chopin waltz, which began on a single, plaintive B flat, played over and over again—quarter note first, two eighth notes, quarter note—leading into a fitful dance that bubbled with hope, the way its chords sparkled intermittently against the edges of melodic minor runs.

And the sonata...wow, the sonata. It dazzled me to hear such beautiful music and know I was at its center. I would play a long run of solo notes—pianissimo at first, gradually building, building to enormous crescendo and then the other piano would respond with a rush of rich, solid chords that filled me with excitement and pleasure. I would wait quietly while Mrs. Brummer played, my head bowed in concentration, fingers poised delicately on keys. Sometimes we played at the same time, neither piano dominating, each issuing forth ornate sounds that blended miraculously.

"You have amazing sensitivity." Mr. Brummer shook my hand in the crush of people that milled around the concert hall right after the recital. David hopped by to say I played so well, he didn't recognize me, and a puffy-check blonde lady in a violet suit asked if I had any musical plans for the future.

"Well, no, I love classical music," I replied, surprised by the question. "But I'm just doing this for my...I'm just doing this for now." I corrected myself, no longer certain I was only doing it for my parents.

"I'd like to get a photograph of all the participants." Mrs. Brummer approached me too, her face flushed with success, her vocabulary returned to normal words. "Let's all meet in the corner of the reception room, opposite the refreshment area."

I smiled for posterity for the second time that day. David hovered around the refreshment table with some kids his own age, while my parents sipped punch, my father pointing me out with rapturous smiles to passing strangers. Then Daddy told Mrs. Brummer he had a celebration planned of his own and didn't have enough energy at his age—he laughed, pulling himself up to his full five foot six height—for two parties. So I never tasted any of the cookies Mr. Brummer had so painstakingly arranged on his silver trays. But I did get to ride home in the front seat of the car, Mommy and David taking an obliging backseat to my sudden turn of fortune.

"Where'd you get the flowers, Marcy?" David asked as we drove past the huge brick mansions along Fairmount Boulevard south of Cedar Road.

"I got them from..."

"Her teacher." My father placed a warning hand on my leg as he finished my sentence. I had never seen my father fib before and

I glanced sideways at his face, almost expecting him to look different.

"Mrs. Brummer gave you flowers!" David exclaimed. "Aren't you the teacher's pet!"

"She gave Gloria Sarafina a corsage too," I said referring to the only other girl who had performed today. "But she didn't want to wear it." I stared straight ahead, afraid to look at Daddy, who knew this was untrue, or at Mommy, who didn't. I felt like I had jumped into a swimming pool with my clothes on and was sinking towards the bottom.

"She should have gotten flowers for the mothers," Mommy piped up, her voice etched with hurt, which made me feel even worse, since Daddy and I had been *trying* to protect her feelings.

Daddy supposed she wouldn't have wanted to stick pins in her beautiful new dress and my mother said, yes that was true, but Mrs. Brummer couldn't have known she'd be wearing it. "And after all we've paid her for lessons..."

"I'll get you flowers, Leah," my father replied in a very polite voice. "I'm going to surprise you with flowers one day very soon. And they're going to be a lot nicer than the ones Mrs. Brummer gave Marcy." I knew he felt badly that he hadn't gotten her any tonight, and therefore had to downgrade mine. He was caught in his lie. We both were.

We gathered by the backyard picnic table in a lovely, moonlit night and Daddy opened a bottle of Italian champagne he'd stashed in the refrigerator. *Asti Spumanti.* The cork made a magical popping sound and flew up toward the stars.

"Thar she blows," David announced, following its white arc into the clear sky. "Thar she blows." We'd seen the movie, "Moby Dick" that spring and both David and my father loved to use that phrase at every opportunity.

"Do you really think the kids ought to drink that?" Mommy ran a worried hand through her damaged hair as Daddy began filling all four fluted glasses he'd carried out from the dining room hutch.

"It's a special occasion, Leah," Daddy reassured her. "How often does my daughter play a Haydn sonata in front of seventy-five people? Anyway they're going to try alcohol sooner or later. They might as well learn to handle it at home."

Daddy sometimes made kiddy cocktails for David and me and we'd gulp them with the same sort of gusto with which we used to approach candy cigarettes. But champagne, actual champagne. Once I'd begged the olive from Mommy's martini, but it tasted horrible—bitter and perfumey—and made me wonder exactly who my mother was that she smacked her lips over the same flavors.

"To the family." Daddy spoke solemnly, standing before us with his glass raised high.

"To the family!" David squealed, knocking my glass so enthusiastically I nearly dropped it.

"To the family!" I clanked David's glass back, the both of us breaking up at the notion of toasting each other.

"Sip it slowly now, kids." Mommy warned, delicately clinking her glass against mine, then Daddy's and David's.

But slowly was not a word I could associate with champagne, not after one, two, then many more acquaintances with its delightful wet fizz. David guzzled it like it *was* a kiddy cocktail, wiping the back of his hand across his mouth with a satisfied sigh.

"I see the cork," he shouted suddenly, pointing at the sky. "I see the cork."

It wasn't the cork, of course; it was the North Star, but David didn't care. He danced around the yard like a little jumping bean, singing at the top of his lungs:"My Dad's a corker, he's a New Yooorker."

"No, David." I bumped him with my glass, sloshing champagne over both of us. "There's the cork. There's the real cork." I waved a dramatic hand at the moon, which smirked large and nearly full over all of us.

"By the light, by the light of the silvery cork," I blurted out and Daddy joined in, then Mommy and David, all of us substituting a lot of lah de dah de dahs where we didn't know the real words.

"Carolina Cork..." Mommy launched us, off-key, into another fractured song, sidling up close to Daddy, while David and I sashayed over to the picnic table to refill our glasses.

"Row, row row your cork, gently down the stream." David was getting really silly. But it didn't matter; we all joined forces, our voices rising above insect choruses, rustling leaves, even the steady whoosh of cars traveling north and south along Coventry Road just beyond our hedges. We sang until long after we'd emptied the bottle of champagne and the moon had bellyflopped over neighbors' rooftops, leaving us in darkness, except for a sliver of light from our kitchen window.

"I'll open another bottle," Daddy volunteered during a lull in the musical entertainment, but Mommy said no. She had no idea what time it was, but it was certainly past time for bed.

"And look at David over there, already asleep on the grass." She indicated a thin, white blob by the cherry tree, and I wondered how long he'd been lying there. I hadn't even missed him.

"Mommy." I unpinned the corsage and followed her over to the tree, feeling the grass cold and dewy around my ankles. "Mommy." She stooped down to wake David and I angled the orchid at her face. It smelled a little sour from spilled champagne. "I don't really need this anymore. I didn't even want it. You can have this, Mommy," I said. "It would look beautiful on *your* dress."

David's eyes popped open, then closed again like a half-dead man on "Gun Smoke."

"No, no Marcy, it's yours," Mommy looked up at me, her eyes as dark and unseeing as the night. "I don't need flowers from Mrs. Brummer. Daddy will get me some."

She had David on his feet by then and began leading him haltingly toward the house. I trailed behind, feeling dizzy. When they disappeared through the back door I took the corsage in both hands and flung it in the air, hoping it would go the way of the cork. But it landed at my feet a moment later with a gentle thud.

"Did you lose something, Marcy?" Daddy swept it up with a courtly bow and positioned it back across my chest. He'd whipped his suit jacket off long ago, along with his tie. His short-sleeved white shirt hung half out of his pants, partly unbuttoned.

"You're very beautiful, Marcy." Daddy wrapped his other arm around my back, and regarded me, his plump face twisted like a lanyard with sadness. "Dance with me," Daddy said and began singing in a more beautiful voice than I ever knew he had. "Moon River," Daddy sang, and the light in our kitchen window went out, turning the yard into total darkness. "Wider than a mile, I'm crossing you in style some day. . ."

I closed my eyes and began moving with him, pretending he was John Coates, a boy I'd danced with to this song a few weeks ago at the ninth grade class party. John had smelled sweet, like clean laundry and his arms felt strong and safe.

"...Oh dreammaker, you heartbreaker, wherever you're goin', I'm goin' your way..."

Daddy pressed against me more urgently than I'd expected. He pressed against me so urgently I stumbled a few times and tripped over his feet.

"That's a very pretty top, Marcy." Daddy still held the corsage close against my new scoop-neck white blouse. It looked like a soggy potato chip now, splattered with sweat and champagne and the beginnings of a squished orchid.

"I can hold the corsage," I suggested hoarsely. I'd begun to feel as if the cork we had sung to all night had landed inside me. I took short, rapid breaths in an effort to expel it, and felt overcome with the aroma of flowers. Not the corsage flowers. I smelled garden flowers—peonies, roses, marigolds, daisies, irises—the flowers my mother planted and tended through the summer, pent up for the night into leaden buds, releasing heady aromas.

"Relax, Marcy. Don't be so tense," Daddy soothed. "I'm your father." He didn't let me hold the corsage, but gripped me so tightly now—both hands suddenly clamping my shoulders—that the corsage stayed in place on its own.

I'd danced with other boys at the ninth grade party, but John Coates had scanned me with his quiet blue eyes and said I looked good. John was the one who wove magic.

"Wherever you're goin', I'm goin' your way." I sang back to Daddy, my eyes squeezed shut. I remembered the frantic, excitement-packed events of this night and thought what a grand thing piano lessons had been after all.

First Kiss

I reached high school without ever kissing a boy, unless you count Teddy Kornblum, who used to thrust himself at me back in third grade, lips puckered for action. I shied away from him then, but by sixth grade I faded into a total wallflower, parking myself in a scratchy green armchair while the rest of the kids played spin-the-bottle at Teddy's birthday party. They played spin-the-bottle at all the birthday parties that year and after a while I stopped getting invited. This left me confused and hurt and at the same time relieved, because I wasn't interested in kissing boys when I was twelve. Even the idea scared me.

I was Mommy's little girl and Daddy's very favorite. And while I can't remember my parents specifically telling me not to kiss, I knew—I JUST KNEW—they wouldn't approve. At night, under the covers, in the darkness of my own room, I masturbated to beat the band. But that was a private secret I never shared. I didn't even know the act had a name until eleventh grade Hygiene when granite-faced Miss Lehmann rattled off the erotic definitions.

Girls had Hygiene on the days they didn't have gym. We didn't call it sex education in 1964. We didn't even have a book, and Miss Lehmann never entertained discussion. We just sat at our desks dutifully recording her words in our three-ring notebooks. She lectured on diet first, dental caries, and acne. Then one day, with all the verve of a mechanical cement mixer, Miss Lehmann started hurling forth the vocabulary of sex.

"Masturbation," she recited grimly, her lean, gym teacher's frame etched darkly into a chair behind a wide, bare desk. "Manual stimulation of the genital organs commonly resulting in orgasm.

"Orgasm," she continued, her stony face freezing into a tragic mask, and we girls wrote, not even the boldest among us daring to giggle. "...the climax of sexual excitement, typically occurring toward the end of coitus or masturbation..."

"Genitalia," she began anew, and though my hand kept moving, my head spun back to the last words.

So that's what it is, I remember thinking, finally knowing at age sixteen that the glorious feeling that blossomed between my legs at my own insistent doing, was indelibly linked to sex.

I was backward, even for my time.

I knew about sex, of course, the way I knew about John F. Kennedy or Mahatma Ghandi. I just never connected it to my own life. At fourteen, I huddled with Bonnie Carroll all one summer afternoon in her backyard pup tent, reading a story from her brother's *Playboy*. The story centered on a young woman traveling by bus and the man who sat next to her. It was hot in Bonnie's tent, the air thick and syrupy. Bonnie and I lay side by side, reading aloud, our breath quickening when the woman let the stranger touch her, at first through her clothes, then little by little in the most forbidden reaches of her flesh.

"Aroused" would be Miss Lehmann's term for the way I felt, hidden away with Bonnie in her tent, greedily learning about things that could happen on a bus. Thinking of it now, I can almost believe Bonnie touched me as we read, her curious hand surging down, down, into my rising heat. But that's imagination at work, not memory, born of the charged energy I can still taste between us in that tent after all these years.

Bonnie fell in love with Matt Aldridge the following fall and didn't have time for girlfriends after that. I had known Matt since Coventry Elementary, could never stop thinking of him as the boy who threw up on his desk in second grade. Bonnie obviously saw different things. Sometimes they passed my house when he walked her home from school and I would stand in the picture window watching. They looked like one person moving, not two, their arms locked around each other's waists, their bodies yearning so close together you couldn't see daylight between them.

"Well, she's certainly turned the corner," my mother said once, wiping her calloused hands on a dish towel as she joined me in the window to watch.

I had my loves too, but always at a distance. In seventh grade I adored Michael Scullini, who brought pizza to school from his father's Italian import store. All the girls liked Michael. He was the smilingest boy I had ever known, with dark curly hair and dancing eyes, a friendly greeting for everyone. Loving Michael was painless. Maybe that's why I lost interest so soon and discovered John Coates, who spoke to me only when he felt like it.

John had blue eyes and brown hair and parents who let him call them by first name. An atheist and iconoclast by age twelve, he refused to say the Pledge of Allegiance. But he got all A's and made varsity basketball. I loved John Coates. In eighth grade I shaved my legs because John stared so disapprovingly at them when I walked into French class. My mother never mentioned my hairless legs, even though she had ordered me repeatedly not to shave them. Looking back on those tormented years, I wish I had disobeyed her more often.

Gary Cohen was the first boy who asked me out and I can't say this thrilled me, especially since I was second choice. An overweight, reticent boy, he had a squarish face that bore a permanent blush, like today's trendy white zinfandel wines. I don't remember ever speaking to him, until the night Anna Silverman called in a panic, asking if I knew Gary's phone number.

"I'm supposed to go out with him on Saturday, but my grandmother's sick," Anna said, her voice wispy and plaintive. If a quieter, more lonely girl than I existed in all of tenth grade it was Anna. "There are so many Cohens in the Cleveland phone book," Anna moaned.

I didn't know Gary's phone number, but he was in my Sunday school class and I had a synagogue directory.

"Try Marvin Cohen," I told Anna, "on Stillman."

Ten minutes after I hung up with Anna the phone rang again.

"Marcy!" My mother's voice shrilled through the entire house. "Telephone!"

It was Gary.

"I have tickets to the Playhouse on Saturday night," he said, foregoing small talk. "Would you like to go?"

Nearly thirty years later I still can't say "no" to such questions. I say, yes, I would like to go, but I have a meeting, a dinner party, a friend I must take to the airport. What was I supposed to tell Gary? I didn't have previous engagements at fifteen. I didn't even baby-sit.

Gary and I saw two plays together—*A Funny Thing Happened on the Way to the Forum* and *How to Succeed in Business without Really Trying*. I loved the plays and the bright, make-believe world they allowed me to enter. I didn't even mind seeing them with Gary's parents, part of the deal when he had a date. Except for Gary's stocky, square-faced father, we could have passed for deaf mutes on an outing. An older version of his son without the blushing, Marvin Cohen never noticed he did all the talking.

"Now 'Oklahoma,' there's an unforgettable story!" he crowed once, saluting us with his corned beef sandwich at Corky & Lenny's. The Cohens and I always went to Corky & Lenny's after the show. Social life in our suburb practically *began* at this bustling delicatessen that smelled sharply of cigarette smoke and briny dill pickles.

"Have you seen 'Oklahoma,' Marcy?" Mr. Cohen asked, as I took a bite of my own corned beef sandwich, which I had slathered a little too generously with mustard.

"Mmmhmmm," I managed, chewing. The youth theater had done it one summer at Cain Park.

"What do you know about that, Florence!" He grinned at his wife, a tiny woman with short hair and long bangs and a penchant for very high heels, which she usually slipped off her feet as soon as we were seated. "She's seen 'Oklahoma.' Now, Marcy, do you remember the part where Annie Oakley shoots the clay pigeons off a fence and sings 'You Can't Get a Man with a Gun?'"

"Mmmmhmmm." I replied again, nearly gasping on pungent mustard. I knew he had that song confused with another play, but I didn't want to correct him. My own father grew furious if you suggested he was wrong.

"Well, you might not have realized it, Marcy, but that was a brilliant move on the part of the writers. Absolutely brilliant, the way it helps move the plot along..."

"Oy, my feet are killing me," Mrs. Cohen observed to no one in particular, and I pictured her rubbing her sheer-stockinged soles together under the table. Gary, concentrating on his chocolate phosphate, made an accidental slurping sound through his straw and reddened to the roots of his crew cut.

My relationship with the Cohens ended after two plays. Maybe Anna's grandmother got better or the theater season ended. It wasn't anything I worried about. I spent Saturday night with my parents again, watching "Perry Como" and "Lawrence Welk," wondering what it felt like to go on a real date.

I found out what it shouldn't feel like in eleventh grade when Miss Lehmann showed the movie. The movie surpassed the *Playboy* article in its ability to excite me. I was embarrassed as much as thrilled to be aroused right in the middle of Hygiene class when I should have been absorbing an important lesson.

I understood the lesson, though. It was obvious. The girl in the movie got pregnant and then her boyfriend, who really did love her—he wasn't just dating her for sex—died in a car wreck. Most of the film showed the desperate teenage heroine struggling to conceal her ripening stomach from her parents, teachers, and friends. It would have sobered the hell out of me if I hadn't been so turned on from the part where they showed her going all the way.

An innocuous scene by today's standards: two teenagers kissing in the back of a parked convertible on a starless summer night. The moment when they *stopped* kissing titillated me, the moment when he silently urged her for more and she silently consented, and then both of them disappearing down, down onto the back seat, leaving just a 1959 Plymouth convertible with the top down and a lot of sound effects from crickets.

I didn't understand the wild feelings that movie pulled from me, but I sensed I could be in deep trouble if they cropped up near a boy. At the time, however, I couldn't imagine that happening. I hadn't been out with anyone since Gary Cohen.

Then second semester senior year, Ira Weiser focused his watery eyes on me in chemistry class. I had noticed him before, but only peripherally, the way I'd taken in the periodic table of elements on the wall or the racks of test tubes and beakers on Mr. Helmer's desk. But one spring day, after glancing my way during a lecture on charged atomic particles, Ira followed me out of the room.

"Did you get the homework assignment?" he drawled, and I turned, even though I wasn't sure he meant me. Ira stopped so suddenly he practically landed on my feet.

"We're supposed to read Chapter Five," I said. "And answer the questions on ionic bonding."

"Thanks." Ira remained rooted, staring at me while students swirled in the hall all around us.

"You're welcome." I stared back, saw a serious, dour-faced boy with a bad case of acne, and a bold way of carrying himself that suggested he thought his skin perfect.

"Could I call you tonight?" he asked purposefully. "And go over the homework?"

Ira didn't mention chemistry when he called. He had another question. Did I want to go out?

Ira was not one of the cute, popular boys I dreamed about having as my own. But he was no Gary Cohen either. He'd been out with girls before. I could tell by the way he talked and moved. He exhaled confidence in a way I never could with a bad complexion. Ira also had a car.

"What does that boy want?" my father's gravelly voice boomed out a few days later from his upstairs study. He addressed my mother, not me, but I sat just around the corner at my bedroom desk. He knew I could hear.

"What do you mean, Jack?" A wicker laundry basket creaked as my mother set the load she'd been carrying down onto the hallway floor. "What do you mean?" I felt my chest tighten as her liquid voice traveled dutifully toward his den.

"I mean, Leah, he's calling her every day and she went riding with him this afternoon in his car." How my father knew these things baffled me; he was either at work all the time or holed up in his study.

"Kids do that, Jack." I let out a slow breath, relieved to have mom on my side. Usually she didn't have any idea *what* kids did.

"But what does he want?" My father sounded angry.

"He's probably just looking for someone to invite to the prom," said my mother, a great one for speculating on motives.

"He better not have anything else in mind," my father intoned meaningfully; then mom was inside his study, closing the door, and I couldn't hear more.

My father's words troubled me. Ira wanted me, of course. And what was wrong with that? I wondered, staring dully at my chemistry book. If he asked me to the prom on top of it, well that was a glorious possibility I had never considered.

Of course I would go to the prom with him. I liked being with Ira because he seemed so pleased to be with me. On the drive we took after school in his brand new used car with all the windows open, I felt the wind soft on my arm, felt my skin tingle. Not the way it did when I read *Playboy* or saw the hygiene movie. It was a simple, exhilarating feeling that filled me with a sense of trees coming into leaf, tulips and forsythia and crocuses exploding with color. I felt larger somehow, the way I must have felt long ago when I pushed through my mother.

Ira must have felt the same excitement, because he said a thrilling, sophisticated thing while we sped along the highway. He fussed a wave of dark hair off his forehead and said, "Why don't we keep driving all night and get married in Pennsylvania?"

He also invited me to see *Goldfinger* with him on Saturday night.

How innocent we all were in those days. *Goldfinger* had a heroine named Pussy Galore and it remained a wholesome movie. But Ira and I didn't discuss Pussy or James Bond afterward at Corky & Lenny's. We talked about him, mostly. He told me about the orientation week he had attended at the University of Cincinnati, where he planned to study engineering in the fall. He told me that his SAT scores in math and science ranked among the highest in the incoming freshman class. And then, when we'd settled into his car for what I thought would be the ride home, Ira told me he knew a good place to park.

"You do?" I tried to sound cavalier so he wouldn't suspect I had absolutely no experience.

"Yes," he declared. "It's perfect, because hardly anyone knows about it and it's totally hidden from the road."

"Where is it?" I asked nervously. I knew he expected me to ask.

"I'll show you."

He drove to a temple parking lot, of all places, three miles at most from my house. A long driveway sloped up to it off of Mayfield Road, with thick stands of trees all around. Ira zipped into the place as if he owned it, which he might as well have that night; we were the only car there.

"Well." He clicked off the engine, then the lights. "What did I tell you?"

"It's private all right," I offered politely, and sat staring into darkness.

"You could move over if you want." Ira sounded polite too.

"I know," I said, but didn't move.

"Do you want me to move over there?" He sounded amused.

"Nooo," I said tentatively, so he wouldn't think me a prude. I knew Ira was supposed to remain behind the wheel.

"Well..." Ira prodded.

"We could just talk..."

"What do you want to talk about?" Ira looked at me, his studious face bathed in shadows. I could no longer tell he had acne. "The situation in Vietnam?"

"Nooo." I had only heard of Vietnam that year, knew it as a faraway, troubled place to which our country sent military advisers. It had to be the last thing Ira would want to talk about now.

"Well..." Ira prodded again, smiling faintly.

I was frozen with uncertainty, and at the same time afraid to let him know I'd never parked before, since he seemed so confident that I had. In the end I let him choreograph the thing; let him tell me to move my feet slightly to the right, my shoulders to the left, swivel my torso around just a little... It was such a strange way for me to act, I think he never knew for sure I wasn't pretending.

When I'd followed his directions and landed—in Ira's arms of course—it felt like I'd plunged from a great, frightening height onto a soft, cushiony cloud drifting in space. Ira wore a sweet/spicy aftershave. I'd smelled it at the movie, but with our bodies hugged against each other, my head on Ira's shoulder, the aroma filled my pores. I had never imagined myself alone in a boy's arms in his car. It tasted delicious and dangerous all in the same breath. What would my parents think? What would Miss Lehmann say? What about my best friend Grace, whose father didn't even let her go out with boys? My younger brother David, when he learned to drive, would never whisk a girl away from Corky & Lenny's to a place like this.

And yet, how could it be *wrong*? I wondered, every molecule in my body standing on end with the joyful excitement of being so close to a person whose molecules butterflied too. I felt good, I felt safe, I felt warm. This wasn't the hygiene movie. This was just Ira and me, dancing a slow dance in his car.

"A penny for your thoughts?" Ira penetrated our dreamy silence with a suddenly husky voice.

"I wasn't thinking anything." There was no way in the world I would answer *that* question.

"Yes, you were," he teased.

"Wasn't."

"Well, anyway..."

Another car pulled into the parking lot. I felt the vibration of its engine with one ear against Ira's chest. When I lifted my head I saw the shadow its headlights cast through the trees onto the large, domed structure of Beth Israel Temple. And in that instant I remembered my father hated Beth Israel, had refused to attend a wedding there because he said the rabbi was Communist.

"It's all right." Ira smoothed my head back onto his shoulder as the other car extinguished its lights and drifted away from us, into another section of parking lot. "What time do you have to be home?" he whispered a few moments later.

"Two o'clock," I murmured, looking up at Ira. It was such a wild number that my mother had thrown out. I don't know why she picked it. She knew we were going to an eight o'clock movie.

"Oh, then..." Ira petted my head again. "We have plenty of time."

Our house nested in total darkness when Ira and I pulled into the driveway a few minutes before two. We sat close together on the front seat, holding hands. I could still feel his body imprinted on mine, my head on his shoulder, his hands in my hair. Time had turned to butter in Ira's amazing used car. Melting, melting, melting into a golden Olympic-size pool we might have drowned in if Ira hadn't checked his watch finally and said, oh so reluctantly, "It's time to go home."

Ira got out of the car, came around to open my side. We walked close together, up the front steps.

"Goodnight," Ira said at the door. Then before I could say anything, he bent forward and kissed me.

Oh, wow! I thought, eyes closed reflexively. Wow! It was so simple, so sweet. I had no idea a kiss felt like this. Ira kissed me again before I could open my eyes. Then the porch light came on, and when I looked, my father opened the door, his face as plump and mysterious as the moon.

For a moment we all three stood there staring. Then I spoke.

"Turn off the light," I told my father through the screen door. I didn't know I would say it. It was a thought that escaped through my lips before registering in my head. I never confronted my father that way.

My father turned off the light and went away in the same silent manner he had appeared. Then Ira kissed me again.

The story doesn't end here; it begins. It begins with me floating into the house after one more kiss, sailing up the stairs—not into the lit study, where I knew my father waited, a cigarette between his lips, but to my bedroom, where I gazed into the dresser mirror, searching my face for indications of change. The girl who stared back at me had the same short brown hair I remembered, curling forward onto hopeful cheeks, the same deep brown eyes, generous eyebrows, the same expectant, trusting lips. I saw wonder on that face, a happiness that hid blemishes better than makeup could. But it was still basically me in that mirror. That's what awed me. Even though I'd crossed a great divide, it was still me.

I heard my father typing before I fell asleep. I heard him come into my room later that night. His heavy footsteps on the maple floorboards woke me. I felt his blazing flashlight on my eyes. In the morning I found his letter.

"Dear Marcy," it began. "Perhaps your mother and I have failed in some way to provide you with the values and high standards that are so important to a girl in this day and age..." The letter went on and on, referring to his disappointment in me at age seventeen, at my apparent eagerness to forget everything they had taught me and sell myself cheap to Ira. "If you think this boy, this skinny, pimply-faced boy can provide for you better than your own parents have provided for you all these years, then marry him," my father wrote. "Marry him and go live with him, and good luck to the both of you, because you don't belong under *our* roof any more, Marcy, not the way you behaved..."

My father might just as well have set fire to my room, the way I felt when I read that letter.

"What does he mean by this? Is he crazy?" I handed the letter to my mother, after a long Sunday at home in which nobody said much to me.

"If you don't know what he means," my mother replied, looking up from her ironing to glance at it briefly. "Read it again if you don't know what it means," she repeated, her dark and delicate face iced with anger.

I did read it again. I took it back upstairs to my room and read it again and again and then tore it into bits because I knew what it meant. I had been right all along, ever since sixth grade. They didn't want me to kiss boys. They didn't want me to have anything to do with them.

"Nothing happened, Mommy, really," I insisted two days later, when I called her from school during lunch period. I had never called my mother from school before. But she would barely talk to me at home. My father wouldn't speak to me either, but his was a deeper freeze I didn't dare try to penetrate. My mother, I hoped, still had warm spots.

"You were out until two a.m.," she said, in this new frozen broccoli voice of hers that made me feel much, much younger than seventeen.

"You told me I could stay out until two."

"What were you doing all that time?"

"Nothing happened, Mommy, really," I repeated, not wanting to tell her exactly what had happened. It seemed so private, so special, so much between Ira and me. "Nothing happened."

"Something happened," my mother insisted. "You wouldn't have talked to your father than way if nothing happened."

"I put my feet out in front of me and kind of swiveled to the left," I began, feeling miserable. Behind me in the school hall, people rushed past, laughing and calling out to each other with abandon. "And then I kind of landed in his arms...I mean that's all we did. I just let him hold me."

"And there was nothing else?"

Nothing else? Nothing else? How could there have been anything else? I couldn't begin to explain it to my mother, how landing in Ira's arms had been so wonderful.

"Nothing happened, Mom. Really. But I'm sorry. I'm so sorry. I'm really sorry I upset you." I knew my mother wanted me to apologize.

"Well, okay, that's better." She said it grudgingly, but her voice melted toward chicken soup. "You're supposed to be a smart girl, Marcy. We don't want you to sell yourself cheap."

"But I like Ira," I moaned. "I really like him."

"Then have some sense when you go out with him. That's all we ask," my mother said soothingly and I knew she would make things right with my father.

I went out with Ira one more time, two Saturdays later. My mother said I could go, if that's what I really wanted, but I would have to be home by midnight. My father was away on business and she promised not to tell him.

We went to another James Bond movie and the Beth Israel parking lot again. Ira said there wasn't time for Corky & Lenny's.

By then I knew Ira had asked another girl to the prom, someone he met during orientation week at the University of Cincinnati. He liked me too, he said. He hadn't known when he asked the other girl that he and I would start dating.

I can still remember sitting alone in the living room that night, waiting for Ira to pick me up. I'd washed my hair and fluffed it carefully around my face. I'd polished my nails and dressed tastefully in a simple white sleeveless blouse and full flowered skirt, a recent acquisition from my cousin Ina. I remember being excited, happy for the chance to sit close to Ira once again, to smell his spicy aftershave and let him touch me with his eyes and his hands.

I also felt uneasy, and a little guilty. Maybe he *was* taking advantage of me and I had sold myself cheap. Maybe I was wrong to want to go out with Ira.

I knew exactly what to do in the Beth Israel parking lot that night. Ira didn't have to tell me how to swivel. But it didn't feel magical when I landed in his arms. It felt like I was sitting too close to a skinny boy wearing too much cheap cologne. I felt angry. Angry at my parents for making me see him this way; angry at Miss Lehmann for showing the hygiene movie; angry at Ira for asking me out under what now seemed like false pretenses.

"I know what you really want," I told Ira, after he had been holding me about five minutes. "I know what this is really about."

"What do you mean, Marcy?" For a flash of a millisecond he looked handsome, his eyes soft and wondering, his complexion restored again by the dark.

"Let's go in the back seat, Ira, and get it over with," I said and actually began trying to climb over him. If I was going to be the girl in the hygiene movie I wanted to *feel* like the girl in the hygiene movie. I wanted to feel like I had felt when I saw the movie.

"Marcy!" He pulled me back. "Marcy, I just want to get to know you."

"Take me home, Ira," I ordered him then. "If you don't want to go into the back seat with me, take me home."

Ira looked at me for a long, silent time, as if he had just divined a new element in the periodic table, a new element which he couldn't be sure was real or fake. I looked at Ira, trying to will forth the wild sexual pull from the movie, not knowing, not knowing...it would be years, many years before I knew that the intractable excitement that movie wrung from me had much more to do with the girl than the boy.

He turned the key reluctantly and started the car.

I almost asked Jerry Grossman to the prom. We were editors together on the school newspaper and one afternoon when we were alone together in the journalism room, making up our pages, I had the perfect opportunity. I looked at Jerry, watched his long, dark eyelashes flicker beautifully as he bent over his work, and I let the moment pass, too petrified to risk rejection.

"Whatever happened to Ira Wisepimple?" my father liked to ask that spring and well into the summer, as I spent Saturday nights at home again, watching television.

I would shrug miserably, unable to look at him.

In Loco Parentis

It was as if Jack intended to go to college with me, the way he right away bought a subscription to the campus daily and jumped into the letters to the editor fray about *in loco parentis*.

I didn't know you could do that. The paper was free, dropped off like so many bulging bales of hay in practically every lobby of every building on campus. I didn't think parents could plop down money and have it mailed to their homes. I thought the *State News* belonged to students only.

"Dear sirs: As a concerned citizen and proud parent, let me be the first to congratulate the administrators of this fine university for its well-thought out policies on the welfare and well being of the young people it serves. . .especially the young <u>coeds</u>, who are at the mercy of male hormones they can neither understand nor control. . ."

What was I supposed to do? Follow the delivery truck around like a gleaner in that famous old painting, tearing out copies of the offending page until I keeled over from exhaustion? I had books to read, papers to write, professors to impress with the fact that I had been an honors student in high school—really I had—even though I couldn't understand the chapters on fruit fly propagation in nat sci or the story in American lit class about the man who turned his wedding ring around and around and *around* on his finger.

"I see your pops has another letter in print, Marcy." My roommate Lolly Quirmbach kept me posted, just in case I'd missed out. Lolly, like Jack, delighted in the rules, but for a different reason. "I get the absolutely biggest rush out of all of us bunched around the door at ten minutes to curfew, French kissing our heads off. It's such a turn-on, don't you think, Marcy?"

"I suppose," I murmured. I trained myself to react noncommittally to Lolly. It was the only way I could live with her. Lolly might not have noticed, but I was never in the one a.m. love-crush at the door. Once a boy I met at an underclass mixer walked me back to the dorm after we'd danced for a while and he'd tried—unsuccessfully— to show me how to do the monkey. He kissed me on the forehead when we reached Wonders Hall. The forehead! And mumbled something about calling me sometime. It wasn't anywhere near curfew. It wasn't even midnight.

"We can always get around the rules," Lolly would insist, with a sly kind of grin that I tried to imitate back at her. "I mean, y'all can screw your brains out for hours and still be back in the dorm by one a.m. Right?"

Right. I could only nod—horrified and secretly pleased at the same time: Lolly was the only person in the world who assumed I had a sex life.

Jack liked Lolly. She was blonde and buxom, rosy-cheeked as a cheerleader and rah rah patriotic. "We're fighting for a good cause over there, Mr. Rosen. I swear." She'd told Dad on move-in day, when he leaned into one of the pictures of her GI boyfriend she'd placed on her desk.

"You better believe it." Dad had beamed and poked Mom in the ribs, as if to say, this kid's all right, she'll be a darn good influence on Marcy.

My father had been a soldier during World War II, though he never got beyond the supply terminals of Camp Perry, Ohio. His biggest act of heroism was going AWOL to visit Leah in Cleveland. But he supported the war, never mind the post-induction eye exam where he couldn't read a thing on the chart, not even the biggest letter. ("An 'E', sir? No sir, I really can't see an E, sir.") And he supported our role in Vietnam, even had his own private theory about why we were there.

"Cinnamon. That's what this is about." Dad had marched through the house one rainy Saturday afternoon, his thumb stuck on the page in the Rand McNally Atlas that held the killer fact he believed Lyndon Baines Johnson *and* the CIA had withheld from us.

"Cinnamon?" Mom hollered from low on the kitchen floor she'd been scrubbing. I flicked off the carpet sweeper and followed Dad into the kitchen.

"You better believe it," Dad had said, his favorite expression through all those years. It was before cinnamon turned into a top-forties hit you could dance to, and I was still open to theories from my father about war. He'd raised me to believe in the absolute propriety of the good guys.

Cinnamon, let me in,
She la, la, la, la, la
La, la la, la, la, la. . .

"It says right here that cinnamon is one of Vietnam's key natural resources," Dad rambled on. "And you've seen how expensive cinnamon has gotten at the A&P."

"I thought they grew a lot of rice there." Leah rose to her feet, a dab of suds clinging to her forehead.

"Of course they grow rice." Jack reverted to his what-a-stupid-idiot-you-are tone. "But who eats rice in this country except for a few Chinese? It's cinnamon we couldn't live without if there were no Vietnam. We could live without the rice."

"Ohhhh, you're right." My mother studied the atlas reverently. It always boded better for everyone if Leah assured Jack he was right.

"You see, Marcy?" Dad flashed the bulging map of Southeast Asia in my direction, as mom renewed her scrubbing with an enlightened flourish. "You see why we have to do everything possible to win in Vietnam?"

Five potato, six potato
Seven potato eight
Give it to me, Cinnamon
I can't wait. . .

Lolly turned her desk top into a kind of living shrine for Cpl. George Wilson Wencel, the nineteen year old marine she had dated since before they were both fourteen. Photos everywhere, a total art gallery, the biggest ones standing in gilded eight by ten frames: George in uniform, alone, and then entwined with Lolly in the grand and stately lobby of a downtown Atlanta hotel.

"We spent the night together there the day before he shipped out," Lolly told me. "It was sooo beautiful, Marcy," she said. "So silky and sweet. The biggest bed we'd ever slept in."

I was dying to know more about Lolly's sex life. I didn't know anyone my age who slept with boys *and* talked about it. My best friend Grace from high school had a stricter father than mine; he didn't let her go out with boys. The two of us spent prom night at her house, playing chess and making double chocolate fudge brownies and devouring the whole panful between us. There were girls I knew who had *reputations*, and all I knew about them was what other people said. Susan Sutter, they said, wouldn't say no to anyone and Deena Berman was who boys went out with if they only wanted sex. I couldn't believe it about Deena. She was Jewish and my mother had told me over and over again that Jewish girls always, always waited for marriage. I was sure when people said that Deena slept with boys, it meant she only *slept,* maybe cuddled up against them.

And here was Lolly Quirmbach, my actual college roommate, come all the way up from the red Baptist soil of Macon, Georgia, to attend Michigan State University—telling me—literally telling me that she not only had sex with the boy she had dated since back in ninth grade, but also with boys she met randomly on campus and barely knew. It was the equivalent of living with the roar of Niagara Falls always in your ear and a daredevil beside you who would gladly ride over it in a barrel.

Sometimes on Saturday nights when she went out with Leonard or Steven or Carl or whoever—it was a revolving door of names I couldn't keep straight—I'd sit at her desk and study the photos, wondering what it would be like to be Lolly. I'd start with the earliest pictures—Lolly and George, the both of them with braces and bangs, pitching a tent on a camping trip or riding the church bus with the Sunday school choir. They looked like friendly cousins or something, both of them smiling and whooping it up. I couldn't imagine them naked and on top of each other.

In the prom pictures things took a different shape. There were four proms—his junior and then hers; her senior and then his. They lived in different neighborhoods, went to different schools. The common denominator, Lolly told me, had been church, where you weren't supposed to smoke, drink, dance or think about sex—even if you were horny.

Oh, Lolly, in your smashing green or red or blue or aquamarine empire-waisted gown, your body filling out the fabric in more delightful ways with each passing prom. Your boyfriend at your side, his body fuller, shoulders broader and stiffer and more soldierly-to-be with every year. If you couldn't dance at the prom, what did you do? Did you sneak away from the party to a bedroom refuge provided by a commiserative friend whose parents had gone out for the night—most likely to chaperone the prom. Did you throw off your grown-up clothes, find the record player, find the Beatles albums, wait for your favorite song of songs, "I Want to Hold Your Hand," before you actually let George inside?

Lolly told me she liked to "do it" to that song. She told me lots of things I always wanted to know about sex but was afraid to ask. She was a regular Dr. David Reuben, before he even wrote his book.

"You can do it standing up, did you know that Marcy?" Lolly once confided, looking up from a textbook she'd been staring at and staring at, pages unturned. Why oh why, did she and I always talk so much about sex? Actually she talked. I nodded, and drank it all in. "And you can do it in the shower, but you don't want to do it in the bathtub or a swimming pool, because if the angle's funny or the pressure not just right, one of you might explode."

Sometimes I'd throw a bathrobe on over my long nightgown as one a.m. approached, and pad into the lounge to watch the boys waltz the girls home. I'd keep my eyes peeled for Lolly, noticing how she lost herself in the arms of the boy she was with. There were always a few girls on the floor who ended their Saturday nights this way, peering through the dark, glassy windows at the spectacle four flights below, every one of us imaging ourselves in someone else's shoes.

Whether I watched or didn't watch, I hightailed it up to my top bunk before Lolly strolled in, pulled the covers up to my chin and feigned sleep. I didn't want her to know I'd been waiting up. She'd step into the room and take off all her clothes—every last stitch—and pad back and forth around the place until she finally fell into bed. If I rolled over quietly onto my stomach, I could peer down through the space between mattress and headboard and watch her light a cigarette, white-blonde hair cascading over the pillow. She'd lie on top of the covers, taking in deep, urgent puffs that practically lit up the whole room. I watched Lolly smoke until she snuffed the last embers out.

I wanted to be Lolly. To go out on dates with different boys every night and be loved by another boy, who was fighting for our country in Vietnam. I wanted to be as cool about it as Lolly, as unconcerned about who called, and how many times, and *thanks for taking messages, Marcy. You're so sweet to do it. Will you tell him I'll call as soon as I have a chance?*

I didn't know how Lolly knew all these boys. I didn't know any, except the one who'd walked me home from the Shaw Hall mixer early fall quarter, and who I hadn't seen since. It was such a huge campus, with its own bus system and networks of bicycle paths and complexes of multi-storied dorms and classrooms. You didn't run into people on a campus this size. You got lost, had to stop every so often your first weeks in school, to look at the map they handed out at freshman orientation.

That's a way to meet a boy, my mother suggested by letter, her new way of providing advice I couldn't use. *Ask him for directions*, my mother wrote, *and try to look sexy.*

Sexy? What did she mean? Stick my chest out? Light a cigarette? The most I could hope for in terms of sexy was skin without oil; hair without frizz; a face that didn't vibrate with lost-girl vibrato. If I could have found the *right* boy, maybe I would have asked: Hey, where's Erickson? Isn't it supposed to be near the chemistry building? And here I am—ha, ha—standing right in front of Shaw, which we both know—ha, ha—is a guy's dorm.

Why couldn't I talk to guys that way? Why did I get so pathetically nervous and scared when it came time to talk to a boy who might possibly like me? I had a brother, after all, and he had friends and I had no trouble talking to *them*...at least until the day David had to pull Arnie Rockawicz off of me, because of an unlucky remark I'd made about Arnie and balls. I'd meant *base*ball, *basket*ball, *foot*ball. I was twelve years old. What did I know about double entendres? But Arnie was younger than I, and he knew.

If I would have run into Kent Hopkins again—the boy from the mixer—I would have asked *him* for directions. He had exquisite blue eyes, sandy hair and a name I'd never heard of on anyone but Superman. Superman! Now, why didn't I say *that* to him? Hey, Kent, why don't you pop into that phone booth over there and change into your Superman clothes? My name is Lois Lane, by the way. You know, Lois Lane, star newspaper reporter, who has the biggest crush on Superman.

Kent grew up on a farm near Owosso, less than forty miles from campus. I looked into Kent's blue eyes and imagined the sweet scent of clover and hay and dairy cows, wondered what it would be like to live on a farm and maybe gather fresh eggs from the chickens in the morning and again at dusk. I had always had a secret desire to run barefoot through tall grass, to lie on my back in the middle of a field and squint up at the sky, to be one of the kids who got to sleep on a cot near the prize-winning animals in the 4H barn at the county fair.

I had already decided that I could live on a farm if my husband wanted to be a farmer, when Kent told me he had come to Michigan State to get away from that life.

"I'm going to get my HRI degree and never look back." Kent had shouted so I could hear him above the roar of Herman's Hermits and the thunder of dancing feet in the big bean shaped room that doubled as Shaw's cafeteria.

"I think it would be wonderful to live on a farm," I yelled back, because this is what I had been thinking, and I couldn't switch gears just because of Kent's sudden interest in hotel, restaurant and institution management.

"Well, it's not," Kent replied and then he asked me to dance, sparing us the task of making further conversation.

HRI was *Lolly's* major. The secret weapon she had used to persuade her Baptist minister dad to let her go to school this far away from Georgia. What if Kent knew Lolly? I thought as Kent and I wriggled around the dance floor with all the others, and the Hermits sang, "Hen er y the Eighth I am I am." What if they had Econ 101 together or wound up working the same shift over at Kellogg Center? Sooner or later all the HRI majors had to put in time prepping food or waiting tables or clerking the front desk at Kellogg Center. What if Kent called our room some day, wanting Lolly, not me? What would I say to him? It wasn't anything I should have worried about. But I did worry about it. I worried so much about what I would say to Kent if he called our room asking for Lolly that I couldn't think of anything to say to him now.

"What's your major, Marcy?" Kent asked, as he walked me back to the dorm from the mixer after a couple more dances, one of them the monkey I couldn't learn to do.

"Undeclared." I shrugged, laughed, hoping he didn't think less of me for being undecided. I hadn't expected him to walk me back to the dorm.

Kent laughed too. "Why'd you come all the way from Ohio to go to MSU?" he asked. "You got relatives in Michigan?"

"No." I shook my head. "I've never even been to Michigan before this year."

"You should have gone to Ohio State," Kent said. "It would have been a lot cheaper." My heart jumped off the high board into an empty swimming pool, drained for the winter. Kent didn't like me. If he liked me, why would he think I should go to Ohio State? If he didn't like me, why was he walking me back to the dorm? Was he just extra polite, from having grown up on a farm?

"My father wanted me to go to MSU." I didn't know what else to say. It was true. I didn't pick this school.

"Your father?" We had come to a woodsy bend in the Red Cedar River, the most romantic part of a campus divided into ivy covered old section; concrete and glass new section; and a gigantic future section way the hell over on Hagedorn Road, devoted to cropland, greenhouses and barns.

"Yeah, my dad decided I should go to Moo U." I used the term the fans from the other side bleated at football games.

"So you could major in ag science and live on a farm?" Kent asked and I couldn't tell if he was making fun of me or just trying to be funny. We had stopped walking, stood on the path near a particularly thick willow, its long weepy branches trailing over us. Kent approached the tree and leaned against it; and I stepped right up beside him.

"My father likes the HRI school," I said, suddenly unable to formulate a sentence without the word "father" in it. "He came here for a meeting a couple of summers ago with a bunch of other accountants, and he and my mom stayed at Kellogg Center and my father was very impressed with the way they ran everything, and he started telling me I should apply here."

"Did you apply anywhere else?" I could discern the vague edges of Kent's friendly face, but not the searching blue of his eyes, as he gazed down at me in the dark.

"My father said I should just apply to MSU. He said I would have a good chance of getting in."

"And what did your father decide you should major in?"

"My father thinks I should major in home economics," I said, a little embarrassed, because I had no interest in home economics. "I decided to try it, because my father's second choice is nursing and I really think I would hate that."

"What would *you* like to major in?" Kent asked politely, moving us away from the tree and back on the path, as if whatever bus we had been waiting for had come and gone.

"Well, English, of course, but my father says college is for learning a trade." I assumed Kent would agree, since he'd chosen HRI. "My father says classes where you only think about things are a waste of time...and anyways I can't for the life of me understand James Joyce or D.H. Lawrence, but my father says he's glad I can't and..."

It went on and on that way until we got back to the dorm and Kent kissed my forehead and said he would call. My father, my father, my father. I couldn't start or end a sentence without those two words. I hated my father. I hated my father for choosing this school where I felt lost all the time and didn't understand what the professors talked about. I hated my father for writing letters to the editor supporting curfews, supporting mandatory sign-out sheets for girls; supporting the feet-must-be-on-the-floor-at-all-times rule for boy-girl dorm room visitations. I hated my father for writing long, single-spaced typewritten letters to me every few days, fishing around for information about exactly how I spent my time. I hated my father. Why then, could I think of nothing else to talk about to Kent besides my father? Everybody else's answer that year was blowing in the wind. How come my answer was always him?

"You really shouldn't be such a grind, Marcy," Lolly said one day at dinner, winter quarter. We didn't usually eat together. We lived in a coed dorm—boys in one wing, girls in the other, cafeteria for everyone right down the middle. Usually Lolly ate at a table of boys. She was the sort of girl who didn't hang out with other girls much.

"You should go out more on weekends," Lolly persisted. "You know, have fun." When she said the word "fun" her whole beautiful face exploded into a kind of soft, carefree cloud, creased with a knowledge of fun as I had never known it. Yes. Of course. I wanted to have fun. I wanted to be happy.

"I have fun." I forced a smile, poking my fork into a Wonders Hall meat cutlet of indeterminate origins.

"You don't mean with Caroline Custer?" Lolly's cloud of a face took a cumulus turn, vapors swirling upon vapors into serious doubt.

"Caroline Custer is fun to be with," I replied. "So are Shellie Paulson and Laura DeVries and Judy Hart and Debbie..." I was developing a circle of friends. Some of them had boyfriends who monopolized their time. But Caroline didn't. And Judy didn't, though she went home to Grand Rapids almost every weekend because she said she had trouble studying on campus.

Caroline didn't go home. She was from Macon, Georgia, just like Lolly, and they had gone to the same high school, the same church.

"I'm who Lolly was *supposed* to be roommates with," Caroline had told me one wintry afternoon, walking across campus after Food Prep 101. "I promised her father I would look after her."

"You did?"

Caroline had her whole life mapped out. She was going to be a missionary in Africa some day and teach people there how to cook macaroni and cheese and sew gingham aprons to wear while preparing it. So of course she chose home economics as a major and, as luck would have it, wound up cooking alongside me, the actual roommate of her ex-friend Lolly.

"Well, yes, we had agreed to list each other as preferred roommates," Caroline said. "Which I did. And Lolly obviously didn't."

"Well, it could have been a mistake." I wondered if this meant we would have to trade, and I would no longer spend Saturday nights at the George Wilson Wencel shrine. There were new pictures now: George in his flak jacket, returning from night patrol; George and a buddy, spooning c-rations from little cans in front of a sandbag bunker; George on top of a steep, rocky hill called Nui Loc Son, longing for the views of Lolly I would lose if we didn't share a room.

"Oh, it was no mistake," Caroline insisted. "I asked her a long time ago if she wanted to switch and she said if she did, she would let me know."

Caroline spent her free time at the Southern Baptist Student Center on Harrison Road, a short walk from our complex of freshmen dorms on the southwest end of campus. All that winter as we cooked together in the home ec kitchen, she would urge me to go over there with her.

"There's never any debauched music blaring to break your concentration," Caroline insisted. "It's a perfect place to study."

"I'll think about it," I said, though it was the furthest thought from my mind as we stood over work tables in our official snap-up-the-front white smocks and mesh hairnets that helped to separate this sort of home economics from the home economics they taught in high school. Girls who took home ec in high school ratted their hair so tall they couldn't put hairnets on it. Girls who took home ec in high school weren't considered college material. In college the stakes were high. Stakes. Not steaks. We never cooked steaks—too expensive, I suppose, even for college, though we did learn how to use a broiler. And how to mix muffins that didn't have tunnels and souffles that didn't fall—until at least a few minutes after they came out of the oven. We learned the difference between sauces thickened with cornstarch and sauces thickened with flour, and the various effects of dry heat and wet heat and French fry heat on chicken (though to this day, I don't know what to do with the used up grease). And we learned how to set a table for a formal tea, never mind that women's consciousness raising was just around the corner.

I embarrassed myself to death the day we made vanilla fondant. I'd never made candy before, had never even seen a candy thermometer. I couldn't tell when one was in a plastic case that should be removed before you plunged it into hot bubbling sugar. I grew up inside a protective case myself, and anything beyond its shiny, concave surface always seemed a little bent and distorted and fogged up. I thought that was the way the world looked, and of course I was plenty near-sighted. Like my father.

"Marcy I don't believe y'all forgot to take that thermometer out of its case," Caroline exclaimed, in a deep southern drawl that was much deeper than Lolly's, even though they came from the exact same place. "Imagine all that plastic smooshing right into your candy!"

"I didn't forget to take it out, Caroline," I said. "I didn't know you were supposed to." We were walking back to the dorms again, crunching along the path that led past Beaumont Tower, its trusty carillon ringing out the five o'clock hour. There was a saying on campus that you weren't really a coed until a boy kissed you under Beaumont Tower at midnight.

"Marcy you are a stitch," Caroline exclaimed again in a voice so loud you could hear it above the bells, and I imagined all the students on the footpaths around us were listening. "You would be so much fun at our get-togethers over at the Baptist Center. You really should come with me sometime."

"Are you an official coed, Caroline?" I asked, as much to change the subject as because I wanted to know. I wanted to know if I wasn't the only one on this whole campus who hadn't been initiated.

"Of course I'm an official coed," Caroline replied at the top of her lungs. But I'm almost positive she had no idea what I was talking about. How could she, considering where she spent so much time?

"Watch out for Caroline Custer," Lolly said that day at dinner, more Georgia inflexion in her voice than usual, as if dredging up Caroline brought her closer to home. "She'll turn you into an asexual like herself."

"Oh I told her from the start I'm not interested in converting," I blurted, realizing too late, that Lolly wasn't talking about religion.

"I don't believe you sometimes, Marcy Rosen," Lolly laughed. She had a beautiful laugh, teeth blazing white against snowy complexion, her voice filled with melt-in-your-mouth pleasure that had no edge to it at all—not the least bit of superiority or condescension. "You don't really know anything about sex, do you? How in the world do you get on with your boyfriend back home?"

"I don't have a boyfriend back home." Lolly's laughter seemed to have an effect on me, like truth serum and I just kept talking and talking, divulging more information than I ever did in the tiny confines of our room. "Well, I mean, I had a boyfriend, if you count Ira Weiser. We went out a few times, but he only had ONE thing on his mind. And we wound up making out in his car in a synagogue parking lot, of all places. And then he took another girl to the prom."

Lolly didn't say anything for a long time, and I began to worry that the Baptist in her considered me blasphemous for necking on synagogue property. Or maybe she just thought it blasphemous that there were synagogues at all. But finally she scrunched her napkin up into a little ball, and made a face that seemed to say, well-who-cares-about-Ira-Weiser-anyway, isn't-he-ancient- history?

"I know plenty of boys who would like to go out with you," Lolly volunteered at last, her long white-blonde hair shimmering against an expression of unguarded friendliness. "I'd be happy to fix you up, you know...if you ever get your fill of dear old Caroline."

It didn't seem like a good time to tell Lolly about the Pat Boone hootenannies they had over at the Baptist Center on Friday nights, and how someone always kept the stone fireplace blazing in the big first floor lounge, and after the singing you could pull the overstuffed couches up to the fire, or sit on blankets and roast marshmallows and drink hot chocolate and talk about anything you wanted to about student life. And how I went there one Thursday to study, and it was quiet enough to concentrate, and a much quicker walk than to the library on a cold winter's night.

I might have made a good Baptist had I been born that way. I could live without all the things they didn't allow—drinking, swearing, smoking, dancing. Oh, I loved dancing, but my body hated it, twisted all over itself like a salted pretzel when I tried to let go to the music.

"Dancing is lascivious," Caroline insisted at one of the little talkabouts, and I silently made note of another word I would have to look up, though as the conversation continued, I began to catch the drift.

"It's not the act itself, but what it makes you think of," offered a buttoned-up girl named Gloria, who had a habit of sitting with her arms pressed against her chest.

"Doesn't everything make you think about IT?" This one boy asked, taking the words right out of *my* mouth. There were about seven other people in the circle and they all just looked at him and groaned, "Oh, Billy," almost in unison. Even Penelope Bly, a squarish faced graduate student with thick auburn hair halfway down her back, released an exasperated sigh. Penelope played the guitar for the singalongs and functioned as an advisor around that place.

"But doesn't it?" Billy persevered, shaking overgrown bangs out of his eyes. Caroline, who happened to be sitting next to him, rapped him on the head with the flat of her palm like in "The Three Stooges." Billy shook his hair again and kind of honked, by way of laughter.

"My English professor finds it everywhere," I ventured, thinking this as good a time as any to broach a topic that had been troubling me. "I mean, he claimed all those passages in D.H. Lawrence about flowers opening, figs bursting through their skins, ripe apples dropping from trees, are about sex, not plant life."

"What a dirty mind *he* has," Gloria exclaimed.

"No wonder your father wrote that letter to the *State News* complaining about the English department," added Caroline.

"My father?" How had we gotten to the subject of Jack Rosen in *this* place? Shouldn't it have been Daddy-proofed by the big cross on the front lawn, the pictures inside of Jesus at various stages of his tortured career?

"That *was* your father who wrote that letter?" Caroline bent her forthright, future missionary face into my line of vision. "I only noticed a couple of other Rosens in the university directory."

"He's kind of a letter writer," I allowed, feeling my face growing hot.

"Don't be embarrassed, Marcy. He was totally justified," Caroline said, and everyone nodded with the solemnity of judges—even Billy.

"We had quite a discussion over your father's letter when it came out," Gloria informed me, arms pressed protectively against her chest.

"You did?"

"Actually all his letters raise important issues about student life," said Penelope Bly, offering a bag of marshmallows around the circle.

All his letters?

"Do you think your father might be interested in speaking to us?" Penelope asked. "The next time he comes up to visit you."

I forced two marshmallows onto a long fork and followed a few of the others over toward the fireplace.

"We could offer a small honorarium."

My marshmallows bloomed with a big jagged flame that I just stared at for several long seconds.

"Would you ask him for us?" Penelope knelt down beside me with her own roasting fork.

"My father is a deaf mute," I said finally, blaspheming myself in front of all those God-fearing people. "He could talk and hear if he wanted to, that's the weird thing. The doctors can't find anything physically wrong with him. Something must have happened to him when he was a child." And with that I pulled the glob of charred, sticky goo off my fork and popped it into my mouth.

When spring quarter rolled around and everything alive started bursting through its skin à la D.H. Lawrence, they substituted bible study for hootenannies at the Baptist Student Center. Caroline forgot to tell me this. I showed up to sing one Friday night and she welcomed me with the most beneficent expression, as if I had just made a miraculous recovery from cancer. I waited until they got into a tizzy over something God said in Genesis to Adam and Eve and I left.

D.H. Lawrence couldn't have created a lusher scene than the MSU campus that spring: Trees turned sweet shades of green. Forsythia yellowed the winding paths along the Red Cedar River; ivy once again insisted its way up the dark brick buildings on the old part of campus. Everywhere, but everywhere, couples sauntered about, arms wrapped around one another with an urgency I had seen on maybe one or two couples back in high school, but never in my wildest dreams, multiplied to the fifteen thousandth power.

Even I cut classes to lie beside Lolly in the field across the street from the dorms, worshipping the sun in our respective bathing suits along with dozens of other coeds on any given day. Lolly camped out in that field almost every afternoon, straps undone on her bikini top, metal reflector trained on her face to intensify the rays. I quickly grew restless and sweaty and bored, unable to concentrate on a book in that heat. But after a few visits my complexion rallied for the first time in months and I told Lolly that if her offer still stood, I was ready to be fixed up.

I don't remember his name. Maybe I do. Maybe I have wanted too much to forget it, even though as we all four piled into the black Volkswagen bug that waited outside Wonders Hall that Saturday night, I worked very hard to memorize the moment.

Lolly looked ravishing as usual, in a mauve wraparound cotton skirt and silky white blouse she had ironed that afternoon, carefully smoothing out the material of each long sleeve before applying heat, so as not to make any irregular creases. The blouse shimmered against her long, white-blonde hair and bronzed face. I wore a pretty blouse and full skirt too. Lolly had told me that's how girls dressed for fraternity parties.

The car belonged to Anders Somerfield, a tall, lanky boy with closely-cropped hair and ears that stuck out just a little. He was a senior, from a well-off suburb near Detroit. Lolly had been seeing him almost exclusively that term, even though other boys called and George still sent letters and photos that pretty much filled up whatever surface area remained of her desk.

Lolly slid into the front seat and this other boy—let's call him Geoffrey. Yes, Geoffrey with a G. Geoff opened the back door for me and bounced in beside me, draping his right arm across the back of the seat, not exactly touching me, but his arm felt heavy on my shoulders nonetheless.

I wanted to ask him to move his arm, but didn't want to get things off on the wrong foot. So I leaned forward a little. Geoffrey leaned forward too, and I sat back because it felt better to have his arm hanging over me than his whole body brushing into me. What can I say? It was my first real date since high school and I was nervous.

"We rent a place in the country for our spring parties," Geoffrey said, as we headed south on Hagedorn Road into cornfield country. "When it's spring time in Michigan, you know," he laughed, "everyone wants to be in the country."

"I'm from Ohio," I said, to keep the conversation rolling. I wasn't sure what to say. And Lolly wasn't much help, since she kept falling over the gearbox, whispering things into Anders' ear that made them both laugh hysterically.

"But when it's springtime in Ohio, Marcy, do you like to be in the country?" Geoffrey pressed. He was self-assured, had the ruddy good looks of a person who pursued wind bent sports like sailing and skiing, and owned all the right clothes for them.

"If I'm ever in Ohio again in the springtime," I said, not having the slightest idea what I meant, "I'll be sure to head for the country."

"I bet you went to Florida over spring break." Geoffrey grinned broadly. "You seem like the sort of girl who could spend a whole week on the beach without a care in the world."

"I do?" I wondered if Geoffrey was teasing me, but I couldn't tell.

"Why didn't I run into you down there?" Geoffrey mused.

"'Where the boys are...'" Lolly started singing à la Sandra Dee. So apparently she had an ear tuned to the backseat after all. She swiveled around to look at us—me leaning back under Geoffrey's arm, him leaning forward. And she flashed this big playful grin at me as if to say, "Aren't you the lucky one, Marcy Rosen, going out with this hunky junior, no less, instead of staying home for the one millionth Saturday night and climbing the lonely cement walls of the room."

"I thought about going to Florida," I lied to Geoffrey finally, after Lolly stuck her lovely nose back into the front seat. "But I didn't want to ask my parents, you know, for more money."

"My dad's well fixed," Geoffrey chimed back. "He makes about twenty grand a year as an engineer for GM. He can afford a few extra bucks to keep me happy for a week after almost a whole year here of hard labor.

"How much does *your* dad make?" Geoffrey asked a few seconds later, more like a kid comparing lunch box sandwiches, than a snob, I think. He just seemed used to conversations about the cost of things.

"My dad's an accountant for a paint company in Cleveland," I said, not really wanting to talk about you-know-who. And I had no idea how much Jack made, though I would have figured it at half as much as Geoffrey's father, based on the difference in the things they could afford.

"So what'd you do for fun spring break, if you didn't go to Lauderdale?"

"Hung around home. Saw my friend Grace. Went shopping downtown with my Mom."

"Fun." Geoffrey said, and again I wondered if he was teasing.

Fortunately we arrived at the party and we didn't have to talk about fun any more or Florida, or about the shopping trip with my Mom which hadn't been fun at all, once we'd sat down face to face in the May Company snack bar and she started grilling me about my nonexistent sex life.

"Your father says we don't have any idea at all what you do in college." Leah peered at me crookedly through her new bifocals.

"I go to classes, Mom. I study. I eat. I sleep. I get up and go to classes." I sipped at my chocolate malted, trying to act nonchalant.

"Don't be flip," Mom said. "You're two hundred fifty miles from home, on your own, and we have no way of knowing what you're doing."

"I go to meetings at the Baptist church." I said. "They talk about the evils of the flesh."

"Don't be flip, Marcy." Mom repeated sadly, pushing her barely touched malted aside. "Your father says we don't have any idea at all what you're doing in college."

"Didn't I call home the night I melted the thermometer?" I demanded brusquely. "Didn't I tell you about that?"

"You've changed, Marcy," my mother said. "You're not the same girl we sent to college."

I'm not? I wondered silently, not having changed so much that I wouldn't let my mother have the last word in a public conversation.

The thing I remember most about the party was the silver keg sitting on the floor in the middle of the room like a giant sun god, and everybody rotating vociferously around it.

"What is this place?" I asked Geoffrey when he brought me some beer in a big plastic cup, foam rising to its lip. I had to shout and even then I couldn't quite hear my own voice above the record player somebody had turned up full blast.

"It's a VFW Hall," Geoffrey shouted back. "An uncle of one of our brothers is a member."

"And he lets you use it for parties?" I sounded like a Baptist, quizzing Geoffrey on the mores and manners of fraternity life. Or worse, I sounded like my mother.

"Why not?" Geoffrey slugged down some beer and leaned into my ear so he wouldn't have to shout. "A lot of the guys will be members some day...*if* they make it back from 'Nam. Me, I'm not going. My grades are good. I'm going to grad school for as long as it takes."

"Lolly has a friend there." I meant Vietnam, not grad school, but Geoffrey got my drift.

"Oh yes," he nodded grimly. "I know all about George. And why don't you drink your beer, Marcy, before it goes flat on you?"

I had never tasted beer before. I'd tasted champagne. On two different occasions. Once after a piano recital when I was fourteen, and the other time at a wedding for a relative I barely knew on my mother's side. They had a fountain at the wedding with pink champagne punch dancing out of arched spigots into crisscrossing rivers that ran back up into the fountain, and even though I was only twelve years old at the time, no adult batted an eye when I held a fluted cup under the spigots again and again. But my father said it wasn't really champagne because by the time it flowed in and out of the spigots so many times it lost all of its kick. And besides, he said, these relatives were so c-h-e-a-p, they wouldn't have added much champagne in the first place. Kool-Aid, Dad said. It was nothing more than Kool-Aid.

I drank the beer Geoffrey handed me, pretending it was like punch from a wedding fountain that wouldn't make me drunk. But even my wild imagination struck a hard place when my mouth filled with a wet, sour fizz that tasted like something you'd washed your socks in.

"Hey, drink up, and let's dance." Geoffrey nudged me with his elbow, and actually tilted the cup up towards my mouth. "Don't be shy. There's plenty more where that came from."

The time I had champagne—real champagne—after my piano recital, my father danced with me at night in our backyard, which sounds strange to tell, but it made sense then and even seemed romantic, the way he held me so close against a world spinning upside down, and I felt like a very little girl and an almost grown woman, both at the same time.

I wasn't a girl anymore. And as my own mother had implied just a few weeks before, I wasn't even a nice one. But I didn't feel at all like a woman, spending night after weekend night in the dorm waiting for the other girls to come home from their good times. And I wanted to be a woman. So I drank the beer and danced with Geoffrey in a crowd of people I didn't know, except for Lolly and possibly Anders, both of whom had long since disappeared into the dark fringes of the room. I saw momentary flashes of Lolly's white blonde hair, heard her laughter plash above the screeching words I couldn't quite make out in the latest song we danced to.

"Don't you *love* Bob Dylan?" Geoffrey asked, his whole body rocking, rocking very close to mine.

"Oh sure," I agreed, thinking, *Bob Dylan, Bob Dylan*. That must be who we're dancing to. "But I always get him confused with Dylan Thomas," the budding English major in me blurted drunkenly and Geoffrey kissed me, actually kissed me on the mouth.

"You're a funny kid," he said, pulling me close to him, pulling me close.

I forgot my fear of slow dancing, forgot my fear of fast dancing, slow dancing, fast dancing.

By the time John Denver started singing ever so sweetly, Geoffrey held me almost as close as my father had held me the night we celebrated my piano recital and drank champagne, and the world spun out from under me in almost the same way. Except instead of the flowers and new grass of our backyard in Cleveland, I smelled spilt beer and eddies of sickness from where somebody had heaved-ho, short of the bathroom.

"I'm leaving on a jet plane, don't know when I'll be back again. Oh, babe, I hate to go..."

"Geoffrey. Geoffrey." I leaned into him now, with the most relaxed casualness, the way he had already been leaning into me. "Geoffrey, I'm not even an official coed and it's spring term and I've never been kissed at Beaumont Tower at midnight."

"Now I know you're putting me on," Geoffrey said, but his eyes sparkled with the cleverness of my idea.

He had to borrow a car. Anders and Lolly were nowhere to be found. I actually thought they might have left without us, but Geoffrey said, no, no, the VW was still in the lot so they must have just gone for a walk. "And don't worry about your roommate, she can take care of herself, believe me." Geoffrey seemed almost angry as he said it, turning the key in the ignition of a big, cozy car that didn't have bucket seats, so of course, I slid as far away from the passenger door as I could and started singing.

I'm Geoffery the Eighth I am
Geoffery the Eighth, I am, I am
I got married to the widow next door.
She's been married seven times before
And ev'ry one was a Geoffery
She wouldn't have a Willie or a Sam
I'm her eighth old man named Geoffery
Geoffery the Eighth I am.

"I'm not drunk, am I?" I kept asking, in between choruses of my favorite Herman's Hermits hit, twisting it back to "Hen er y the Eighth" on a few go 'rounds, with just the slightest twinge of regret for Kent, who had asked me to dance when they played that song at the Shaw Hall mixer.

So we stood at the base of Beaumont Tower, the only couple there on that balmy spring night and Geoffrey kissed me and kissed me again when the bells chimed out midnight and kissed me again when the bells finished ringing, dusting his tongue into my half open mouth and I jumped a bit because it was the first time anyone had French kissed me.

"C'mon," Geoffrey urged throatily and took my hand and I let him lead, the way I had done when we'd danced together, and I shouldn't have been surprised—should I have been surprised?—that instead of heading up Stadium Road toward the dorm, he turned onto West Circle Path toward the ag building and the journalism school, and the large wooded expanse beyond that bordered the Red Cedar River.

This is the part where there's nothing more to tell, unless I want to remember that his name wasn't Geoffrey and that I don't remember what his name was. And what was he doing on top of me so suddenly, and me lying on my back in the grass and trying to squirm out from under him, until he soothed me with his lips and his tongue and his hand moving down my breasts and under my skirt and up my legs and me thinking, this is what everyone does, what every boy wants, and it must be my turn, and why not get it over with, and find out what it's like, and him pushing and pushing into me and saying, *thank god you're not a technical virgin like your roommate,* and whispering, *Oh, oh, god, oh yes, yes, ohhhh...*

And once when I was thirteen years old, walking home from school, a man passed me in his car on the quiet, darkening street and then turned around and parked, and got out of his car and walked toward me with something very white and very large and wrong protruding from his pants. I had never seen anything like it and didn't know it could get so big and fleshy, and when he got close enough for me to understand exactly what it was, he said, "Do you like it?" I started running and running and didn't stop for two blocks until I arrived, panting and aching at my own front door.

And that's all I could think about in however long or short a time it took for Geoffrey to finish saying, *oh god, oh, yes, ohhh...*

That's all I could think about: the man from five years ago saying, "Do you like it?"

I called my parents the next day. How could I not? The dorm was as still as a tomb, and it hurt when I walked and it hurt when I looked inside a book or didn't look inside a book, and I forgot to go to the cafeteria for breakfast or lunch and didn't eat anything until five o'clock when I bought a strawberry shake in the grill, half expecting to see Anders and Lolly at one of the tables, their books sprawled all over the place, their bare feet tapping against one another, as they drank coffee and smoked and talked about everything but the chapters they were supposed to be reading.

"There's been a terrible accident," I told my mother, who answered the phone, and she right away started screaming for my father to pick up, and I had to repeat it when he got on the line with a cheerful, "Hello, dere."

"There's been a terrible accident," I said.

Nobody had ever told me that Volkswagens had an engine in the back instead of a trunk, an engine that could explode like a bomb if you were rushing down Hagedorn Road to get back to the dorm before curfew and then the light started to change and you almost went through it, but slammed on the brakes instead and the car behind you, rushing too, crashed into you with more firepower than the bouncing Betty land mine that George Wilson Wencel would step on just a few weeks later.

"There wasn't anything left of anyone," I said.

"Stay in Cleveland next year," my mother said. "You can go to Western Reserve."

"Reserve doesn't have a home ec school," my father said.

"I'm not going to major in home ec any more," I said, relieved to follow my parents onto this inconsequential tangent, because I would never, never tell them what had happened to *me*, and how it had happened without even a definite struggle. If my parents knew, I might as well have been in that Volkswagen too. I would have been as dead to them as Lolly.

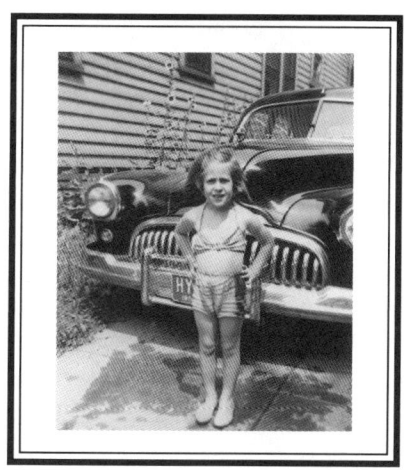

Policeman's Wife

Marriage made me homesick. Gregory worked nights and I worked days and his free time rotated, so he only had weekends off every six weeks. In the beginning, whenever this occurred, we visited my parents in Cleveland. Gregory didn't mind. He never seemed to notice that they didn't like him.

It was the height of the Watergate scandal and Gregory and my father would stay up late talking politics. They both adored Nixon, Haldeman, Erhlichman, and the whole break-in crew, especially G. Gordon Liddy, the spy who refused to talk and went proudly to jail. I wonder what Gregory thinks now that Liddy's a radio jock with a national call-in show. Maybe he phones in all the time, championing conservatism in his ghetto guise the way he did on other shows when we were dating. I envision him clutching the phone with one hand, scratching himself through his Fruit of the Looms with the other—for the benefit of his latest girlfriend.

"Now y'all see here," he begins in a resonant southern drawl that no one could mistake for a white voice. "Ahm jus a po' ol' man so maybe mah word don' count fo' much. But ah invites any of them white lib'rals to come down to *this* neihbrohood and get they own fill of them young welfare mothers churning out childrens like they some kind of gran' tribute to the gross national product..."

He probably goes on about the gangbangers too, "refusin' to work and cryin' out brutality all the times when the pohleese tries to do his job." That's the script Gregory used twenty years ago when he called the Howard Miller morning show in Chicago. So why wouldn't he follow it still, now that his viewpoint is fashionable?

No one I met after I turned thirty and joined the peace movement could believe I'd married a cop. Nobody who ever met Gregory could believe I'd married that one. It wasn't our religious differences people noticed—Jewish for me versus his Roman Catholic—though it troubled my parents. It was our disparate sensibilities. I told everyone—and still do—that Gregory was inevitable, in light of my father. If I hadn't met Gregory, I would have invented him, there in that trendy Chicago singles' bar that April night, just down the street from my tiny studio apartment.

Gregory was standing towards the back of the bar, sifting through mug shots. Not that he expected to find any of those faces in Friar Tuck's. It took me years, but I figured it out; he was using them as bait to attract working girls—that's the term Gregory used—working girls like me. My friend Crystal Mason found him first, and urged me over to meet him.

"Ohhh," I exclaimed looking round-eyed at the photos, then Gregory, who was wearing a navy blue raincoat I would one day come to hate. "What are those people wanted for?"

"Murder," Gregory intoned heavily, lips twitching into a superior smile. He was a tall stocky man, with brown hair, brown eyes, cheeks slack from an ongoing battle with his weight.

"Murder!" I brushed a glass of white wine to my lips. "You think they all killed people?"

"I *know* they killed people," Gregory proclaimed, and at my side Crystal laughed nervously. "You are looking at a two-legged predator." Gregory flashed one of the photos in front of me. The man in the picture had a thick scrub brush of hair, inky skin, and a left eye that in profile looked swollen. "He raped a woman with a broken Coke bottle before he killed her," Gregory proclaimed grandly. "If you ever see him lurking around your apartment building, be sure to call 9-1-1 *immediately*." He tucked the pictures into a pocket of his coat and pulled forth a package of Winstons, which he offered all around. I didn't smoke but I took one anyway, because it seemed to fit the occasion.

"So do you girls come here often?" Gregory asked, cigarette between his own lips as he leaned forward to light mine and Crystal's.

"No, but we'll have to now, won't we, Marcy?" Crystal breathed a long practiced stream of smoke in my direction, and dabbed a scrap of tobacco off her tongue. "We didn't know there were so many cute guys here," she added as a sandy haired man, also in overcoat, joined our circle.

Crystal hit it off with this other guy. His name was Roy. He was a cop too, Gregory's partner that night, in fact. The two of them, both plain-clothes detectives, had stopped by the bar on an unauthorized break. She went out with Roy for four months, until his ex-girlfriend resurfaced and wooed him back.

Gregory also had an ex-girlfriend. Her name was Marcy, too, of all things. Gregory referred to her as "the other Marcy." The other Marcy never returned to the little apartment they had shared above a shabby travel agency near the Jefferson Park train station. Gregory still kept the place, but didn't live there. When she'd left, he had moved back into the apartment his parents rented in the same neighborhood. Gregory was an only child with a doting mother who alternately cooked for him and bellowed about his surging weight, and an ailing, retired police officer father, who bellowed at Gregory about everything.

He was only too happy to show up at my place every night after we started sleeping together, which wasn't very long after we met.

"Why don't you ever stay at your own apartment?" I asked once, out of curiosity, not desire for Gregory to go elsewhere. I had been jilted too—a few months before I met Gregory—by someone who spent little time with me. It flattered me to have Gregory so anxious for my company. Right away I'd thrown out the *Nation* magazines my old boyfriend had left behind, and started reading the *National Review*, so I could understand the world from Gregory's perspective.

"I want to stay here with *you*," Gregory had replied after only a brief pause, tossing cigarettes and matches on the bedside table in preparation for climbing in with me. I was almost always in bed when Gregory arrived, usually asleep. He worked four to midnight, his favorite shift. I had given him keys early on, so he wouldn't have to ring the doorbell.

"I know you want to stay with *me*," I'd persisted. "And I know you're at your parents' when you're not here. So why do you pay rent on a place and not stay there?"

"I keep things there," Gregory said cryptically, easing his warm, flabby body in next to me. He started kissing me right away and I didn't ask any more questions.

When he had known me another month, Gregory told me what he kept at this other apartment. He kept cats.

"Cats?"

"Well, the other Marcy liked cats," he confessed. "When we started living together she brought home two kittens."

"Oh, that's sweet. But aren't they lonely all by themselves in that apartment? Maybe you ought to bring them to your folks'."

No, Gregory said, no he couldn't do that. His parents hated cats. Anyway the kittens were cats now and they weren't lonely. They'd had kittens themselves. There were other cats to keep them company.

"How many other cats?" I sat upright in bed, where we had most of our conversations, spent most of our time.

"I don't really know anymore." Gregory sat up too and switched on the lamp, then reached for his cigarettes. I took one, though Gregory no longer encouraged this. He didn't want me to darken my lungs.

"You don't know?"

"There are a lot." He took a deep drag into what must have been very black lungs. Gregory was a heavy smoker.

"What are you going to do about them?"

"I feed them," he said. "I stop every day on my way in to work."

"You can't keep feeding them forever."

"I want them to live out their lives. I wouldn't want to see any of them hurt."

"Take me there," I said. "I want to see them."

Gregory sighed and I concentrated on my cigarette. It tasted good. I didn't buy cigarettes for myself because I didn't *really* want to start smoking. I borrowed Gregory's. Sometimes the best moment of the day was hearing Gregory's key turn in the lock and knowing I could soon have a smoke.

There were twelve cats in all, seventeen counting the latest batch of kittens. Gregory no longer knew who was related. He thought a couple were strays who'd wandered into the backyard because of the food he left there. The only ones he allowed inside were Cinders and Sandy, the original pair, and their grown son Stanley. The two males didn't get along and had taken to marking their territory. The whole place smelled of cat.

This would have been a good time to walk away from Gregory. But nothing in my life had prepared me to gauge the strangeness of the situation. I watched Gregory move through the tall weeds of that yard, counting cats, a huge bag of cat chow in his arms. I watched his dark blue raincoat, which he never buttoned—it no longer fit him well enough to button—flapping at his thighs. I felt only one thing: Sympathy. Sympathy for Gregory and his fruitful cats who seemed destined to multiply in biblical proportions while Gregory paid rent forever on his otherwise unused apartment.

He needed my help. Gregory could pull thieves out of stolen cars every night on the gang-ridden west side, but he couldn't face down the problem the other Marcy had started.

"We have to find homes for all these cats," I told Gregory, as he filled large plastic tubs with water from an outside tap. "We can run ads in the newspaper."

"I don't have time to find homes for them," Gregory said.

"But look how much it's costing you." I had already learned where Gregory's soul burned brightest. "If we find homes for these cats you could give up the apartment."

"This is true, Marcy." He looked at me with grateful brown eyes.

Gregory started bringing cats to my place in the middle of the night. My landlord objected to pets of any kind, even goldfish. Gregory said we would have to break the rules, because the cats had to be accessible when people called. Gregory enforced rules for a living and broke them on his time off. One of his favorite games was driving the wrong way down a one-way residential street, then flashing his badge at any motorist who passed from the other direction. "One way!" he would shout out the window in his most authoritative voice. "This is a one way street."

I found homes for all the cats, except Cinders and Sandy. They found homes with me. Gregory said he couldn't part with them; they were like family. I had one spayed and the other neutered and they settled into our routine, trotting to the door each night when Gregory's key turned in the lock.

Gregory brought me along the October night he moved out of his apartment. There wasn't much to move. He said the furniture belonged to the other Marcy. He only wanted some papers stashed in a rickety old bureau. While Gregory sorted his papers into two cardboard boxes, I lay on the sofa contemplating my next project.

"Gregory," I began, as he lingered a long time over one batch of papers. "The landlord says I have to get rid of Cinders and Sandy."

Gregory looked up with round watery eyes. "No, Marcy, you can't do that," he said. "Sandy and Cinders don't cause any trouble." This was true because I hadn't let Gregory bring them to my place until I'd adopted out Stanley.

"The landlord doesn't care." I sat up on the moth-eaten sofa that belonged to the other Marcy. "He doesn't want pets in the building."

"I'll talk to him," Gregory announced, tilting backward onto two legs of his chair, as if to prove he could accomplish anything.

"No, Gregory," I said, "Don't." I didn't want Gregory flashing his badge to make everything all right. I wanted to move to a bigger apartment where cats were allowed and where Gregory could move in, with his clothes this time too, and then marry me. I was twenty-six years old and I wanted a husband and children, because I had been raised to believe they were my due. Gregory had stepped into my life with the proprietary air of someone who intended to take care of me. I was afraid enough then of doing so myself to assume that he must, therefore, be "the one."

"Gregory," I began again, after he'd settled back onto four legs. "I want to live in a place where I don't have to keep the curtains drawn so the neighbors can't see in. The lady next door is very hostile. I think *she's* who told the landlord."

"Actually." Gregory rifled through the last of his papers. "I don't like you living in that neighborhood. The crime rate is astronomical."

We didn't discuss it further that night because Gregory went outside to burn some of his papers in the trash barrel. He posted me in front of the building in case the landlord showed up. It wasn't a well thought out plan. I had no idea what the landlord looked like, and

Gregory knew nothing about building fires. The flames shot so high that somebody called the fire department, and as the truck pulled up, I raced into the yard in time to see Gregory escaping through the hole in the fence that the cats had formerly used to get in. What could I do, but flee with him, an inadvertent accomplice to a crime whose purpose I knew nothing about.

In the spring, almost exactly a year after we'd met, Gregory helped me move into a roomy one bedroom apartment near O'Hare. Airplanes thundered so low overhead in their landing patterns, you had to suspend conversations, even indoors. But I was safe here, Gregory insisted. Safe from murderers, rapists and gangbangers, in this complex with a swimming pool, located miles from the nearest bus stop. The cats were safe too, from hostile landlords.

"But I don't feel totally safe," I'd tell Gregory. He still kept his clothes at his parents' place, and had refused to put his name on the lease. "I can't feel safe," I'd remind him night after night when he'd crawl naked and horny, into my new queen-sized bed. "I won't be safe," I'd explain ever so patiently, "until you marry me."

He eventually picked a month—though not a day—and I wrote to my parents, joyfully announcing our engagement. They headed for Chicago almost as soon as they got the news, determined to break us up.

"It looks like you're going to *have* to marry him, Marcy," my mother chided under her breath when she saw the outsized bed. But she was friendly to Gregory.

"We never wanted Marcy living in that neighborhood anyway," she announced over dinner at the drop leaf maple table I'd found chairless and cheap in Marshall Field's basement. "We're glad you encouraged her to move out here, away from all the weirdos." Even in her fifties, Mom had a lost kitten face—long, sad and delicate, her eyes perennially misting over with incomprehension. My mother had been raised by a series of stepmothers. She did not view the world as a safe place.

"Mrs. Rosen and I were very worried about Marcy moving to Chicago," my father put in, sounding like someone in a Jane Austen novel. I'd heard him call my mother many things, but never "Mrs. Rosen."

"Yes." Gregory grinned, first at Leah, then Jack, each of whom looked smaller than usual, sitting on ladderback chairs that were a little too low for the table.

"Yes." Gregory began again. "But if Stouffer Foods hadn't offered Marcy a job in Chicago…" He looked shrunken himself, as he stretched for the bread basket.

"We thought she should have found a job with Stouffer's in Cleveland." My mother handed Gregory a slice of bread, as if this would prevent him from finishing his sentence. I looked down at my plate, remembering the huge fight my mother and I had had over this still touchy issue.

"Marcy and I would have never met if she hadn't moved to Chicago," Gregory persisted.

"Yes." My mother smiled sweetly, but I think even Gregory noticed the forlorn tilt of her nose, the disappointed droop of her shoulders.

"I take good care of her, Mrs. Rosen." Gregory flashed the exuberant, boyish smile that melted my insides when he directed it at me. "You can be sure she's in good hands with me."

"Pass the lasagne, please." My father hefted himself up in his chair, his rotund chest thrusting forward. Here was something else about my father Gregory couldn't know: My father said "please" about as often as he called my mother Mrs. Rosen.

"Marcy is a wonderful cook, Mr. Rosen, isn't she?" Gregory persevered for my benefit. I couldn't cook at all. Gregory *knew* the dinner had come out of colorful cardboard cartons I'd brought home from work.

"Marcy is my daughter." My father's broad nostrils flared as if he were exhaling smoke. His was a round, authoritative face, the face of a man who could have ghostwritten the bible. His face was as certain as my mother's was tentative. He, too, believed the world was unsafe, the brunt of its dangers aimed at me.

"Yes," Gregory nodded enthusiastically, punching up the oblivious grin and closing his eyes to parental fine print. "Marcy tells me you're a wonderful cook."

I had never told Gregory that. My father didn't cook; he couldn't even boil water.

"Everything Marcy knows," my father barred his teeth as if he were facing down a dentist. "Marcy learned everything she knows from me...or Mrs. Rosen."

"Congratulations!" Gregory lifted his water glass while my parents stared at each other, forks frozen in mid-air. "You raised a magnificent daughter."

That was how Gregory bonded with my parents. He was a policeman, after all, who dealt with far rougher elements every day. I, on the other hand, had not yet progressed beyond lopsided wrestling matches with Leah and Jack.

"Look at the way he dresses." My father began pacing between dining alcove and kitchen as soon as Gregory went home to get ready for work. Dad looked tall again, out from the ladderback chair, and without Gregory looming over him. My father had always looked tall to me, all five feet six of him.

"The way he dresses?" I repeated cautiously, from over by the kitchen sink.

"That boy wears cheap pants he has to keep yanking up." My father circled about like a plane in a holding pattern, barrel chest protruding. "Why doesn't he wear a belt?"

"He wears a belt at work, Dad." I drew in a pained breath, my fingers shriveling in hot dishwater. I had *asked* Gregory to wear a belt for my parents' visit. "Belts make him uncomfortable."

"And why doesn't he tuck in his shirt?" My mother chimed in, as she rearranged one of my cupboards. I had *asked* her to just dry the dishes and stack them on the counter.

"As soon as he loses a few pounds he's going to dress differently." Why couldn't they understand? My father had always been overweight. He never bought new clothes. My mother shopped for him.

"Well, he can do something about that raincoat," my mother asserted, putting coffee cups on the shelf where the glasses used to be.

My stomach curled in on itself. Gregory's raincoat was misshapen and grease-splotched now from crawling under cars to look for VIN numbers. But he wouldn't hear of getting a new one.

"It brings him good luck, Mom," I said quietly, inventing excuses for Gregory the way he had invented my cooking. "Gregory met me while he was wearing it, you know; he thinks that getting rid of the raincoat would be like getting rid of me."

My father stopped moving. My mother walked over to where he stood, beside the maple table. She draped an arm around his waist, and he wrapped an arm around her shoulder. Entwined like a sudden vine in my kitchen, they eyed me accusingly. They both seemed to realize, finally, that I intended to marry Gregory.

"What kind of husband do you think Gregory is going to make?" My father fished in his pocket for a cigarette with his free hand. "Working nights all the time. He'll never be around when you are."

"You work nights," I offered softly, turning around to lean against the sink. My father fluffed his hand through my mother's salt and peppery hair, which she wore short these days, cropped close against her face. She called it her swimmer's style. She couldn't swim though. My mother had been in the same beginners' swim class for years.

"That's different." My mother swayed closer against my father. "Your father has an office at home. I know where he is at night."

Hah! I wanted to shout, remembering the sleeper-couch my father had installed in his study years ago, and all the many nights my mother went to bed alone. But I held my tongue. This was too new for me, my bickering parents united in a loving front against me.

"Well Marcy, it's *your* life." The unlit cigarette bobbed up and down in my father's mouth. "You're the one who's going to have to sleep with him. Your mother thinks you may have done so already." He put meaningful weight on every syllable. "I told her, 'No, that's impossible. Marcy is a nice girl. She has more respect for herself than that. She wouldn't spread her legs for a man like a common whore.'"

"I don't sleep with him!" I screamed so forcefully that Cinders and Sandy jumped out suddenly from under the bargain basement table and started running.

But I did sleep with him. Oh, did I sleep with him, more than ever, it seemed, since I'd moved into the new apartment. I'd drink coffee by the bucketful in the morning at work, trying to stay awake.

"You look a little piqued, Marcy," Crystal Mason would tease. She and I worked together at Stouffer Foods, internal communications—writing newsletters and updating employee handbooks. "Did you watch the sun rise again?"

"Just about," I might laugh and then blush, looking up from my notes from an interview with one corporate vice president or another. "Watching the sun rise" was a code phrase between Crystal and me, ever since I'd dropped a few hints to her about Gregory's stamina. I'd exaggerated slightly, for Crystal's benefit. We'd gone at it until the sky lightened once, but that was the night he brought home some grass he'd confiscated from a car thief, the night we both went a little crazy.

Mostly what I loved about sex with Gregory was lying in bed together *after* sex, talking and smoking cigarettes.

"I worry about you, Marcy." Gregory would always fret, no matter what I'd tell him about each day's activities.

"Gregory, I had dinner with Crystal Mason at her apartment in Lincoln Park. How could that possibly be dangerous?" I complained, secretly pleased that he cared so much about my welfare.

"There's a rapist on the prowl in that neighborhood, little duck." Gregory invoked his favorite nickname for me. "You really shouldn't be anywhere in the downtown area after dark."

I promised him I would find some other way to socialize with Crystal, knowing she didn't like driving all the way out to where we lived, knowing I would probably see less of her.

"I worry about you, too," I'd tell Gregory, lying in the pillowy crook of his arm. "You're the one who faces real danger."

"Don't you worry about me, little Marcy," Gregory's voice was pillowy soft, too. "You know I always draw my gun when I stop a suspicious-looking car. I never know who's going to be inside; I never know what kind of weapons they might have with them. I'm very careful that way."

"I hope you never have to *use* your gun," I would say, contemplating the growing embers of my cigarette. I hated that Gregory's job involved guns.

"I'd never shoot anyone if I could help it," Gregory would reassure me time and time again. "That's the last thing I'd want to do, you can be sure of that, little duck."

Gregory never did shoot anyone, while we were together. But a man in his unit named Jerry O'Connell did. Jerry O'Connell heard someone creeping behind him on a dark stairwell one night, just after he entered a building on a domestic violence call.

"Domestics are the most dangerous calls," Gregory had moaned, unable to sleep that night, unable to stop talking. "Coppers show up to stop an attack, and the next thing you know the woman withdraws her complaint and the perpetrator turns on the cops."

Jerry O'Connell saw the shadow of a man and the glint of a gun in the stairwell's silver light and he fired his own gun.

"Bam, bam, bam," Gregory groaned to me in bed that night. "Just like that, Marcy. Bam bam, bam. Jerry killed his own partner."

"Oh, Gregory, oh, Gregory." I kissed Gregory, kissed his flushed cheeks, his stunned mouth, his smooth innocent forehead, and then I kissed him further down, lest Gregory go permanently limp and die like one policeman had in one way that night and like Jerry O'Connell had died in another.

Gregory and I made slow, languid, silent love, celebrating our aliveness, our ability to evade death. It was afterward, as we lay spent and exhilarated in one another's arms, that Gregory had asked me to marry him.

"October would be a good month," he had murmured, as we puffed our post-coital cigarettes.

"A good month for what, Gregory?" I lifted my head, straining to make out his face in the bedroom's darkness.

"For getting married, Marcy." He caressed my head back down onto his arm. "Isn't that what you want to do?"

And then, two weeks later, my parents had visited, working their primal dark magic, turning me into their child again, into their obedient and shameful little girl.

"Gregory," I breathed as he reached for me the night after Leah and Jack had finally departed for Cleveland. "We shouldn't have sex anymore, Gregory. It isn't right. We should wait until after the wedding."

Gregory rolled off of me and lit a cigarette.

"You're very close to your parents, aren't you, little duck?"

"It's the other way around, really," I stammered, the cigarette tasting rancid as I faced the sour truth of it for the first time. "My parents are close to me."

"Dear Mom and Dad, Having a wonderful time, glad you're not here! (hah! hah!, just kidding!) California is beautiful. Sunny and warm—flowers everywhere, mountains on one horizon, ocean on the other. Went to the beach today. May go again tomorrow! The water's great! Last one in is a—(fill in the blank!) Love, Marcy and Gregory."

That's the sort of postcard I mailed to Cleveland on our honeymoon that fall. Full of exclamation points and superlatives. This particular one boasted an aerial view of the craggy coastline north of San Diego where we were spending most of our time. I liked the wide-open blueness in the picture. Blue sky, blue water, bluish-green haze of tall and scrubby Torrey pines for which the area is famous. I praised the California scenery in all my messages home. The scenery fascinated me, and I hoped it would fascinate my parents and Gregory's parents and that no one—especially not Gregory or I—would have to face the real truth of our honeymoon.

"Gregory." I set this postcard on the table beside our endless motel bed and flopped belly down across the mattress. "I don't want to go to that beach again today, Gregory. Let's do something else."

"What do you want to do, little duck?" Gregory called through the open bathroom door. He was shaving—more methodically, more meticulously than he ever did at home. I didn't have to watch to know that this was true, though I could see him in the bathroom mirror from where I lay, could see the careful, admiring way he flexed his chin and stretched his neck so as not to miss a spot. Leah and Jack should see him now. And Marline and Gregory Senior. Or maybe just Marline. Nothing Gregory did ever seemed to please his father.

"I'd like to, you know, see the sights," I replied, staring down at the honey-brown carpet, tracing curlicues in it with a finger.

"Torrey Pines State Beach is one of the greatest wonders of the area," Gregory sang out brightly. "'Backed to the sea by 10,000 years of a warming climate and by 200 years of encroaching human civilization, the rare Torrey pine has nowhere else to go.'" Gregory had been memorizing facts like that. He'd read in bed, maps and guidebooks spread out between us like a crinkly river. The light glared when I fell asleep each night. I had to bury my head under the covers.

"Well, then let's *see* the Torrey pines," I crooned back darkly. "Let's take a real hike today and have a picnic on the bluffs."

"'Along the coast the trees are stunted and bent into shapes reminiscent of the Japanese art of bonsai,'" Gregory continued to recite as if I hadn't spoken. "'Inland the more sheltered trees grow taller and straighter.'"

"Let's go to the zoo at least, Gregory. San Diego has a famous zoo."

"Don't you worry, Marcy. I told your parents I would take good care of you and I will."

"I hate that beach," I wailed, summoning up the tears that had been a closer friend to me than Gregory in the last few days. "I hate that beach."

"Now, now little duck." Gregory emerged from the bathroom finally, in undershirt and boxer shorts, and sat down next to me on the bed, began massaging my shoulders. I sniffed away my tears and inhaled a kingdom of fragrances born of breath freshener and soap, shampoo and aftershave. But I didn't smell tanning lotion. For once I got no whiff of coconut among the melange of minty, peachy, appley, orange-spicy scents that accompanied his newly improved hygiene routine. Maybe we weren't going to the beach today. Maybe Gregory had a secret up his sleeve, was planning something we would both enjoy.

I turned over onto my back and looked up at Gregory. His round, fleshy face shone down upon me, comforting and dependable, like the California sun, which generally started the day fogged in by clouds and steadily burned its way into brightness. His brown eyes glinted with an electricity that I recognized, as from a far off place. It had been four days since we were married, his parents and my parents, and a handful of other people converging on what was now *our* apartment for dainty tea sandwiches, wedding cake, and champagne. It had been more than three months since my parents met Gregory and warned me of the life I'd spend with him, three months since I'd made Gregory prove his love for me by swearing off sex. When, I wondered, contemplating Gregory's eager, cherubic, upside down gaze—when would Gregory swear off celibacy?

"Put a bee in my bonnet, Gregory," I cooed up at him from our round honeymoon bed, a full fertile moon of a bed with a boundless circumference. Who would have thought that a squat stucco place called the Budget Mate Motel would have a honeymoon suite? But Gregory had found it, asked for it and a "police discount" too, while I'd stood silently beside him, overcome with shyness and fatigue.

"We don't have police discounts," the plump, orange-haired manager had informed Gregory solemnly, studying me with wide curiosity, like a librarian trying to catalogue a book. But she was no librarian; her hair alone—a reckless mass of flyaway curls that cast an orange pallor on her face—was too loud for that job. She looked more like a movie star hopeful whom time had passed by, weighted down with makeup, especially around the eyes. She had long fingernails too, each sculpted perfectly and painted the same startling orange as her hair.

"We have a bridal suite." She wore long, silvery earrings that shimmered in the stark fluorescent light of the wedge-shaped motel office. "But it's forty dollars a night for everyone, regardless of what you do for a living." She tapped her elaborate fingernails on the counter, and smiled corrosively. "Take it or leave it."

This was the fourth motel we'd tried. Gregory's parents had given us cash for our honeymoon. But Gregory believed in saving money. After the first two motels, he'd made me come in with him, saying it would improve our chances.

"You never know when it might come in handy to have a policeman on the premises," Gregory pulled himself up to his full, burly height, ignoring the manager's ultimatum.

"We've got in-house security," she replied, looking bored.

"I can add to that." Gregory grabbed his billfold from his hip pocket and flashed the silver badge embedded in the leather. "I can patrol the parking lot after hours. This place will be extra safe while I'm here."

"You really are a cop!" She leaned over the counter to get a closer view. She wasn't so much overweight, I saw then, as wearing too-small clothes. Her breasts bulged insistently against a lemon-colored shirt, and her hips pushed the limits of her bright aqua stretch pants.

"I've got a weapon too." Gregory smiled triumphantly, tucking his wallet back in his pocket. "It's in our rental car now, locked up with the luggage."

This was true. Gregory couldn't seem to go anywhere without his gun, had worked out the details of transporting it in advance with airport security. I hadn't found this any stranger than anything else Gregory did, but the orange motel lady burst out laughing. She had a screechy laugh that sounded like a traffic accident.

"You can't really be on your honeymoon!" She arched her penciled brows, her only thin feature and scrutinized Gregory as through a microscope.

"I never mind helping people out." Gregory produced the boy scout grin he reserved, like a spare tire, for emergencies.

"If you're really on your honeymoon, you're the one in need of help." She released her curdled laugh again. "I'll give you ten dollars off on the honeymoon suite," she said, "*if* you stay at least four days." She handed Gregory a check-in form. "And *don't* patrol the parking lot."

"I wouldn't mind patrolling it," Gregory murmured oh-so cordially, taking up a pen.

"Married sex can't hold a candle to single sex," she suddenly declared, staring at me as if she knew a good deal more about Gregory than I ever would, and for that reason alone she was coming out ahead, never mind the price break. Gregory kept writing without looking up. I stared straight ahead at bare paneled walls, but the room kept filling up with the manager's wild orange hair and all-knowing, makeup-heavy eyes.

"C'mon Gregory," I stretched out luxuriously on our amazingly large bed, trying to exclude the manager's face from this room. It was an ordinary room really, except for the massive bed—which practically brushed against the walls—and a round mirror above the bed on the ceiling. There was a little alcove near the door where they'd installed a TV along with a couple of small tables and a tiny couch. I suppose that's why they called it a suite. Gregory had complained that there was no TV by the bed, and I'd suggested they might have thought honeymooners wouldn't notice.

"Put a bee in my bonnet, Gregory," I urged again. Gregory had stopped massaging my shoulders after I'd rolled onto my back, had let his hands drop into his lap. "C'mon, Gregory." I placed my hands over his. "Gregory, light my fire."

"We don't have time for that, Marcy!" He grimaced like I'd told a bad joke.

"It's our honeymoon, Gregory." My hands started roaming. "What else do we have time for if not that?"

"Later, Marcy." He pushed my hands away.

"No, Gregory, now!" I fairly shouted in frustration, and Gregory laughed condescendingly, as if I were a child he'd have to set straight.

"Aw, Marcy, you little duck." He leaned over and put his hand on my mouth, as if to shush me.

"We have all the time in the world, Gregory." I wanted to prove the motel manager wrong. I wanted to reach for the phone and call the front desk, scream ecstatically into the receiver, let that snotty woman think what she might. The walls were so thin, I wouldn't even need the phone. I'd heard people banging around in the regular rooms every night. I'd heard them laughing and giggling and yelping with joy as I lay under the covers waiting for Gregory to finish reading his travel guides.

There had been nothing but silence from the honeymoon suite in the three nights since we'd checked in, and I wanted to change that.

"Put a bee in my bonnet, Gregory," I screamed into the hand he'd placed on my mouth, but Gregory pressed down harder.

"Wewewee," I said, trying to say "Gregory" through his hand. Trying to say, "Gregory, cut it out."

"Wewewee." I flailed at him with fists that bounced off his chest and arms like harmless raindrops.

"No, Marcy, no." Gregory wasn't smiling, hadn't been smiling for several long seconds. "I'm the one who decides when we make love. We're married now, Marcy. I'm the one who makes the decisions."

Gregory pressed his hand down harder on my mouth, his whole hand, hard, just under my nose, pinching up against my nostrils so that I almost couldn't breathe.

Let go of me, let go of me, Gregory, I willed him with my eyes, punching him with flaccid fists.

Gregory kept bearing down until I stopped flailing. When I lay absolutely still, he started stroking me with his free hand. Gregory stroked my breasts and my thighs and he yanked my shorts and panties far enough down to stroke between my thighs. I began to grow excited. To my dismay, I grew wet.

Gregory rolled on top of me then, loosening up the hand on my mouth as he eased himself into me. I began moving too, not looking at Gregory with his eyes squinted shut, his hand covering my mouth. I looked at the round mirror on the ceiling and watched the two of us move together on our giant honeymoon bed, more observer than participant in my own strange passion.

"Yeeahhhhhh!" Gregory moaned after not so very long and heaved himself off of me, pulling me close to him, into the soft crook of his arm that he had long ago designated as my nesting place.

"You sweet little duck," Gregory reached across the mattress and grabbed his cigarettes from the bedside table. "We're married now, Marcy. We're going to be together forever."

He lit two cigarettes, one after the other. I didn't want the one he handed me. I took it anyway, half choking on the smoke, but afraid to think what might happen if I refused it.

"Dear Marline and Gregory Senior, California is wonderful. San Diego especially. We're spending more time here than we had originally planned, but there's a beautiful beach and we've been going there every day. Just relaxing on the sand under the delicious October sun, which is not the same sun you have in Chicago this time of year. Not the same son at all..."

I set the pen down on the rosy round bedspread we had transported to the beach from our cut-rate honeymoon suite. I reread what I had just written, frowning disappointedly. "Dear Marline and Gregory Senior..." It seemed too formal a salutation for my in-laws (who I had yet to address in person by any name at all). But it was the most honest part of the letter. That and "not the same son at all..." which I didn't notice at first. I stared at those few scratchy lines a long time before my little slip jumped out at me.

"Marcy..." the son stood over me suddenly, camera dangling from his sunburned neck on a long black strap. "Marcy, I'm going beachcombing again and I'm going to take some pictures this time. I want you to come with me."

I squinted up at him, at his tall bulky frame silhouetted against the burning blue California sky. Gregory's thick legs poked out of his swimming trunks, milky white under a dark layer of hair. This was our third day at Black's Beach, but only the first day Gregory wore his bathing suit instead of long pants, and even still he worried so much about how he looked that he kept his shirt on. Which was a sorry joke, considering how little anyone at this oddball beach seemed to care about appearances.

"I'm writing postcards, Gregory." I stared at his bulging white belly that peeked out of his unbuttoned sportshirt. "Go by yourself."

"Come with me, Marcy." Gregory spoke firmly.

"No." I looked away from Gregory, back toward his parents' postcard, which needed one more line to fill it out, one more bright line about how much fun we were having on our honeymoon. I couldn't mail it as is. There was too much white space left in the message section.

"Marcy..." Gregory squatted down on the sand and grabbed my upper arm with one hand, grabbed it tightly.

"Owww, that hurts. That really hurts." I retorted loudly, too loudly, but I knew he wasn't going to try to silence me the way he had silenced me a few hours ago in our room. Gregory wasn't going to smash his hand over my mouth in front of all these people. He didn't have that much nerve.

"Marcy," Gregory knelt onto the sand and actually whispered, whispered politely while squeezing my arm. "People are looking at you, Marcy," he said. "Sound carries on the beach. You're going to have to stop fussing."

"Then let go of my arm," I whispered back, sucking in my breath to keep from shrieking. I was angry at Gregory for what he had done to me in our room, and for bringing me to this place day after day. But I was also angry at myself because I thought it was my fault somehow that Gregory had turned weird on me, my fault that I had gotten excited and wet, having sex with Gregory while he hurt me.

"Are you coming with me?" Gregory loosened his hold and flashed the winsome smile that had worked on me the way his badge worked on other people, made me churn all soft inside and forgive his transgressions, made me refuse to believe he had meant any harm.

"Yes, Gregory." I stuffed his parents' postcard into my white straw bag and rose to my feet, slipping into beach thongs and the striped blue cover-up that matched my blue swimsuit.

Gregory and I were the most overdressed people on this beach, a fact I had tried to erase up to now by burying my head in postcards, in *Redbook* magazines, and in the same travel guides Gregory read in bed every night while I waited for sleep. I'd stretch out prone on our round bedspread/beach blanket, while Gregory sat upright, surveying the beach with the diligent enthusiasm of a watchdog. Or he'd walk up and down and around the beach admiring the startling scenery. Beachcombing, he called it. "I'm going beachcombing, Marcy," he would announce, as he had announced just now, and off he would go, straining to get a closer look at all the flesh.

Because, yes, it was a nude beach. One long, golden strand of sand blanketed with naked bodies, baking like so many cookies in the oven, into various degrees of doneness. There were evenly browned bodies and blotchy bodies, their untanned parts revealing the outlines of bathing suits that must have only recently been tossed aside. There were doughy white bodies and crispy bodies, burning in unspeakable places. Gregory hadn't been able to take his eyes off any of them, any more than I had been able to look, really look, at anyone.

"Is this legal? Can people do this?" I'd demanded of Gregory three days before when we'd first stumbled onto this place.

"Maybe it's legal, maybe it's not." Gregory had brought field glasses along. He held them up to his eyes as we stood above the beach on one of the steep oceanfront paths in the state park described so eloquently in Gregory's guidebook. "But you know how crazy people are in California." Gregory scanned the sand in the vicinity of where we had seen our first naked sunbathers. "They'll do anything for a thrill."

"Shouldn't we turn back, Gregory?" Crazy or not, I didn't see how a nude beach fit into our plans.

"Not yet, Marcy." Gregory had effected the sort of brave, shoulders-high stance a great explorer might display, crossing into dangerous territory. "I've never seen anything like this. I want to get a closer look."

We didn't turn back, of course. We kept easing forward. We kept easing toward the beach. Gregory said we would only stay a little while. We wouldn't take *our* clothes off, of course. It was okay to watch, Gregory said, as long as we didn't take *our* clothes off.

I felt naked anyway. I felt naked that first afternoon sitting next to Gregory on the hot sand while he studied the crowd through field glasses. I felt naked in my bathing suit and matching blue cover-up, parading across the beach with Gregory and his camera. I thought everyone was looking at me...me, who had been self-conscious about my body even before I started growing breasts.

"Give me some homemade milk, Marcy," my little brother David had piped up one day when I was nearly eight and he was six and we were still taking baths together. "Give me some homemade milk." He'd pointed at my chest with one hand, dumped a plastic cup full of water over my head with the other.

"No!" I'd shouted and left the tub, never to return to it again in David's presence, never to have the same nonchalance about my body.

"But that's the whole idea," my mother had instructed some years later when my figure did fill out and I'd confessed to her, at fourteen, that I thought I looked "too sexy" in a bathing suit. "You're supposed to look sexy in a bathing suit," my mother had said. "Sex is what you're selling."

And now, here were naked bodies everywhere. In front of me—behind me—to the side as far I could see: naked bodies. In repose, playing checkers, chasing Frisbees, diving into waves that came splashing saltily to shore. And was this about sex too? I knew Gregory thought so, trekking across the sand like a horny Lawrence of Arabia on a photo shoot.

"Stand over there, Marcy!" he decided suddenly, after we had traveled about fifty feet, picking our way carefully around the baking bodies. "Stand over there by that couple."

"Which couple, Gregory?" I whispered hoarsely. There were couples everywhere. In pairs, in groups. Or did he mean that skinny, bearded, dark-haired man with the very beautiful, very pregnant blonde, dead to the world on her back, her belly as swollen as a pan of E-Z Pop popcorn. How was I supposed to know which couple Gregory wanted me up against?

"Over anywhere, Marcy." Gregory smirked. "It's all fertile territory. Stand over here. Stand over there." He held the camera to his eye, fiddled with the focus and the F-stops. "Just keep posing, don't worry about me. I'll get the picture."

"I'm not a fashion model, Gregory," I complained, but I followed his instructions anyway, his dutiful, fearful, self-conscious wife.

I wasn't in many of the pictures. Gregory shot three rolls of film on that beach, thirty-six exposures each. You could see a piece of me in some photos—right side, left side, the back of my head, a generous portion of my beach bag.

Gregory carried those pictures with him everywhere when we returned to Chicago after six days at Black's Beach. He became a walking travelogue.

"Get a load of that one!" He would pluck a photo—any photo—from the pile and wave it at the guy sitting next to him in whatever trendy bar we'd happen to drop into. Gregory was a big one for dropping into bars on his time off. It was either that or stay home watching television, and I was glad for the opportunity to drive to the Near North Side for some nightlife. Gregory absolutely forbid me to drive in by myself. "I wouldn't want anything to happen to you while I'm at work," he used to say. "Your friends should come out here if they want to see you. There is way too much crime in the city."

So there we'd be in the River Shannon, Yaksie's or maybe Friar Tuck's, the New Town fern bar where we'd met two years earlier, and it would be *deja vu* all over again—Gregory in his raincoat and superior grin, sifting through photos. Only of course, the coat was abysmal now and Gregory had progressed to a very different type of mug shot.

"Oh baby, where'd you go on *your* vacation? Polynesia?" a stranger would exclaim, glancing sideways at the photo Gregory held up in the room's dense, smoky light, and pretty soon a crowd would form around Gregory—men and women both. Everyone would crane to get a closer look, making the sort of lascivious remarks you'd expect from people who'd been drinking.

"Knockers, man! Would you puhlease check out those knockers!"

Or, "If that's what he looks like limp, I'd like to see his pecker when it's stiff!"

Or, "Check out that pregnant chick. What a bush she's got on *her*!"

"We just stumbled onto the place." Gregory would grin and swig some beer, or offer cigarettes all around, except not to me, his wife, who he no longer believed should smoke in public. Which was okay with me. I had lost total taste for cigarettes on our honeymoon.

"It's right outside San Diego, near that rich town, La Jolla." Gregory would begin the long explanation of how we had been admiring the stunted Torrey pines in a perfectly tranquil park when he'd spotted a naked man walking along the beach far below us, then another and another.

"If I hadn't brought the field glasses along," Gregory was fond of saying, "We might have missed it entirely."

I sat by silently through all of this or smiled and laughed at the pictures along with the rest of them, especially after I'd downed some beer. I didn't think anyone *expected* me to speak, certainly not Gregory, who needed me there the same way he'd needed me on that beach in California. With his quiet, demure wife along, who could accuse Gregory of deviant behavior? All those people hooting beside us in the dark, smoky fern bar couldn't say they would have acted differently had they been in our place with a camera.

One wintry night we ran into a friend of a friend of Gregory's in one of the bars. Martin O'Reilly was his name and he burst into Gregory's little photo show, cigarette in one hand, bottle of beer in the other, like a needle sidling up to a balloon.

"So you *did* find that nudie beach after all," Martin O'Reilly began, and took a drag on his cigarette. "Jimmy Mulligan told me he'd given you directions, although he didn't think you'd have much time for it on your *honeymoon*."

"Your *honeymoon*!" A tall, skinny woman with wavy blonde hair down her back exclaimed loudly. She'd been hanging over Gregory's shoulder, making me feel invisible. But now she turned to me with a stupefied expression that reminded me of the orange-haired lady in the San Diego motel. "He took you to that beach on your honeymoon!" she shrilled above the room's heavy facade of sound. "Whoooaaa!" she exclaimed as if there were wild horses in this room instead of people stampeding all over themselves to get a look at Gregory's pictures.

"We did other things on our honeymoon," I smiled coyly at this woman, defending my honor, defending Gregory, even as my mind whirled a million miles away from her, whirled itself into a black suck hole.

"You *knew* about it Gregory? You knew about the beach all along?" I confronted him almost as soon as we settled into the car, more than an hour later—not when I wanted to leave, but when Gregory was good and ready to leave—for the ride home.

"I *heard* about it, Marcy," Gregory equivocated, making the tires squeal as he swiftly pulled the car out of our parking space and into traffic. "But I didn't know *where* it was."

"Your friend said differently, Gregory."

"O'Reilly doesn't know what he's talking about."

"He said Jimmy Mulligan gave you directions."

"What difference does it make now, little duck?" Gregory resorted to his soft, cajoling tone. "We found it one way or another. We had a good time."

"I didn't want to spend my whole honeymoon on that beach, Gregory."

"We did other things on our honeymoon, Marcy," Gregory grinned suggestively. "Didn't I hear you say so tonight yourself?"

"Fuck you, Gregory, fuck you." I'd been smiling too long in that bar for Gregory's sake. My anger had been festering. "Fuck you Gregory!" I half screamed, half wailed at Gregory. Gregory said nothing. He turned on the radio and fiddled with the dial to find his favorite rock sound. "You're so vain, you probably think this song is about you, don't you don't you?" The music came in loud, and Gregory turned it up even higher. "You're so vain..." I had to wail above it. I wailed like a police siren that was following us home. I had to wonder as I wailed, if maybe I was crazy.

"Marcy," Gregory said finally, when we pulled into our apartment complex nearly forty minutes later. I had quieted down, but Gregory and I hadn't spoken for the entire ride home. I hunched unhappily in my seat, my body hugging the door, as far away as I could get from Gregory. The radio still blared, the song about Jo-Jo now. "Jo-Jo was a boy in Tucson, Arizona... Get back Jo-Jo, get back to where you once belonged..." I hated that song. I never could figure out who Jo-Jo was and what he needed to go back to.

"Marcy," Gregory said again, downshifting into first as we drifted past two eight-story apartment buildings and then the darkened, fenced-in pool, before winding around a bend to our building in the back. "Marcy, next weekend I have off." Gregory turned the radio way down so that the Jo-Jo song became a scratchy buzz, like backyard crickets. "Do you want to go to Cleveland?"

"Cleveland?" This took me by surprise. "We went to Cleveland last time you had the weekend off."

"I know, little duck." Gregory reached across the seat and pressed my leg. "And I know how close you are to your parents..."

"They're close to *me,* Gregory," I snapped, feeling foolish. I wrote to my parents at least twice a week since we'd returned from California. I called them every Sunday after Gregory left for work. The marriage I described to them was far different from the lonely life I lived with Gregory, but I needed for them to think that I had made the absolutely perfect choice.

"Well, they're looking forward to our visit, Marcy." Gregory smiled slyly. We had pulled into one of the parking spaces near the back entrance to our building. It was dark back there. The orangey light from the lone street lamp danced dimly across his face.

"What do you mean, Gregory?" I asked, though I sensed from his ominous tone what was coming.

"I called your parents yesterday while you were at work." Gregory's hand still rested on my leg. "I told them we were coming."

"You didn't, Gregory!" He wasn't pressing hard, but his hand felt heavy through my jeans where he touched me, just below the bottom of my heavy green parka.

"I did." He nodded solemnly.

I had no idea whether he was telling the truth or not. But it didn't matter, I thought, as he gripped a corner of my parka with his other hand and tugged me toward him. My mother was always urging me to come "home" whenever I could. We would go.

"Gregory...What are you doing? Not here, Gregory. Someone might see. Gregory, let's go inside."

"Shhh, little duck. No one's here. We're all alone. It's just you and me."

He had lifted his hand from my leg, and was unbuckling his belt, unzipping his pants, reaching inside to expose himself to me.

"Gregory..." I knew he would thrash about if I refused him, thrash about and maybe hold me down when we got inside, hold me down and this time hit me. He would thrash about like a drowning person and pull me under with him, into dark, deep, deadly waters.

"Yes, Marcy, yes, that's it, that's the way..."

It wasn't so awful, what he was asking of me. It wasn't so difficult. I could close my eyes, burrow my head against his spongy belly and do what he wanted me to do. Against the sour smell of his sorry raincoat, the sour smell of sweat and tobacco and fern bar beer that permeated his clothes and mine, I could shut my eyes and imagine us sitting around the dining room table in my parents' house in another ten days.

Maybe my mother would cook prime rib again, and my father would carve it into thick, juicy slabs that we would each in turn slice into quick, eager bites. Bites of rich, beef to consume with baked potato, spicy Caesar salad, and a cheap sparkling wine, as we all chatted merrily about the joys of married life.

"Yes, Marcy, keep going, faster now, faster."

Afterward maybe the men would go upstairs to my father's study and ogle the beach pictures again before settling into a pep rally for politicos I was already, secretly, beginning to hate.

"Don't stop, Marcy, oh, ohhh, you're so good, you're so good at it."

And my mother and I would carry the dishes into the kitchen and she would talk and I would listen—long after we finished washing and drying the last dish. She would talk about my father and how she didn't know where he was half the time, how he wouldn't speak to her for days, even when he was there, how I had to come home—as often as possible—I had to come home—my father missed me so much and it made everything so much better when I came home.

"Swallow, Marcy." It was a command even as he whispered it.

I left Gregory before we were married three years. One Saturday morning while he slept, I wadded his raincoat into a miserable ball and tossed it down the trash chute in our sixth floor hallway. I dumped his gun down there too. I wasn't afraid that Gregory might shoot me. I ran away from Gregory when I decided I might shoot *him*. I fled to Crystal Mason's place, and eventually to my own apartment back in the heart of the city. I fended off phone calls for a long time after that from Gregory *and* my parents, all of them calling to remind me that every marriage had its problems.

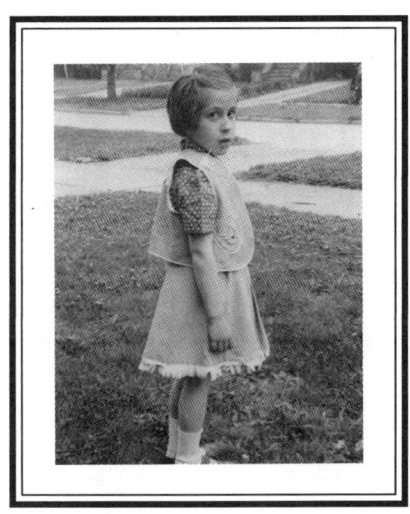

Love Is My Drug of Choice

Maybe it wouldn't have happened if Crystal Mason had come with me as we'd originally planned. Or if the hibiscus hadn't been in bloom, tender, lush blossoms strutting their stuff like silken manifestations of so many deep and passionate sighs. But what was Martinique without hibiscus? Or bougainvillea, starry orchids, moon-white ginger lilies fluttering coquettishly in the soft breeze. And oh yes, anthurium, their stiff yellow spikes poking out of waxen red leaves like a sexy joke.

Even if Crystal had been there I might have succumbed, might have breathed in the vision and aroma of the little inn's terraced lawns overlooking a clear sky and endless sea and remembered a longing, my mouth filling with salty need, my lips demanding quenching. Quenching.

Was it the flowers or the horizon that caused me to fixate like a sudden mermaid on my own two breasts, triggering the amazing chain of events that led to my delirious downward slide?

You should have come with me, Crystal, how could you have bowed out at the last minute? I lay on a lonely twin bed that first night in a pale yellow room, lacy white curtains on a window that looked onto a bubbly blue soda pop sea. Two twin beds in this room. One for Crystal, one for me. She'd tried to blame it on Ray Fedorowicz, our boss at Stouffer Foods: Only one person from the same department allowed off at a time.

"He didn't tell you that!" I'd studied Crystal's face, watched her already soft, undefined chin spin into mush. "He wouldn't have said that." We'd cleared it with him ages ago. Slow time of the year, wasn't it? Annual report deadline months away, company magazine just put to bed.

"Well he did." Crystal had begun, her hazel eyes hardening, then dissolving toward tears. She didn't cry though. She didn't have to. She knew I saw through her, looking across a Formica-topped table in the break room at work. She knew I knew it was really Terry not Ray. Terry Turner, boy wonder, attorney at law, who'd bought her a beer at the John Barleycorn that spring and now thought he owned her.

"It's just for five nights, Crystal." She and I had been through a lot. How could I hate her? "Can't you tell Terry you'll be back in five nights?"

"He wants to take me to the Caribbean himself, Marcy, this winter." She brushed a shock of frosted hair off her forehead, lit a cigarette, blew smoke toward a creaky fluorescent light fixture on the faraway ceiling. "You know we get so little vacation time. He says, who goes to Martinique in August?"

How could I hate her? When I fled my marriage the summer before, I'd moved in with Crystal and stayed for three months. I slept on her couch, ate off her dishes, borrowed her clothes and her laissez-faire disposition until I mustered the courage to get my own place and serve papers on Gregory.

"I'm going to Martinique in August," I said.

I went. I saw. I felt hollow inside, like a drinking straw through which somebody sucks up the last drops in a glass. No one should be alone on an island like this, I thought, combing the beach before breakfast that first morning, bone white sand seeping deliciously through my toes, the newly risen sun soft on my back. Coconut trees, mango trees bulging with fruit, waved in agreement from the sandy sidelines. The turquoise sea burbled and burped. Get a companion, find a companion, invent a companion they all seemed to say. Nobody should be alone on an island like this.

I returned from my walk with Edward, Gerard and Bernard, a handsome set of triplets if ever there was, each with a plausible excuse for his invisibility. Edward the poet, swept away by a tidal wave of inspiration for this lush place had dashed into the rain forest with his notebook and pens. Gerard the intrepid explorer had vowed to climb Mt. Pelée before he mounted me. And off he had trekked toward the dormant volcano, which—who knows—could erupt again unexpectedly in 1980 as it had so destructively back in 1902.

And Bernard? "Bernard has the bends," I explained ever so patiently to the cocoa-skinned waiter who poured coffee *au lait* that first morning on the patio.

"The Benz?" He had asked, one long stream of coffee blending into a hot river of milk, and frothing like the sea in my oversized cup.

"They're giving him oxygen at the hospital in Fort de France even as we speak." I eyed the waiter intently, watched beads of sweat gather on his furrowed brow. "They're hoping to save his potency at least." I smiled apologetically. "If not his brain."

"The Benz?" the waiter echoed dimly, retreating, his silvery, French-patois accent causing me to shiver in the escalating island heat. "The Mercedez Benz?"

The breakfast amazed me. Glistening wedges of papaya, pineapple, mango, melon and custard apple forming wild geometric patterns on a white crockery plate. A thick and creamy omelet oozing Gruyere cheese. Crusty baguette hacked into neat, even, tender slices, butter so sweet, so devoid of salt I wanted to personally find and thank the cow.

I summoned Edward back from his poetic wanderings. Surely a man mad for metaphors would appreciate a spread like this.

"Pass the butter, Edward. Pass the guava jelly." I prodded Edward, his eyes wandering already around this breezy outdoor dining room speckled with rampant ferns, white-clothed tables and billing and cooing couples. "You must not stare, Edward. You must particularly not stare at love or it will blind you like the sun."

I ordered Edward around as I'd ordered no other man, but he didn't notice, didn't even look at me, speak, eat. He pulled a monogrammed fountain pen from the pocket of his baggy Bermuda shorts, plucked forth his poet's notebook and scribbled, scribbled:

Alone my love, alone at last
with the wind at our back

> *the sea at our feet*
> *your face a complex conch shell*
> *on a deep coral reef...*

Edward stank as a poet. He was derivative actually, and lost in the nineteenth century with the other hopeless romantics who doted on form, meter and tragic endings. But the finer, most ethereal journals published him and fueled his foolish obsession with verse.

"You'll burn, Edward," I warned him testily, not one hour later, as we lounged in sagging canvas chairs between the bougainvillea-covered trellises that bound the little beach-side patio just outside my bedroom door. "You'll burn in hell."

Edward fiddled with his pen and refused to accept the bottle of tanning lotion I thrust in his face, and I refused to see that he was turning me into a common nag. I tilted the bottle toward my own skin, massaged the creamy oil into my arms, neck, legs, thighs, chest, deep into the heart-shaped crevice of my breasts just above the sloping upper lines of my bikini.

Itsy-bitsy teeny weenie, red, yellow, and blue balloon bikini. Amazingly similar to the plastic wrap on the Wonder Bread my mother had always steadfastly refused to buy, and which I consequently never bought, despite what Buffalo Bob insisted years ago on "Howdy Doody."

"Now remember kids, tell your mom to look for the bread with the red, yellow and blue balloons on the wrapper."

"Do my back, Edward," I held out the bottle again toward my literary lover. "Please, if I turn over, will you do my back?"

But such is the disadvantage of an invisible companion. He doesn't drink too much, shout, pout, or run off with another more flirtatious or curvaceous woman. But he will not rub sun tan lotion on your back, across your spine, over the most unreachable, unseeable places of your body.

I did my best. With a man, without a man, I was good at doing my best. I filled my right palm with lotion and lifted it high above my head then down, down onto stony, stubborn vertebrae. I met the right hand with the left, swiping, sliding, sloshing oil around until I believed I had the whole back covered.

"You see, Edward," I gloated. "You see."

But I didn't turn over to brown my back. I found something else to fret about: Tan lines. I didn't want tan lines interfering with my perfect Martinique vacation. I undid the buttons on my red, yellow and blue bikini bra. Lifted the straps up off my chest, pushed them away, above my shoulders, and sent Edward packing, back to the lush fronds of the rain forest. He was the wrong man for this job. I needed someone who could eye my unstrapped bikini and ask for more.

This was a French island, after all, freckled with sophisticated travelers from Paris and Montreal, Lyons and Grenoble, Quebec City and even golden Monaco according to the guidebook that had captivated Crystal and me way last winter when we'd planned this trip. We'd dreamed of exotica, erotica, and not just among the plant life.

"Topless means nothing to French women," Crystal had declared over thick crust pizza at her place one cold and snowy February night. "They're totally blasé about their bodies."

"How do you know about French women?" I'd never imagined Crystal traveled much beyond the twenty-fourth floor of the downtown office building where the two of us earned our corporate communications bread.

"I knew a French woman in college," Crystal had replied, taking an enthusiastic bite out of her current wedge of anchovy and black olive pizza.

"And?" Crystal was a great one for leaving me hanging, as witness my Crystal-less vacation on that lovely Martinique beach.

"And she told me a few things," Crystal had laughed, helped herself to another slice of pizza before she'd finished the one on her plate, the way she sometimes lit up a cigarette while she still had another one going.

"Such as?"

It was no use. I wasn't going to get anything more out of Crystal about her French friend in college. She'd smiled devilishly and chewed and flipped through a few more pages in the Arthur Frommer's *Caribbbean* we'd found in the library. "Here we go," she'd said, her forefinger leaving a faint circle of tomato sauce just above a photo bright with little fishing boats and nets drying under a tangle of sea grapes on a sparkling shore. "Here's the hotel I want to stay in...'unpretentious seaside inn with a summery decor...bougainvillea climbing white stucco walls...one of the most beautiful sections of the island...Don't be surprised by the topless bathers lounging around the pool...around pools and beaches all over this glorious island...'"

I hadn't been to the swimming pool yet. I had wandered past it, heard the music of French conversation across a thick fence of hibiscus and frangipani, women's voices floating above men's like bells above timpani. I'd sniffed the de rigueur clouds of Gauloise smoke, glimpsed the chemical blue blur of the pool, the spidery web of deck chairs and body parts—arms, legs, heads, necks, breasts. Yes, I could tell, even in my haste not to see, that Crystal and Frommer had been right. French women *were* blasé about their bodies. As blasé and silvery-shimmery as fish.

Turn me into a poem, Edward, I prayed from my solo canvas beach chair, balloon bikini cloth heavy and hot upon my chest. Wherever you are, Edward, with your notepads and pens, turn me into a lyrical, spherical, miracle poem, so that I too may be free in my body and mind to sit by the pool with the others.

"It's not about bodies, it's about sex," hammered a voice inside my head, Gregory's voice. Gregory, who I'd married in the dark ages of my life, and then divorced because he'd grown like a major toenail into something that catches and clutches on everything. I'd hacked him off and tossed him away after two and a half fitful years in the nest and he wasn't supposed to follow me here, to Martinique of all places.

I'd seen acres of nudity on my honeymoon with Gregory. Acres of legalized California nudity on a beautiful beach, but I hadn't so much as lifted a strap off my bathing suit—a proper one-piece job that year—because Gregory had forbidden it.

"I forbid you Marcy, to show these people one more inch of skin than your bathing suit allows," Gregory had said when he wasn't racing around the hot sand of that California beach, taking photographs of all the skinny and not so skinny dippers. "I forbid you, Marcy, to do so now."

"Go fish!" I told Gregory, not then, but now, in my head. "I'll whip them out if I want to, let them dance in the wind, enjoy the tropical breeze. I want them to be free, Gregory. Do you hear me? Free!"

But I couldn't. I wouldn't. How could I bare my breasts in a public place, never mind all those tinkly-voiced French women shimmering like big-eyed fish by the pool.

"Just one little glimpse, Marcy. Just one little peek. There's nobody around. Nobody who can see. They're all by the pool or sitting way down the beach. Please, please. We want to see the seashore too. 'All day, all night, sitting by the seashore sifting sand...'"

They had started to sing. My breasts had actually started to sing to me from inside the cups of my Wonder Bread bikini so it was the least I could do, the smallest, itty-bittyist little favor I could do for my darling, loving cooped-up twins who'd stood by me during good times and bad more than Gregory ever had, or any man for that matter.

"Just a little peek, puhhuleeese, just to see what it's like out there in the beautiful, fruitiful tropical world," they cajoled, and I couldn't bear to turn them into common nags too. I thought that maybe if I unleashed them for just a split second or so they would get it out of their system and leave me alone for the rest of the trip and I could wear my bikini with impunity.

So I did. Yes I did, and of course that's when Victoire just happened to amble along a deserted path leading towards the beach from the swimming pool and front part of the inn. Victoire, from Trinité on the eastern side of the island, where Atlantic waters roil up fierce and unswimmable, calling out a cheery *"Allo! Ça va?"* approaching at the precise moment of my unveiling.

"Allo!" As if he'd mistaken me for a long-lost friend. *"Ça va?"* And where were my yearning-to-be-free, singing breasts now? They collapsed into silence like clams, that's what they did, leaving me to deal with the bronzed stranger who'd stepped like an eclipse between me and the sun. The sky crusted with clouds, the sea jelly-rolled into itself and nearly disappeared. The wind hissed like a pressure cooker and shifted course, blowing in from Mt. Pelée and other points north. It's going to rain, I thought. It's going to storm cats and pheromones. And I'm going to drown. Right here, like a naked loaf of bread, in front of this unknown man.

"Are there hurricanes this time of year?" I wondered aloud as Victoire drew closer. Those were my first words to him, my first attempt at small talk: "Are there hurricanes?" And me ever mindful of my breasts, but refusing to look at them. I studied the gathering storm clouds instead, and Victoire whose face seemed to emulate the sky the way it blinked with both light and danger and a certain grace that spoke of lofty possibilities and insurgent feelings.

"Hurricanes? Oh, no. It rains, of course it rains sometimes in August, but it is rare, a total rarity, to have hurricanes this time of year."

Victoire smiled and didn't look at my breasts as Gregory would have done or my father. Oy, oy, oy, my father, who used to stumble into my girlhood room under one pretext or another, never knocking or announcing himself. Just coming towards me and towards me, inspecting my blooming body up and down like it was his own private cornfield.

"Last fall Hurricane David terrorized the islands for awhile," Victoire continued blithely, the most oblivious man I had encountered in a long while, given the fact that my breasts rose up from my chest like beacons of light from the sea. They were lovely breasts—not extravagantly large—but luscious and shapely as ripe pears. Even Edward would have set aside his ambitious pen—I was almost sure of it—to admire this unprecedented view.

"But luckily David did not wreak great damage on Martinique, not like the one years ago that destroyed *La Pagérie*..."

"*La Pagérie?*" I met his earnest and steady aquamarine gaze, still straining to keep my own eyes level. *Don't look down, whatever you do don't look down*, I ordered my brain, as if I traversed a narrow ledge above a steep and rocky gorge. One false step and he will have to look too and then we will both plunge towards oblivion.

"*La Pagérie*," Victoire repeated, a piece of work himself in a minimalist bikini that clung to his hips and a few other key body parts like buckling terrain to a cliff.

Don't look down, don't look down, don't look down I repeated to myself. I grew dizzy with the effort of it.

"*La Pagérie* is of course the birthplace of Empress Josephine," he exclaimed with practiced aplomb. "A high and mighty sugar plantation gone with the wind." He made a dismissive little spitting sound with his lips. "Only the kitchen still stands, and it has been turned into a museum. Worth a visit, as they say, if you're in the neighborhood."

"I wasn't planning to visit museums," I replied, daring irony with Victoire for the first time, "when the outdoor scenery is so dazzling."

"There is a letter in this museum from Napoleon himself," he prattled on, meeting my irony and raising it to new levels. "A deeply passionate letter, promising kisses to Josephine." He leaned closer to me, and finally lowered his eyes. The storm clouds dissipated and sunshine returned; the gorge folded in on itself like a healing wound.

"*Mille baisers amoureux, partout, partout*...a thousand love-filled kisses," Victoire translated though he didn't need to, not with the lovely way he spoke French, "A thousand kisses everywhere, everywhere...

"I am a tour guide," he added quickly. "I can take you there tomorrow on my day off." And from the suddenly silken turn of his voice, I knew—we both knew, didn't we?—that he wasn't just speaking about museums.

"And the Benz...how is the man with the Benz?" The cocoa-skinned waiter surveyed me with dark and curious eyes even though I came fully dressed to the lunch table, my breasts perky and safe inside a backless pink sundress. "The man with the Mercedez Benz he is recovering?"

"Oh, yes," I nodded briefly, perfunctorily, accepting the cold crab plate he handed me. "Oh yes," I elaborated for the benefit of a waiter who understood more English than I'd first supposed. "Bernard is doing much better, thank you. The doctors say he should be on his feet again soon."

"The Benz?" Victoire eyed me dubiously. Victoire from the beach, who I'd invited to join me at my table for two on the flower-filled terrace, despite—or should I say because of—his languid suggestiveness.

"My fiancé is in the hospital," I offered breathily as the waiter tippytoed away. "It's his gallbladder actually," I said because I couldn't deal with the bends any further; it was too preposterous. I had only invented the bends for the benefit of the waiter, who had intruded into my life that morning at breakfast, with one too many questions. "The waiter misunderstood me. He thought it had something to do with a car."

"Ah," exclaimed Victoire, who had not dressed for lunch, so that he *might* have been naked for all I saw of him across our magnificent lunch table. I saw his beautiful bare, nutty brown chest rising into capable shoulders and neck and then the hungry, sensuous face that had both startled and amazed me at first glance and caused all those disturbing climatic conditions.

"I told Bernard it would be all right with me if we turned around and went right back to Chicago so he could see his regular doctor, but he said, why should we after all? Shouldn't one of us, at least, enjoy this vacation?" Victoire eyed me as calmly and understandingly as if he heard stories like this every day from women sunning themselves alone on the beach. "Of course I feel bad for him..."

Reaching the point where fiction and reality converged, I wasn't sure how to continue. Should I also tell him about Gerard on the mountain top or Edward with his poems and how I'd invented all three of them to shelter and console me from the brunt of my own internal storms. Should I tell him about Crystal and her change of heart; Gregory and his controlling heart; should I go back even further to my childhood and how maybe it had shaped my faint-hearted way of being alone?

"It is all right, I can take you there...on the way to the other places," said Victoire, forking crab salad, oblivious to the uncertainties coagulating like egg yolk in my head.

"There?" I looked at him questioningly. I hadn't thought I'd agreed to go anywhere with him.

"To the hospital, of course," Victoire continued carelessly. "We can stop at the hospital in Fort de France after we visit *La Pagérie*. I will be happy to take you to see your husband."

"Fiancé," I corrected, needing to keep the fabrication straight. I wasn't the sort of person who would go off with another man as soon as her husband's gall bladder churned. Was I?

"Thank you. That would be wonderful," I said, because what could I say?—I don't want to see him? I assumed that if Victoire resembled other men—and why wouldn't he—he'd forget we ever had this conversation long before tomorrow.

"I would very much like to see Bernard," I said, digging into a luncheon salad that held exquisite lumps of crab meat mingling with toasted almond, sliced mango, sweet radishes and celery root in a lemony homemade mayonnaise.

"Good. It is settled then. We can leave in the morning after breakfast," Victoire offered then. "I am booked with another tour this afternoon, but tomorrow," he smiled, the smile of a fisher, an extremely patient fisher who could wait as long as it took to catch the fish of his dreams, so long as the fish dreamed of being caught. "Tomorrow I will be totally at your service."

He didn't forget. Victoire came for me the next morning and we headed south in his banged-up, dust-coated jeep, away from *La Pagérie*, away from Fort de France, through the little village of St. Anne just a few kilometers down the bay from the hotel.

"I want you to see my special beach," Victoire announced after we'd cleared the last little ramshackle house at the edge of the village and entered a glorious stretch of terrain filled with sky, water, sand on one side, rustling cane fields and forested hills on the other.

"What about Josephine...and Napoleon?" I swiveled in my seat to glimpse Victoire in profile. He looked regal and emperor-like himself, except for his thick crown of bluish-black hair blowing every which way in the wind.

"On the islands we try not to hurry things." Victoire cleared a thatch of hair from his eyes, but the breeze slapped it back. "Unlike your friend with the bends."

"Gallbladder," I whispered back.

I should have been frightened. I barely knew Victoire, though he seemed to be known at the hotel. He'd signed for his lunch rather than paid for it, chatted pleasantly with the owner's wife when he'd collected me in the peachy-orange lobby this morning after breakfast. I didn't know what they said to one another, though she smiled and he smiled and she smiled and he smiled. They'd spoken rapid, spitfire French, a language I understood only minimally from many years ago in high school: *La table est rouge; la maison est blanche.* You had to speak French slooowly if you expected me to get it, you had to say *mille baisers partout partout* with the plodding enunciation of an elephant.

"I have taken many people on this tour," Victoire offered suddenly as if reading my mind. "From your hotel and from other hotels I have many satisfied customers."

"Well, then." I leaned back in the seat and tasted the frenzied breeze on my face, on my arms, in my own short, wavy hair, tasted a sudden electricity that I'd known with other men and which had always led to other things besides the destinations we pretended to be headed for. "Well then." I tried to approximate the sophisticated smile of the French hotel keeper conversing with Victoire that morning beneath the arched entranceway of the hushed little papaya-colored lobby. "Bring on the beach."

We couldn't get there by jeep. We had to park behind a wooden rice and beans stand that popped up out of a sloping dune and hop into a little motor boat anchored alongside a flimsy quay.

I should have been really frightened. Beach, beach, beach lay everywhere, as far as the eye could see and here was Victoire, slipping a few coins to the balding old man who raced out of the shop so we could putt-putt away in search of more crystalline pasture.

"It is a very special place," Victoire assured me as I buckled into an orange life vest and received a rough handshake from the rock and rolling sea.

"I like special places," I replied nincompoop-style, beginning to struggle with an unwelcome queasiness. Who would have thought all this lemon-lime fizz could twist and shout like Chubby Checker just a few hundred feet off shore.

"Focus on a single point ahead of you. That's the trick." Victoire studied my face, which must have turned as green as the sea. "I have brought many tourists to this little cove and not one of them, how do you say, ever cashed in his chocolate chip cookies."

I laughed. What could I do but laugh at his musical French voice producing this stateside colloquialism in the middle of a tilt-a-whirl sea. I laughed and searched for something to focus on as I had searched the horizon many months ago with Crystal and found this vacation.

"Divorce isn't all it's cracked up to be," I'd told Crystal, at her apartment again, on one of those cold and dark nights between Thanksgiving and New Years, when it doesn't matter which holiday you celebrate: Christmas, Hanukkah, Kwanzaa.

"There's no joy in any of it," I'd said, "unless you have someone to love."

"You're getting maudlin again," Crystal had observed, and dug out some travel books she stockpiled for moments like this, the way some people stored whiskey and gin.

"Focus, Marcy," Victoire cried again over the sound of the motor and the waves, but I sat in the bow facing Victoire, and all that lay ahead of me was empty sea. So I trained my gaze on him, on steady, sturdy Victoire, steering us to an unknown shore, and wondered what life might be like on this island year 'round and around.

Dear Crystal: I composed in my head, still struggling valiantly to keep my breakfast down. *"It's too bad you decided not to come on this vacation, because now you may never meet Victoire, who only yesterday washed up on the beach outside my hotel, and already we are great friends, going places together. And Crystal, I'm not sure, but I think maybe he will ask me to stay here and live with him. I can see it in his eyes, and though it will mean the end of employee discounts on Stouffer frozen foods, how can I say no to Victoire, Crystal? How can I say no when love is finally at hand?"*

And then Victoire was killing the motor and jumping out of the little boat to guide us onto a miraculous shoulder of sand that jutted gracefully into the sea on two sides. I folded Crystal's imaginary note into an imaginary bottle and floated it onto a wave, just in time, I might add, to begin wrestling Victoire off of me.

"No, Victoire, no," I protested meaning yes, because no one had touched me like that in quite some time. There had been one man since Gregory, or rather during Gregory. There had been Mark, who had kissed and caressed me in the front seat of his car in the parking lot of a restaurant where I had met him for dinner and a few too many drinks.

"You have lovely hands, Marcy," he had murmured during one of those quiet intervals in which we came up for air, slowly, languidly. "You have the long and graceful fingers of a pianist."

I'd chuckled softly to myself as Mark threaded and rethreaded his own thick and stubby fingers into mine. I had played the piano as a girl and daydreamed about becoming a pianist, because my father wanted me to be a pianist, but I never considered it seriously. I didn't have the strength for it or the stomach for recitals.

"I'll become a pianist if that's what you'd like," I'd replied, smiling into his eyes and waiting for him to begin our little beguine all over again. Which of course he did, probing my mouth with his tongue for a long delicious time, before he pulled away to study me with the longing of a river seeking its source. But Mark didn't say anything about pianists again or whether he wanted me to become one.

He said in a very throaty, half broken voice: "The next time we go out, we're going to make love."

But we didn't make love because we never went out again.

"No Victoire, no." I tried to push him away from me, the two of us squooshing our bare toes into cool wet sand and gently lapping surf, my insides right side up again now that we'd hit land.

"I am only trying to welcome you to my special cove." Victoire smiled a shiny seashell smile, then backed away to retrieve his khaki rucksack from the boat. "Fortunately the cruise ships have not yet discovered it."

It was quite a sandbox: A white canvas hammock floated between two coconut palms that shaded a little thatch-roofed shack with a beaded curtain door. And down the strand a bit stood more trees, including a giant ficus with a roughhewn platform laid across its expansive, lowest limbs.

"This is *my La Pagérie.*" Victoire crooked the rucksack over his shoulder with one hand and came to stand beside me in the feather-pillow soft sand. "The sweetest plantation on the island," he murmured, regarding me with eyes that said: "I conduct serious business here, and only with those who pass muster."

"Get a load of those coconuts," was all I could say, my eyes leaping away from his, into the trees. "It's a good thing Isaac Newton never slept here." I laughed.

"Nutonne?" He looked puzzled, as if trying to place the name of a tour guide competitor.

"You know, the guy who discovered gravity when an apple fell on his head. But if it had been a COCONUT, an actual COCONUT...Yadda yadda yadda." I was trying to talk smart to camouflage my nervousness, because Victoire was all over me again, and I knew we were going to make love. I'd known it yesterday, and this morning and if I hadn't wanted to make love I wouldn't have climbed into his jeep, but now that it was actually about to happen I considered my other options and there weren't very many: I could run into the ocean and swim until I disappeared. Or I could bore him with stories about my life with Gregory until *he* ran into the ocean and disappeared.

But why play Scheherazade with a man who only wanted to take me in his arms, run his hands up and down my arms, kiss me, kiss me, hold me, kiss me...turn a big pile of pure white sand into a sugar plantation?

Gregory had barely touched me in two and a half long years and Mark had turned tail and run when I called to inform him a few days after our one and only date that we wouldn't have to meet in parking lots anymore. I was going to leave Gregory.

So I didn't leave Gregory then. But at least I had begun to know I wanted someone to make love to me.

"Come here Marcy Rosen." Victoire said in a voice that reminded me of all my favorite foods piled high atop each other on a freshly baked bun, the world's best and biggest Dagwood sandwich.

"You don't need these, do you?" He swept his hand up and down the fitted white tee shirt and striped red and blue shorts I had thrown on that morning, no bikini underneath, having assumed we weren't headed for the beach.

"I didn't bring my bathing suit," I said. "I didn't know we were going to go swimming."

Victoire laughed. Oh Victoire laughed, and displayed such beautiful, happy teeth that I laughed too, the too hearty way you laugh at a joke you don't quite get.

"We can go swimming, if you like." Victoire pressed his thin, muscular body so close against mine that the blood coursing through his veins felt like the blood coursing through mine. It was the closest I'd been to anybody in a long time.

Victoire stepped away, just long enough to dance out of his clothes and start peeling me out of mine, as casually as if I were a banana.

"No," I protested reflexively as he unhooked my bra. "No," I repeated in a squished fruit voice I didn't recognize.

"C'mon, now." Victoire half-smiled, squinting at me with insouciant eyes that said, 'It's not like I haven't already seen them.'

We made love off and on, deep into the afternoon. In the hammock first, where I almost got seasick again until I remembered to focus, focus on Victoire, and his bronzed, blissful face floating over me like a precious coin. I felt his warm, weightless texture above me, beside me, inside me, the both of us swimming headlong toward deep and urgent needs. No coconuts would fall on *our* heads, not the way we defied gravity in our swinging bed.

"Just think what might have happened if Napoleon had met Josephine in a topless state," I mused, during one of our dreamy intermissions.

Victoire laughed, merry teeth shining on me again like bright light. "He would have never needed to conquer Europe. That's for sure." He ran his hands ever so softly over my breasts.

"Make love, not war!" I said, and we both cried out with laughter.

He'd packed food in his rucksack. Cold wheat pancakes to spread with orange marmalade and salted sunflower seeds; a mango we took turns sucking on until we'd extracted the last delicious juices from its enormous pit. There was cold curried chicken too, and a bottle of red wine which he chilled in the sea anchored securely under a rock.

We ate lunch in the ficus tree, reclining like nymphs in a painting on straw mats he'd unearthed from a creaky old chest in the shack. That chest held snorkeling gear too. I have memories of us drifting naked through a shallow coral reef, blowing bubbles out of long tubes, splendid, bright colors flashing across the sides and dorsal fins of tiny fish. But soon after Victoire rummaged deep into the rucksack and produced a see-through plastic hashish pouch, the colors began pirouetting everywhere—in the water, out of the water. On the fish, on Victoire's face, on my legs entwined longingly around his—it was one big never-ending kaleidoscope.

"I don't ordinarily do marijuana," I confessed, lying on my back up in the tree, watching an elongated blue fish, then a phosphorescent red and gold one dip past a cloud.

"No?" Victoire mouthed sadly, sitting cross-legged beside me, penis temporarily flaccid, like a curled worm. "No Mary Jane?" He accepted the stubby pipe I handed out to him and pulled on it greedily, holding the smoke in his lungs for an extra long time. I waited silently, fearing he thought me self-righteous.

"So?" Victoire fairly gasped, his face a contorted balloon when he finally breathed the smoke out. "What *is* your drug of choice?"

"Love." I blurted, not knowing I was going to say it, but realizing in the same instant that it was absolutely true and hysterically amusing at the same time. "Love is my drug of choice," I said and dissolved into laughter.

"Well, then, Marcy, *ma chérie*." Victoire set the pipe aside and reached for me again. "We will have to *do* something about that, won't we?"

"Yes," I replied, growing even giddier at the little French term of endearment he'd pinned to my name, which he had trouble pronouncing in the first place. He always made my name sound like Mahshy.

"Mahshy, masherie, mahshy masherie," I repeated over and over, melting into a tittering waterfall in his arms and making Victoire smile, too, though I could tell from the silvery-green fish that swam across his face that he didn't totally get it.

I didn't get sick in the boat on the way back. Victoire credited the reefer.

"Your government." He made another little spitting noise, the way he had when we'd met outside my bungalow the day before and he'd first mentioned the Empress Josephine. "Your government tries to make people forget the medicinal value of hashish."

I thought it was the love-making that had cured me, but didn't say so. I focused instead on Victoire's vanishing playground, marveling to myself at how well we already knew each other after only one day.

"We can go there again tomorrow." Victoire turned toward me in the jeep on the way back through St. Anne, his hair a windblown rain forest across his face. "Or, of course," he hesitated, smiled facetiously under all that hair. "We can go to Fort de France instead. Have lunch in the big city and let you visit your fiancé...if he still burns so deeply in your mind."

My fiancé? He'd remembered. More than I remembered, actually, spoke like he believed Bernard existed. I should have said: *I want to be with you Victoire, no one else but you burns in my mind.* That would have been the easy answer, the one he wanted to hear. Instead, I crashed headlong into my own obstacle course.

"Things really aren't so good with Bernard and me anymore," I said, temporarily blinded by the wind. "We took this vacation to try to find out if we still loved each other, but..."

"Love, it is so important to you, mahshy mahsherie?" he interrupted, in a tone that transformed his playful French name for me into a prickly jab.

"Well, yes," I said softly, staring at my hands through a veil of hair. "If I sleep with a man I want to love him."

The car made a frightening, skidding sound on the narrow black-topped road as we rounded a sudden curve and veered uncomfortably close to a wobbly old *Renault Cinq* chugging along from the other direction. Victoire laid his fist on the horn, even though he was the one who'd crossed over the center.

"Love is a drug, Marcy, like you say," Victoire informed me as we hit straightaway again—ocean, sky and sand spread out to forever on the driver's side of the car. "It is a drug that wears off like every other drug, leaving side effects."

"Well, it takes time to get to know somebody." I backpedaled furiously, trying to keep up with him and the forest of coconut palms flying by on the right.

"Love," Victoire said, "is not my drug of choice."

And then the white stucco, bougainvillea-covered hotel loomed up in front of us from high on a shaded oceanside hill, just the way the guidebook described it.

"I'd like to go with you tomorrow," I said as the jeep rolled to a halt, thinking that love was also a game I would never master.

"I'll have to see about tomorrow." Victoire smiled wryly, and stared straight ahead, waiting for me to alight.

"What about dinner? Would you like to join me for dinner tonight?" Victoire said he had to get home, and I realized as I stepped from his car and felt myself falling, falling, that I had no idea what he meant by home.

I waited for him in the morning by a bubbling tiled fish pond in the papaya fruit lobby, until the hotelkeeper's wife came up to me in a long, crisp pink flowered dress.

"He has already come and gone," she said.

"What?" I pretended I didn't know who she meant.

"There was someone who wanted to visit St. Pierre." She looked at me with dark eyes I couldn't read, and because of this I knew there were other things she knew and wouldn't tell me.

I wanted to run into the ocean and retrieve the imaginary bottle I'd floated out to Crystal, proclaiming my happiness over Victoire. Instead I asked if she knew of a driver I could hire, and she telephoned for one. He was young, barely more than a boy, thinner than Victoire if that was possible, with beautiful copper-colored skin, and a soft, ingenuous face that regarded me with a combination of awe and curiosity. He didn't talk much. I had to draw him out, as we hairpinned inland, up, up past pineapple fields and banana groves, then, at last, into drizzling rain forest, awash with magnificent flowers, baby ferns, plumed bamboo, and from occasional majestic vantage points, deep, deep green, queenly valleys.

"Yes, I have always lived here," he replied to my first tentative stab at conversation.

"Yes, I have seen the United States," he responded to the next question. "My grandmother lives in the Bronx. I visited her every summer when I was young."

You are young now, I wanted to say, but complimented him instead on his English, which, I supposed aloud, he must have perfected in New York.

"No," he said, "I studied English here, in school."

He answered questions, but didn't ask them. Didn't ask the obvious question that the waiter had asked right away. So I didn't need to tell him about Bernard, Gerard and Edward. Or Victoire, who I didn't expect to find on this journey north, but didn't expect to stop thinking about either.

"This is St. Pierre," the boy announced when we at last descended to sea level, sunlight, and a humble little town with a sleepy main street and generous harbor. "Once it flourished like a little Paris." He was gaining momentum, volunteering information without prodding, and I thought maybe he could be something more than a driver.

"The beach is black like me," he turned to look at me from the front seat of the car, a smile on his face as wide as the island. "Because of the lava.

"There is a museum," he said, but not in the spitting, scoffing way Victoire had mentioned *La Pagérie*. "Most people go to the beach and then visit the museum. There is a little place near the church ruins that serves conch pie." He parked the car and looked at his watch. "I can meet you there after lunch," he said. "Whatever time you like."

"You don't have to leave me," I said, surprised by the urgency in my voice.

"There is no danger of it erupting," the boy replied politely, as if he thought I feared *that*. "But then of course, that's what the authorities promised just before the volcano vaporized the whole town." He laughed, the honest, weightless laugh of those who live quiet, contented lives outside the muddled pronunciations of their governments.

"Thirty thousand people killed in one stroke. But don't worry," he said, following me across the street to the beach. "The mountain has not been spitting out ash or steam lately."

He was like one of my invisible lovers, the way he sat apart from me on the warm, black sand and studied my Arthur Frommer guidebook, not looking up when I stripped to my bathing suit and dashed into the cool, redeeming surf.

"'It rains frequently on *Montagne Pelée*.'" he read aloud, as I toweled off. "'Temperatures can drop very low, and there are sudden deep crevices in the earth, hidden by tropical growth. Unless you are an experienced climber, you should not attempt to reach the summit on your own.'

"I have been up there many times," he said, turning a page. "It is not so difficult a climb. I can take you."

"Take me to the museum," I said, slipping on dry clothes over my still damp bathing suit. "I didn't wear my hiking boots today."

Inside the museum, which was dark and dank and stifling, I brushed close to the boy and asked him to read from the French placards that explained the history of the town and the volcano.

"But it is also in English." He pointed to the lower half of the sign we stood in front of.

"I like to hear French," I said. "I have never actually been to a country before where people speak French."

"Most people here speak in patois," he said. But he read to me anyway in a voice and an accent that sounded nothing like Victoire's, a different sort of music entirely.

Victoire, of course, was not at the museum, as he had not been at the beach and would not be on the shady veranda of the simple little restaurant where the boy and I ate spicy conch in fluted tart shells and sipped intoxicating glasses of rum punch.

"I don't like museums," the boy said. "I'd much rather climb *Mont Pelée*."

"I don't even know your name," I said, realizing the subject had not yet come up.

"Call me Nadie." He tilted his head quizzically in my direction.

"Call me Marcella," I offered, and now we had something elegant and exotic to chew on besides the conch.

Victoire was not at the museum. But because I visited the museum and viewed its petrified relics and musty old photographs, listened to Nadie recount the story in French, and followed the story in English with my eyes, I learned that one person survived the molten lava bath that wiped out an entire city. A man locked underground, within the thick walls of the prison.

In memory of this man, I invited Nadie into my little yellow room when we arrived back at the inn near St. Anne.

"I think maybe he looked like you," I told Nadie, handing him the fee he'd requested for his services. He pocketed the money and headed towards the door; as if he had no idea what more I could want from him.

"The *Mont Pelée* survivor might have looked like you," I explained, wanting to hold him in this room. "He would have had your sort of calm, trusting face, even while he was still in prison."

Nadie stared at me as if I had invented a new, unintelligible form of English. He stepped toward the bed that would have been Crystal's and picked up a newspaper I had carried with me on the plane from Chicago. "'Day 283 for the American hostages in Iran,'" he read aloud.

I moved toward him, took the paper out of his hand, not wanting to be reminded of a world outside the pretty little one in this room at the inn.

I wanted Nadie to be the man who survived the wrath of *Mont Pelée*, and I...I would be the woman from that movie, "The Summer of '42," who mourned the death of her husband in a faraway war, by comforting herself with a boy.

Nadie acted like he didn't know what I wanted, but he did know, he did know, moving slowly and insistently on top of me until he, I, we, the both of us erupted and erupted and erupted.

"Goodbye, Nadie," I said when he told me his mother expected him home for dinner. Godspeed, Nadie.

"Goodbye, Marcella," I whispered sadly, when he'd tread silently away.

"Her husband, he is sick too." The waiter clucked his tongue commiseratively that night, as he delivered a platter bearing a beautifully grilled whole red snapper, rimmed by a scalloped mousse of sweet potatoes.

Whose husband? I almost blurted. But I was learning to look before I spoke.

"He has blisters." The waiter slit my fish down the middle as he prepared to filet it. "He has hurt his feet climbing *Mont Pelée*."

The waiter wielded the knife expertly, separating tender white fish from the bone with a few deft strokes that left the skeleton intact, head and all. I peered past the silvery rib cage he dangled in front of me and saw the woman he was speaking of, a huge, fashionable straw hat hiding much of her face, as she leaned close to Victoire. Victoire with his catch of the day, and his back turned toward me. She had a dispassionate, cat-like face, from what I could see of it. She apparently did hats, not love, and had made it with Victoire all the way to dinner.

"Her husband should try Dr. Scholl's," I murmured as the waiter laid the skeleton onto a little dish he'd set beside my larger plate. "Dr. Scholl's helped Gerard when he climbed Mt. Pelée. He especially likes those little medicated pads shaped like O's."

"Gerard?" the waiter drew in a sudden, steep breath. "Gerard?"

I ignored him of course, just as I ignored Victoire. As much as I could ignore a man whose very name reminded me of what I'd lost. Whose presence on that enchanted, flower-filled terrace overlooking the sea made me feel like a blooming hibiscus tree yanked up at the roots.

"Bernard, he knows about Gerard?" the waiter asked, the round-faced, cocoa-skinned waiter, sweeping away my untouched fish in exchange for bibb lettuce and hearts of palm, glistening under a light olive oil and balsamic vinegar dressing.

I said nothing, could only nod dumbly as he spun a giant pepper grinder above the salad, wanting to indicate to him that he'd spun enough.

"My living quarters, they are right behind the kitchen," the waiter said not many minutes later, replacing the salad with an airy *crême brulée*, which he anointed with flaming rum.

I ignored him, eyeing Victoire through the blue flames that licked my dessert, watched the fire subsume his body but not consume it.

I ignored the waiter all that night while I slept fitfully, waking periodically to remember dreams of assorted skeletonized fish swimming lazily through colorless waters, past dangerous looking reefs that sparkled with red, yellow, and blue balloon-like rocks.

I ignored the waiter all the next day, which I spent in Fort de France. I took the public bus, a noisy, beaten down, smoke-spewing vehicle that couldn't ascend certain hills without every passenger, every yapping dog and clucking chicken, getting off first.

I spent the day in Fort de France, wandering through crowded, narrow streets lined with open-air cafes, charming restaurants and tiny boutiques displaying Parisian couture and perfumes, crystal, silver and china. In the bustling street market, near the cruise ship-lined waterfront, I lingered at the stall of a woman selling local jewelry.

"How much for this one?" I asked, feeling dizzy with the need to speak to someone.

"Thirty francs," she replied, tossing in a smile for the same price, a magnificent smile that shimmered against her dark skin, liquid eyes, and bright madras headdress. "Very pretty," she added shyly when I hesitated, contemplating the silver necklace in my hand.

"Twenty-five francs," she said, when I continued staring. But I gave her thirty and put it on. She smiled again, handing me a mirror so I could see the way the fish-skeleton pendant danced elegantly on its chain. "Very pretty," she said again.

"My room, it has no locks on the door," the waiter said that night, bringing a stew that bubbled with crayfish and shrimp, mussels, tuna, and codfish in a thick, aromatic broth.

"You should get a lock," I said, looking not at him, but at the show across the way: Victoire and his lady friend with the broad-brimmed hat, billing and cooing like the other kewpie dolls in this place. Even if they hadn't been there, I would have seen them.

"It is called blaff," the waiter said.

"Blaff?"

"The stew," he said. "It contains a little bit of everything for your last night on the island."

"It is delicious," I said, tasting a soup blessed with basil, oregano, garlic, and fennel, and wondering how he knew I was leaving.

"I am called Cadasse," he said, bringing me a complimentary glass of red wine.

"Nobody should be alone on an island like this," he said, bringing me another.

I looked up at him finally, from the crayfish I was pulling apart, realizing that he referred not to me, but himself.

His room smelled salty like the sea, spicy like the food he carried forth every day from the kitchen. It was a small room and clean, walls the color of vanilla taffy. He'd changed out of his white waiter's jacket and long linen pants. He sat near the bed in khaki shorts and navy tee shirt, bare feet propped up on a low wooden table, a partially worked jigsaw puzzle spread out before him. He lifted up one of the pieces as I walked in the door, and turned it around. But I knew, from the light in his eyes, the sudden tilt of his head, that he had been waiting for me.

"You really should get a lock for that door," I quipped, trying to cover up my embarrassment at being there. "Anybody could barge in on you."

"Nobody will come," he smiled shyly. "I did not invite anyone else." He understood English, but not all its nuances.

There was a framed photo on the wall above his bed, a close-up of three beautiful island birds perched in the bowers of ferns that looked massive by comparison. I gazed at the picture a long time, until I could no longer bear the weight of his eyes on my back, watching me.

"This one also has birds." He indicated the puzzle he'd been working on.

"Yes, yes, so it does." I turned around finally to look at it. He'd pieced the border together, had several little circles going in the center, revealing a wing here, tail there of a tiny bright bird.

"I make it and break it and make it all over again," he said. "That is the way you say it? Make it and break it?" he asked, eyes bubbling with laughter.

"Yes," I said, but then my eyes caught on a silver frame on a simple chest of drawers near the bed. I looked again and saw a woman in a bright orange and green dress. She had high, regal cheekbones, melting eyes, the same innocent, lush beauty of the woman I'd bought the fish necklace from in Fort de France,

"That is Viviana," he said.

"Viviana?"

"My wife"

"Why did you invite me here?" I asked, something churning up in me that was neither anger nor sadness. Just something big and full of resolve, like the sea.

"To make love to you, of course,"

"But she is here with you."

"I will turn it around then."

"It is too late for that. She is already here."

"Mar Sea Mar Sea." He sighed, pronouncing my name like it was a great body of water that could carry him to a place where he would not be so alone. "Did you come here to find love with me, Mar Sea?"

"Love makes me forget things, Cadasse," I said, using his name for the first time and thinking how it sounded like poetry. "Love makes me forget what I don't want to remember."

He laughed and sighed again. "I think you are like that great painter, Go Ga, who also visited this island and saw love everywhere."

Go Ga? It was a name I did not remember from the guidebooks. Then I realized he meant Gaugin.

"I am not a painter," I said.

"But you are very beautiful, Mar Sea," he said. "If you weren't married already and if I weren't married already, I would marry you.

"My wife, she lives on Guadeloupe," he continued, as if he needed to keep talking so I couldn't speak. "As you see, she is also very beautiful. We have two babies, boy babies. If you ever want a boy baby you should come back to Martinique and sleep with me." His eyes crinkled at the thought of it. "I am very good at boys."

I laughed, wanting to bare myself to him, tell him I had no husband. I wanted to tell him the truth about Gerard and Bernard and Edward, Victoire and Nadie, and how they had all provided the shelter I had needed at the proper moments. I wanted to tell him that I still longed for Victoire despite what he couldn't give me. That I didn't want to return to my monotonous life, churning out nice words for a big company that made nice frozen foods. That I didn't want *anything* to do with frozen things any more. But if I told him the truth about myself, the whole truth, I feared we would end up in each other's arms after all.

"Will you go back to your wife someday?" I asked instead. "And to your babies?"

"I go back when I can. When I can't I send the money."

"I leave tomorrow," I said. "After lunch."

"Fly away, then Mar Sea," he said. "Fly to the place where you can be most free, and where love makes you remember instead of forget." He cupped my face in his dark hands, kissed me on first one cheek then the other. I smiled and said I would come back to Martinique someday. I would come back for the babies.

And then I left.

In the morning he wore his white waiter's smock again over long pants and poured *café au lait*—thick stream of milk melting a hot river of coffee, and frothing like the sea in my cup.

"Your husband, he has recovered enough for the travelling?" he asked.

"Yes," I nodded. "He will be perfectly fine for this trip."

Dashing through a hot, crowded corridor at Lamentin that afternoon I thought I saw Victoire, blue-black hair floating above a face as certain and cool as a mint. But then he was gone and I was at the gate and on the little forty-seat plane that would go to San Juan, where I would change to a Chicago-bound jet.

Fly away, Cadasse had said, but I was afraid to fly. So I gathered them all around me again one last time: Bernard, Gerard and Edward, Nadie and his mother, Cadasse and his Viviana, even Victoire and the woman whose face I never saw because of her hats. I buckled them all in with an extra quick tug on my seat belt: those I had tried to love, those I had tried to hate, those I *had* loved and would not forget.

Engines rumbled and roared, rumbled beneath my seat. Engines rumbling, engines rumbling, the whole plane vibrating with such tremendous force that at the exact moment we lost touch with the ground my body shuddered too, my body shuddering as in the ecstasies of love. We ascended and ascended, the plane shuddering, my body shuddering and shuddering, as it had shuddered with first Victoire, then Nadie, the plane tilting sharply over palm trees, water and sand, the island disappearing, disappearing into the sea, leaving nothing in its wake but sky.

An Adult Child's Christmas in Ohio

December 23, 4 p.m.

Traffic is light heading into Illinois. The heavy flow honors the other side of the highway; everyone must be going to Wisconsin for Christmas. Jerry and I spent Christmas in Wisconsin last year at his parents' house. He didn't tell me so many people in his family smoked. I had a cold, the only thing that saved me from asphyxiation. I couldn't breathe anyway.

I don't have a cold this year. I'm going south to Columbus, Ohio, where there's an uncle I want to see. Jerry is going north to his brother's gathering. Once upon a time I thought a boyfriend should accommodate me on holidays. I'm more flexible now, more open to alternatives. Jerry is understanding, too; he never asked why I didn't invite him to go with me. It felt strange saying good-bye to Jerry two days before Christmas. We agreed we would exchange presents the day I got home. I made him promise to save New Year's for me, even though I know he is saving it. There was some turbulence between us during the early part of December, Jerry's need for space again conflicting with my need for closeness. We have been dealing with it this time, neither one of us abusing the other with anger or distance.

I mull these thoughts over like a spicy wine as I breeze along I-90. I have never driven to Columbus before. When I lived in Chicago,

I flew. I moved to Madison, Wisconsin, a year ago for a teaching position, and even though that's only one hundred fifty miles further, it's not as easy by air. You have to take ground transportation to Chicago, or take connecting flights, which cost a bundle and tend to drop you off miles from your next gate. I'm a white knuckle flyer anyway; I figure if I'm going to take pavement to Chicago, I might as well take pavement all the way. It's a 530-mile trek, more than I have ever driven alone in one stretch. I plan to break up the trip on the way down by spending the night in Chicago.

6 p.m.

I make a pit stop at the toll plaza near O'Hare, look around for something to munch on. Before I can tell the elderly clerk I want popcorn, she bursts forth with information of her own.

"They've discovered something in South America that makes you younger," she asserts. "You shoot it into your veins. I saw it on television."

The National Enquirer Channel? I want to ask, but bite my tongue. She's round-eyed with wonder and very serious.

"You have to keep taking it or you get old again," she notes. "That's the only problem."

"Sounds expensive," I offer.

"Well, you never know." She finally bags my popcorn. "Maybe the President will get a health plan through that covers it."

"Yes, maybe," I agree.

7 p.m.

I have my choice of parking spots near Crystal Mason's Lincoln Park high-rise. No 'round and 'round the block circuits this time. It is definitely Christmas. Crystal takes me to the new discount pet emporium on Halsted Street, a vast space formerly occupied by a theater complex; I saw "The Heidi Chronicles" there. The economy never falters in this neighborhood. One business gives up, another moves in. New people with financial backers always come along. Crystal looks at dog carriers. She doesn't have a dog, but she wants something big enough to hold two cats and a litter box when she moves to New York in a few months, after she sells her condo. "Why do you want to move to New York?" the young salesman asks. "It's a rat race there; you'll need three locks on your door."

I smile to myself. In Madison you'd get the same wisecrack if you suggested moving to Chicago.

"Stay here," the salesman half-flirts. "And you won't have to buy a carrier."

7:30 p.m.
Crystal and I cross the street for dinner at La Piñata, our favorite Mexican restaurant. We call it Felipe's, for the Mexican waiter Crystal goes bonkers over after one margarita. The margaritas are the beauty of La Piñata. I don't know what they've discovered in South America, but one margarita at La Pinata peels years away from me.

"I didn't know you were close to this uncle, Marcy," Crystal says as we munch giant tortilla chips and pack our potent cocktails with ice. She and I go back to when I first moved to Chicago after college. She knows about my marriage, my divorce, even my hospitalization nearly seven years ago, which I rarely speak of to anyone.

"Oh yes," I say. "We've developed a wonderful friendship in the last couple of years. We've both grown a lot as adults. We like to sit around and discuss our therapy." This makes us laugh for some reason—probably the margaritas.

Crystal tells me the latest on Brian Banwell, the fellow she's moving to New York for, and who flew to Vermont for Christmas to be with his ex-wife and kids.

"He hasn't asked me to move in with him yet," she confides, her usually animated face momentarily perturbed. "But I know he will once I'm there."

If anyone has had more difficulty with men than I over the years, it's Crystal, though I can never understand why. At forty-two she's still blonde and beautiful, with the sort of classic, heart-shaped face you see on women in Renaissance paintings. I wonder what Crystal would think if I told her about my current desires. Crystal's a very straight arrow. I don't think she would understand. For all the trouble she's had with relationships, I don't think she could envision love without a man.

"And I'm sure I'll have no trouble landing a good job in Manhattan," Crystal continues, fumbling for cigarettes. "I mean in *public relations,* Marcy, it's like I'm moving to Mecca!" She squints at me euphorically through the room's hazy air and I smile supportively, even though we swore to each other back in our corporate communications days, that we would never make PR a career. Crystal asks Felipe what he's doing for Christmas. "Watching television," he replies and makes a sad face.

"His family's in Mexico," she explains as Felipe walks away. "Maybe I should take him with me to my boss' house." Then she thinks better of it. Her boss lives a tony life in the far western suburbs.

10 p.m.
Crystal gets me settled in her friend Lisa's apartment, a tidy little studio three flights above her own two-bedroom unit. I lived with Crystal for a few months when I left my husband years ago, before Crystal's building went condo. Crystal has back problems now, doesn't feel up to an overnight guest. She's feeding Lisa's cat while she visits her folks in Seattle, and even though Lisa doesn't know me she has agreed I could use her place. Lisa's pleased Misty will have company, and I'm glad for the breathable environment. Crystal's my only friend who still smokes.

The place is just big enough for a double-sized futon, desk, and kitchen table. A photo of Lisa and her family fills the window ledge. It's a big family. Three girls, two boys, two parents, the mother looking not much older than me. Everyone wears bright sweaters and matching smiles. Crystal points out Lisa, among the cookie-cutter trio of pretty sisters.

"They look happy," Crystal says. "Maybe it's a functional family."

December 24, midnight
Misty is dysfunctional, gnaws a computer keyboard box into jigsaw puzzle pieces. When I approach her, she hisses. I zip myself into my sleeping bag and leave her alone. I'm exhausted from driving, from Christmas, the margarita. I sleep well, waking occasionally during the night to hear Misty chew.

9 a.m.
We breakfast on hot cakes and eggs at a neighborhood pancake house, notable less for its food than for making people pay in advance late at night. It reminds me of the gas stations in this town, which require pre-payment at all hours.

Crystal's back hurts too much to hug good-bye. We smile and wave at each other on a street corner. Then she's off to the chiropractor, and I'm in my car, not remembering the route out of town.

It comes back to me though. I take Fullerton Avenue to the Kennedy Expressway, which becomes the Dan Ryan south of downtown. Traffic is light, the weather dry and I hit Indiana within an hour, wondering how much of Crystal's illness is psychosomatic.

It's a long, uneventful ride, the land flattening out south of Gary like a penny squooshed by a freight train. Everything is gray—sky, trees, plowed-under fields. Sometimes, above the loud hum of my aged Toyota, it feels like I *am* in an airplane, the only difference being I can't close my eyes. Here and there snow swirls onto the windshield and drifts across the road, but there's no accumulation or slippery spots. Once I pass a parked burning car, no driver in sight, just a cloud of black, noxious smoke billowing out from under the hood. I wonder where Jerry is and what he's doing. He wasn't sure when he would leave for the little town near Minneapolis where his brother lives. I wonder if he misses me. I wonder if we are ever going to try the "cure" Jerry thinks will save our relationship. My current shrink didn't find it so shocking when I told her what Jerry wanted and that he had the other couple all picked out. "Just be sure the two of you are very solid," she had said, "before you indulge."

But Jerry never brought it up again after I told him, a few months ago, that I would do it. I can't stop thinking about what it would be like. Not with the other guy. Who needs that? It's the woman, the possibility of a women in my bed that I can't get out of my mind.

It's nothing Jerry has said about it, per se. Something just makes me think that for him, the big excitement is the man.

4 p.m.

Beyond the bigger towns I can't find much on the radio I want to hear. Near Bloomington, Indiana, and later, Yellow Springs, Ohio, public radio comes in. I enjoy classical music for awhile, an interview with an ex-union buster turned author. Otherwise, it's Jesus and Jingle Bells. I think about my uncle, who I last saw in April. "We are looking forward to seeing you soon," he wrote in reply to my tentative query about a visit. I don't even know if Uncle Paul and Aunt Laura celebrate Christmas. My parents embraced it in a limited way, perhaps because they weren't totally comfortable in the Jewish world.

I've always observed it in some fashion, but I'm not really making this trip in search of Christmas.

6:30 p.m.
Just outside the Columbus city limits I pull into a gas station to tank up and call for directions. It snows steadily now and is colder than I'd expected this far south. I have not made great time, but it took me half an hour to revive at the last pit stop, and of course I lost an hour passing into eastern time. A gas station attendant sees me studying my map and offers assistance. He spreads the map on a crowded counter-top, compares the directions my aunt just gave me with what he believes is a better route. "Where is it you're going now?" he asks, and I tell him only approximately. It *is* Christmas Eve, but I have heard too many horror stories to trust a stranger completely.

His directions turn out to be clearer than my aunt's and there is nobody following me.

7 p.m.
Uncle Paul and Aunt Laura urge me to the kitchen table almost as soon as I enter their door. They bring out a big tray of deli meats, three kinds of bread, coleslaw, potato salad. They have something with me, even though they've already eaten. There were eleven years and many differences separating my father and his youngest brother, but they shared a reverence for food. Jerry teases me because I never go long without wanting something to eat. When I am with my family I understand where this need comes from. It's not that we eat that much at one sitting. We simply crave sustenance in all its literal and metaphoric forms. Food is the way we are best able to give and receive it.

They don't celebrate Christmas. They don't celebrate much of anything any more, my aunt tells me lightly. I know this has to do with my cousin Warren's death on a motorcycle almost five years ago.

Laura is surprised when I say my father allowed Christmas at our house. Our families lived in separate cities. I didn't meet the Columbus side until I was thirteen. My grandmother died and then everyone forgot animosities. My father and Paul remembered a special affection. Both men had quick tempers, demons they couldn't shake, but they were on best behavior around each other's families. Growing up, my brother and I knew a visit to Uncle Paul's would be a magical time.

My father has been dead nearly two years, but as I sit at the glass-topped kitchen table in my uncle's warm and spacious house, an old, old memory comes to mind: My father on Christmas Eve, sprawled on the living room floor with the electric train he bought for my brother when he was three. It was a wonderful train, complete with coal car, caboose and hoary tunnel. You could put pellets in the engine and make it smoke. My father loved that train, never lost his temper with it. In the memory I am wearing pajamas with feet, watching my father play.

Laura and Paul and I discuss the usual subjects as we eat: My brother David in Chagrin Falls, who has taken his family to Cancun again for Christmas; my mother in Cleveland, who they saw two weeks ago at my brother's Chanukah party. She attended only after much coaxing, I am told. At seventy-six she has her health, but feels only truly comfortable in her own home. I last saw my brother and mother in April. Paul knows how that went; when I returned to his house afterwards with the car he had lent me I was tense, read ill will into his simplest comments.

"You seem to be in a better place now than you were last summer," he observes matter-of-factly, and I smile.

"Maybe I'll come in again this summer when David and Rhoda are around," I suggest, thinking that by then I might bring Jerry and finally impress my mother with my taste in men. "We can all have a reunion."

December 25, 10 a.m.

The heavily curtained guest room is conducive to sleeping and I take advantage of the opportunity, exhausted from the drive. Paul comes in from outside soon after I begin rummaging in the kitchen. He's been shoveling the driveway. The snow that began on the last miles of my trip fell heavily all night. The world outside sparkles like a Christmas card.

Laura appears from another part of the house and they begin all over again the ritual of making sure I'm fed. Do I want eggs? How about cereal? Fresh grapefruit or orange juice? And of course there's lots of breads.

We spend the day lazing around and it's a wonderful house for it, the living room full of sunlight, cushy sofas and my uncle's own colorful paintings. Paul wrote to me recently that he enjoys the fact that he is learning to enjoy lazing around. He officially retired from his optometry business, yet keeps going back. They wintered in Florida last year, rented a place again for the coming season. But something has come up at work that needs his attention; he's not sure if or when he'll get away.

I've brought a book along, but Paul hands me Kurt Vonnegut's *Palm Sunday*, which he read recently and loved. It's an unconventional memoir, a pastiche of speeches, letters, essays. I'm intrigued by the writing and the author. I especially like learning that Vonnegut majored in anthropology at his father's behest despite the fact he had no talent for it. His true talent triumphed, of course. Vonnegut reports that he got retroactive thesis credit in anthropology for his novel, *Cat's Cradle*. I congratulate myself, as I read, for entering graduate school in my mid-thirties without parental approval. "You'll wipe out your chances of finding another husband," my mother had said. "You're going to wake up one day and realize it's too late to have children."

3 p.m.

Paul's a walker, has mapped out a hilly, three-mile track around his subdivision, which he follows once, sometimes twice a day. I invite myself on his afternoon foray. The air is icy, the snowy streets silent except for the whoosh of traffic along a highway near one part of the course. An airplane flies overhead, its engine loud and lonely in this white Christmas stillness. Paul and I have had our moments, our misunderstandings. Sometimes on the phone he is abrupt or impatient, triggering within me the fears or anxieties that accompanied conversations with my father. But Paul is not my father. He is much more introspective, infinitely more willing to be aware of how he affects people. Always we have come back to each other to share a deep affection—and yes, as I told Crystal—to discuss what we have learned in therapy.

Today as we walk we are both relaxed, both comfortable with our silences. When we talk it seems deeper than usual, more intimate. He speaks about himself more, maybe that's why, is less the reserved, patriarchal uncle. He tells me he is nearing seventy now, but not feeling his age. I tell him we are all staying younger longer these days, that forty-two is far less intimidating than I'd expected. He expresses amazement at my age. "You look so young," he says. "Whenever I look at you I still see a girl."

I can't imagine what Uncle Paul would think if I mentioned my current preoccupation with girls. But of course I won't bring it up, just as I didn't with Crystal. I haven't done anything yet. I've only thought about it. And thought about it. I'm not going to risk jeopardizing my relationship with Uncle Paul because of something I haven't done.

"I don't mind that we may not get to Florida this winter," Uncle Paul is saying, oblivious to my thoughts... "It's mostly tennis and bridge." He shakes his head. That's not how he wants to spend his days. I tell him how happy I am to be teaching communications at the University of Wisconsin, though I haven't quite finished my Ph.D. "It's good to have a job to go to, isn't it?" he asks and I concur. There may be other things in my life that are not quite settled, but at least I know I've found the right profession.

7 p.m.

We drive to the Meyers' for pizza. Les, a retired NBC executive, asks a lot of questions about my research on how children perceive family conflict on television. He and Paul meet for breakfast once a week with a couple of other friends and I get the feeling my uncle's been bragging.

"Send me a copy of your dissertation when you finish it," Les suggests, helping himself to another slice of veggie pan pizza. "You may have hit on something that could influence future programming, or inspire a documentary. I still have a few friends in the business."

"It's almost done," I reply, taking Les' enthusiasm for the way people talk under the influence of good food and friendship. I like his intensity though, and his interest.

I especially like his wife, Betty. She and I share a few moments alone in the living room after dinner while Paul and Les talk politics in the kitchen and Laura wanders upstairs to visit with Bennett, the Meyers' forty year-old autistic son.

Betty launches into a discussion of her bout with depression some years back, and how even electric shock couldn't jar her. "I just one day decided that none of the things I hated about my life would ever change," she confides. "I decided to snap out of it."

"Yes," I nod, amazed that Betty can speak so candidly about such a dark and personal time. I rarely tell anyone about the depression that paralyzed me at one point. I had to drop out of graduate school for a year. The only family members I've told are Paul and Laura, and then only vaguely. I feel as if I've known Betty for years.

December 26, 10 a.m.
There is a fight between my aunt and uncle today. I'm embarrassed to be privy to it, but my aunt doesn't mind. You need to know that we're not perfect, she tells me; we have the same warts and blemishes your parents had; they're just in different places.

The argument has to do with my cousin who died. There is so much pain from this death, so much sadness. A raw agony hangs between Paul and Laura: If one of them—Paul, she maintains; Warren, he insists—had been different, had behaved differently, maybe Warren wouldn't have died.

I don't walk with my uncle today. Disquieted by the argument, I visit the Columbus Art Museum alone. A man enters the Pre-Columbian room, carrying a small boy in either arm. "This art goes back before Christopher Columbus," he tells the boys. "It is important for us to see it because we can tell what people are thinking from their art." The man looks like art himself, the way his arms bulge lovingly with boys.

The American collection speaks to me, particularly work by Ohio artist George Bellows. I gaze a long time at his painting of two farm boys and a calf kicking up their heels under an ominous sky.

1 p.m.
My cousin Randy meets me at the museum and we go to lunch in the Short North neighborhood a few minutes away. It's a strip of galleries, boutiques and restaurants, all of them closed on the day after Christmas except for a deli called the Bermuda Onion. They've got lox lasagne, George Bush salad (with broccoli), stuffed grape leaves and other Middle Eastern fare, along with more standard selections.

Randy orders tuna on whole wheat, pulls out his wallet before I can pay for my salad plate. We help ourselves to cookies leftover from the morning buffet. It's the first time Randy and I have gotten together like this and it's comfortable. I mention his parents, but he steers the discussion to other things, which is fine with me. Paul and Laura told me yesterday that Randy has distanced himself from them lately. "He's angry about the past; I suppose that sounds familiar," Uncle Paul had said bitterly, and I felt bad for all of us. But I don't want to take sides, or compare it to the rift I had with my parents some years ago that changed our status quo forever.

"What's new with you?" Randy asks and I look at him for a moment and see an open, receptive face, a face I suddenly decide to trust.

"Well to tell the truth," I begin, a faint smile on my lips. "Lately I've been thinking I might be bisexual." I can't bring myself to say the word, "lesbian," which is something I've also been thinking I might be.

Randy chews on his sandwich, takes another bite. "Go for it," he says, as easily as if I had just asked for advice on a mutual fund. "Be who you are."

3 p.m.
Randy and I are due back at the parents' (his term) for dinner. I suggest we rent a movie for later because I'm thinking, how will we get through the evening otherwise? At the video store, he stands back and lets me choose. "It's a lose-lose situation," he deadpans, as I search for one that would please us all. "Just pick one you like."

I don't like seeing Paul and Laura through Randy's eyes, for the same reason, I suppose, that their argument upset me: I want them to be the magical aunt and uncle.

But the evening goes surprisingly well. Randy doesn't spar with his father, the way I've seen him do in the past. And Laura doesn't have to soothe ruffled feelings. The table groans with roast turkey, salads and other trimmings, and Uncle Paul's memory jogs back fifty years to his Army days in Europe. "I would go to the church in little towns we passed through and ask the priest about eligible girls," he recalls. "It always got me an invitation to dinner at someone's house."

"Didn't these young women have fathers?" I tease.

"Sure they did, but I was just interested in the meal."

"It's the truth." Aunt Laura laughs. "He was a late bloomer. But he sure made up for lost time."

We all laugh at this, alive and happy in the moment.

The movie is "A New Leaf," starring Walter Matthau and Elaine May. Most people I know never heard of it, but it's one of my favorites. May plays the klutzy, timid heiress Matthau plans to marry, then kill for her money. I don't identify with the May character as much as I used to, but I still like her. She reminds me of me, pretherapy.

Uncle Paul doesn't like the movie, doesn't even stay in the room long enough to see Jack Weston come on, the actor he knew from high school.

"He walks out of a lot of movies," Aunt Laura shrugs.

"I couldn't stand that simpering character Elaine May plays," Uncle Paul notes when we regroup after the movie. I tell him Randy chose the film, can see from Randy's face he doesn't find this funny. I quickly assure everyone I'm kidding.

Aunt Laura digs out a tape of Jackie Mason's New York show and we all see this one through. The guy knocks politicians, ethnic groups, his own in particular; which is ours. He's hilarious. We end the evening in fine spirits.

December 27, 8 a.m.

Uncle Paul kisses me when he leaves for work. "We love you very much," he says. "I love you too," I say, letting his words and touch become a part of me. I never had such moments with my father. Aunt Laura insists I make three turkey sandwiches for the road. I can't imagine being hungry again for one sandwich, but I obey, enjoying the child this makes me feel like. If she were my mother, though, would I tolerate it?

"Randy's going to be okay," I tell her before I leave. "He's just doing what he needs to do for now. He seems more comfortable with himself somehow."

"I hope you're right," she says sadly, then reflects on bygone years, before my uncle's therapy, when her boys were small. "Paul was not so different from your father," she says.

10:30 a.m.

There's a big accident east of Indianapolis, about one hundred thirty miles from Columbus. Traffic on both sides of the interstate stops. A helicopter circles loud and low above us, lands in the westbound lane. Our side starts moving first. I can't tell what happened; the highway is blanketed with vehicles—two semis, several cars, a fire truck, squad cars. Red lights flicker over everything. An empty stretcher waits next to the helicopter.

Noon

I eat the first turkey sandwich and study the display map at a rest stop. "Gary, Indiana, Gary Indiana..." another traveler croons. "Hey," she pokes her companion in the side. "There really is a Gary, Indiana!" I ponder the "You are here" arrow. Randy gave me directions from his motor club for the trip back. This route avoids Chicago. From where I am now it looks like a roundabout way.

The car radio goes limp again. Deep in the Indiana hinterlands they're reading the *Book of Esther,* the part about wifely obedience. Elsewhere on the dial, an announcer stammers through the news. "Yes Sir Air Fit met with Egyptian leaders today..." he reads. "Present Clinton went duck hunting. He shot one duck."

A mileage sign flies by, and I see it's about sixty miles farther to Champaign, Illinois (my next point of reference) than I'd expected. I pull off I-74 at the next exit, head north, thinking I'll hook up with an interstate to Chicago. Heavy traffic or no, it's got to be the faster way. After a few miles I stop, dig out a map. I can't find the road I'm traveling on; I fold up the map and turn back. I get off I-74 again ten miles later looking for a phone. I want to call Jerry. All I find is a rundown restaurant with abandoned gas pumps. I don't even know if I'm in Indiana or Illinois, and I don't feel like going inside to ask.

2 p.m.

"I lost forty-five minutes just wondering what to do," I tell Jerry from a different interchange. I'm still not sure which state I'm in. Jerry thinks it's Illinois, advises me to stay with the motor club route. "You would probably hit Chicago at rush hour," he says.

He sounds happy to hear from me. He says he spent Christmas in a house with "Fuzzy was here" written on the living room ceiling. A motorcycle gang used to live there, he says; his brother is remodeling. Jerry says the cigarette smoke really got to him this time, and that outside it was thirty below. The fresh vegetables he brought with him to counteract his family's all-meat-and-starch diet froze on his way up. Otherwise, he says, his Christmas was okay.

"Mine was okay, too," I say.

6 p.m.

I *was* still in Indiana. Illinois is flatter—if that's possible—with exits far and few between along I-39 north of Bloomington. I push the speedometer on this leg and get my worst mileage, buy a large bag of potato chips with the next fill-up. There's one turkey sandwich left, but I crave junk food. The bag's almost empty by the time I enter Wisconsin. I've traveled five hundred ten miles, still have almost seventy to go. The road is endless. North of Janesville, where the hills begin, I start to cry. I am suddenly overwhelmed by exhaustion, by the emotions of the visit, by what might happen to Jerry and me. I force back the tears; they're blinding me.

Postscript

Uncle Paul died three weeks later, on January 17. It was twenty below zero in Columbus that morning and he had shoveled snow. A big earthquake hit Los Angeles the same day. He called his two sisters there that afternoon to make sure they were all right. A few hours later he suffered a massive heart attack.

Jerry and I drove to Columbus for the funeral, already knowing that we would soon go our separate ways. It just seemed important to both of us to be together now. It was twenty-seven below zero the morning we left Madison. Everything was frozen: the gates along the Illinois toll road; the pop we bought from a machine in a glass-enclosed shelter; my memory of Uncle Paul and me walking side by side on Christmas day, sharing our warmest moments.

Reinventing Leah

It's my mother's fault that I can't write this story. She is old and feeble, but still strong enough to remind me at every turn that she is my mother, has always been my mother, will always be my mother, even after she dies.

"I am not dead yet," my mother told me when she lived alone in the house where I grew up, with all its memories and ghosts. Like the cherry tree, the beautiful little tree whose sour fruit sweetened our summers because Leah knew just how much sugar to add to a pie, just how much thick cream to stir into a borscht.

"How did you make that cherry soup?" I will ask when I visit her again some day, when I am ready to tell her who I am. "Do you still have the recipe for that wonderful cold soup you used to make with the cherries we picked from our tree?"

"I never used a recipe for that soup," she will say, urging me into the kitchen to show me how to make it. The dog, an old dog—its flanks bulging from many insistent, extra feedings—will follow at my mother's heels and flop down beside the table on the smooth, cool floor.

"Oh," I will gush with true enthusiasm, watching my mother magically produce the tree and the fruit and the other ingredients necessary for recreating my favorite girlhood soup.

I cannot write the story, I can only write versions of it. In this version Leah and I become two cheery women in a timeless kitchen, making cherry soup. We fill our bowls and our spoons and then our mouths with the bright, tangy concoction, savoring carefully so as not to swallow stones. Among the joys of my mother's cherry soup, you don't have to pit the cherries before you make it. But you must guard against swallowing them later.

In the story my mother and I remove the pits from our mouths smoothly and gracefully, pile them genteelly upon the saucers in which our soup bowls sit. We talk about other foods as we eat. My mother pulls her recipe box down from a high cupboard shelf and thumbs through its collection of faded notecards. She tells me how she makes cheese blintzes and potato latkes, matzo balls, and noodle kugel. She tells me just how lightly you must flick your wrist when you fold the thickly-beaten yolks and the sifted matzo flour into the whites of a Passover sponge cake.

"You must always start with the flour and end with the flour," she will instruct, just the faintest pinch of bossiness in her voice. "Otherwise you will not blend the batter properly." She prides herself on that sponge cake. She tells me—but not everyone—that she adds a splash of Mogen David wine to lend it the sweet holiday zest other cakes lack.

From sponge cakes we move on to chicken fat, without which you can not bake Leah's startling noodle kugel and achieve the properly crisp, golden brown crust. Leah tells me how to render chicken fat, though I know how to do it. I watched her so many times when I was small and eager to eat the crunchy cracklings that remained. The *grivinitz*, my mother called them, arranging them on a plate lined with paper toweling, so at least some of their grease oozed away. "Marcy, the *grivinitz* are ready. Come and eat."

Leah tells me how to render chicken fat even though the chickens at the grocery store no longer have fat worth rendering. Even though I would never want to render chicken fat and already know how to render chicken fat, I ask her to tell me. In this version of the story, I have no concept of cholesterol or saturated fat; no aversion to eating meat or meat products, no fear of growing old or dying young.

This version of the story could continue on and on, conjuring up enough fragrant aromas to pull my brother in from his backyard batting practice, lure my father away from his upstairs ledger books and adding machines, meld us into a young, untarnished family whose meals boil over with laughter and good-natured jokes. But my mother has her memory in this version and sooner or later she will remember that the cherry tree stopped bearing fruit when I left for college, and that the year I graduated and moved away from Cleveland, the tree fell over in a wind storm and perished.

"We can't make cherry soup without the cherries," my mother will remind me suddenly, and remember in the same breath that I rarely write to her anymore, rarely call. Her lost kitten face, sunken but still supple into her deep seventies, will contort in anger, then pain and she will close the recipe box and freeze in her kitchen chair, the same kitchen chair she chose when the family ate meals together years ago. She will stare at me coldly, elbows on the table, chin cocked pointedly, until I can think of nothing to say, so that this version of the story dies with the cherry tree.

I could let the cherry tree live; that tree was thin and delicate when my parents planted it, just after we'd moved into this house. Its branches fanned out like so many long, slender fingers that seemed incapable of sprouting leaves in spring, let alone flowers and then luminous, ruby red fruit. My father promised me that that tree would grow tall and thick around the middle, develop sturdy limbs and deep crotches into which children could eventually scamper.

"It won't happen in time for you to climb it, Marcy," my father said, even though I was only six. "But your children will climb it some day. Your children will play in this tree and pick fruit from the highest branches."

I don't have children. I am forty-three years old and it is too late to suppose I ever will have children. But that is not my mother's fault. It is only her fault that I cannot write the story.

If I keep the cherry tree alive I could invent children for myself, and also a husband, shaped out of clay that Leah could choose. He would be Jewish, of course, with thick glasses, bookish nose, an expandable waistline sympathetic to *her* cooking, perhaps more than mine. He would treat me well. Leah would get that right. She wouldn't want the life for me that she'd had with Jack.

He would treat me well, but he would bore me for reasons I couldn't understand. I would sit at the kitchen table, watching my children through the window's flouncy, tie-backed curtains—one boy, one girl—scrambling up the cherry tree. I would listen to Leah's recitative on cooking and watch my children play and wonder how to tell my mother that Leon (that would be his name of course—Leon or Leonard or Lester—any masculine derivative of Leah would do). I would wonder how to tell my mother that Leon doesn't make me happy.

I don't let the cherry tree live because what I want to tell my mother concerns me, not Leon. It won't work in the version with the cherry tree. I want to tell my mother who I am, and for that I need textbooks, not recipes. I need the dissertation I wrote for my Ph.D., the dissertation I researched and wrestled with for years and very nearly didn't finish. I have to kill the cherry tree. Even if the windstorm hadn't toppled it, I would have to kill it.

"So who are you?" my mother asks, helping me begin again. "Who are you? Who?" She asks this question in her lady-of-the theater, owl-commanding voice, emphasizing whoooo? whhoooo? in a way that makes me shudder. She also asks this question with her body—lips taut, chest rigid, back arched away from me.

We move into the living room, so we can face each other across a wide space. My mother chooses the purple love seat, a narrow, high-backed perch, designed for two people who want to be close to one another. I don't remember more than one person in our family using it at a time. I sit on the beige couch against a far wall, several yards of gray floral carpet away from my mother. The dog stretches out, wet nose to the floor beside the love seat, loyal to the hand that overfeeds it.

My father is dead, but the dog is still alive. We didn't have a dog when I lived in this house. This dog, a gentle, reasonably intelligent Golden Retriever, wandered into the yard one day, wearing no collar, no tags. My mother fed the dog and named it Ginger. My father fed the dog too, and did not complain when the dog moved in with them. They both liked caring for a creature that obeyed them without questions.

"You know," my mother begins again, even though I haven't responded to her question. "There are mothers and grown daughters who live together."

My mother has told me this before. She told me this when I graduated from college and took a job in Chicago. She told me this when I divorced Gregory and when I broke up with the boyfriend after that. She didn't understand why I enrolled in graduate school in Chicago to study communications, or why I accepted a teaching position in yet another state, instead of seeking one in Cleveland.

"I always assumed you would live here until you married," Leah says, starting all over again, because I have not responded. "I thought you would marry a nice Jewish man like your father and have children and live maybe one, two miles from here and I thought we would see each other often."

"None of that happened," I tell my mother, inwardly blaming the cherry tree. If the cherry tree had lived I would have married Leonard or Leon and given birth to children who would explore its highest branches. Instead I married Gregory the cop and divorced him three years later. I have dated other men since Gregory; I have tried to love too many of them. "None of that worked out," I offer sadly.

"I want to see you settled, Marcy. My life won't be complete until you're settled."

It's as if she needs for me to shoulder her disappointment as well as mine. I want to make her happy. I have tried to make her happy. I tried to make her happy by saying yes to all those men instead of no.

"Can't you find another way to make your life complete?"

"What did I do wrong, Marcy?" my mother asks. "I know you think I was a terrible mother. But what did I do wrong?"

I stare at my mother for a long time. Leah stares back, her aged face pale as an orchid in the room's fading light. The dog stirs where it sleeps, front paws twitching, then its outsized flank, as if chasing something—or being chased—in its dreams. Dogs dream. I know dogs dream. But who can say for sure what they dream of?

My mother's face turns to stone, still an orchid, but carved now from something hard and pure. Ivory, or maybe alabaster. You did nothing wrong, I'm supposed to say. It's not your fault. It's mine.

That's better, my mother will blurt, her face softening again into a flower moist with dew. That's more like it.

But I don't speak. I can't speak. I can't even continue with the story. It's old, cliched. You see people like us on television every day of the week, any time of day. We are in conflict with each other and we are in conflict with life, and we are running out of things to say.

Conflict is process, not product, I tell the students who take my introductory class. In front of students, in my own classroom, I am a doctor of communication arts who knows everything about the way people do, can't, could relate. I don't tell my students about the Rosen family conflict or how, after I divorced Gregory, my need to end it led me to this new career. I tell them about conflict-solving techniques like listening and finding common goals or stepping away when it's a hot conflict, until the blaze burns itself out.

I tell them that you can not solve a problem at the same level of consciousness that created it. Albert Einstein said that, I tell them, not I.

"Dance with me, Leah," I say, rather than erase everything I have written so far and start anew. "You and I have never danced together." I stand up and walk over to the purple love seat, stand before her like a nervous suitor. "Pretend you are young again and that I am young too. Dance with me."

"Two women can't dance with each other." She cuts to the heart of the matter with inimitable skill.

"Maybe they can." I suggest.

"Who will lead?" My mother has all the right questions.

"I don't know." I stare at her blankly. I hadn't gotten that far; it was difficult enough to walk across the room. "Maybe we can both lead."

"At the same time? That is impossible," my mother says. "We will go nowhere."

"We can take turns." I propose. "We can see where that takes us."

"Without music? We can't dance without music." My mother insists. "I'll put on some Guy Lombardo. Your father and I loved to dance to that."

My mother and father loved to dance. They didn't move to the same rhythms in ordinary life, but they danced well together, maybe because—on the infrequent occasions when they went dancing—they didn't struggle with each other about who would lead.

"No, not Guy Lombardo," I say. "That was your era."

"But that's what we have in this house," Leah sighs. "Guy Lombardo, Jimmy Dorsey, Frank Sinatra."

"We can improvise," I suggest, remembering a gentle childhood song. "I'll sing to you as we dance."

My mother bares her teeth and releases a doubtful little laugh. But she rises and stands before me, a scrawny bird, shorter than I by several inches. A spreading age spot dominates one cheek, a mole I've never seen before rides her upper lip. Her hair's a simple cottony thatch swept up off her forehead, cut short around the ears. She used to change her hairstyle almost every time my father shifted moods. He died three years ago. She's worn it this way since he sickened.

If I didn't know Leah, if I'd somehow wandered into this house a stranger, I would urge her to sit, get more sleep, eat more nutritious meals, do anything she can to subvert the weary anxiety of her face. But she is my mother and I want to dance with her.

"I'll lead first," I say, afraid I may not otherwise get a crack at it. Before my mother can respond, I place my right hand against her back, offer up my left. To my surprise, she takes it. I have never led before, in any dance. I stumble a couple of times, not sure which way to step, then finally just start moving.

"Lullaby, and good night, sleep tender and tight." I sing, not considering why I choose this song. It just comes to me, a song I played on the piano years ago when I first started lessons. It's in every beginner's book.

The music calms me, and I glide more purposefully around the room. The dog awakens, takes one look at the four-legged animal we have become and scuttles over to a spot beneath the love seat. "Lullaby and good night..."

Leah feels brittle in my arms, as if she could crumble with the slightest pressure and turn to dust. She was always small, has been shrinking. The Brahms melody melts my fears. I step closer to Leah, and ever so lightly, urge her closer to me. I want her to lay her head on my chest, the starry-eyed way I danced with boys when I was young, the way she must have once, long ago, danced with my father. Lay your head on my chest and dream of how we could be, I want to tell Leah. But after two turns around the room, she wriggles from my grasp.

"You're doing it wrong, Marcy," she says. "That's not how you fox trot. Let me show you."

My students do not respond to me this way in Communications 101. Why does my mother refuse to let me teach?

She holds me rigidly, an arm's length away, presses so imperceptibly on my back I can't tell which way she wants me to move. I falter at first, stumble again, but eventually we find a groove. We box-step around the living room, several times, Leah leading, the dog watching, transfixed, from underneath the love seat.

"This is how you fox trot, Marcy," she says above the music, which I've altered to a hum. "You've lived so long without a man you wouldn't know."

I let go of Leah and stop dancing. The story folds in on itself, but Leah continues dancing, waltzes around the room to music I can't hear, hands poised against an invisible partner.

The dog watches. The dog is alive, but during the following winter it will release a long, loud howl in the middle of the night and roll over dead on the living room floor. My mother will leave Ginger lying where she fell, thinking—she will tell my brother David two days later when he calls—thinking that the dog was only *playing* dead.

She left my father lying in the middle of the living room floor for an entire night, a month before he died.

"He could have gotten up if he wanted to," she told David then. "He knows where the bedroom is. He knows where I sleep."

Leah abandons her invisible partner and flings herself into a fast dance.

"Charleston, Charleston," she sings, stepping high, pumping her arms like fire hoses. It is her dance, from her era, her time, and she does it well. "Charleston, Charleston," She bends over and bangs her hands back and forth against her waving knees, affecting proper flapper style.

"C'mon, Marcy. You know this one," she commands, more energy in her sharp voice than I thought remained in her. "I sent you to dancing school."

I stand, rooted to the floor, as transfixed as the dog, who is not dead yet. I want to tell her who I am. I want her to listen.

What should I do? she asked David five years ago when my father, feeble-minded but not yet physically sick, poured gasoline into the bird bath.

Take it away from him, David said. And he took it away from both of them the next time he visited.

My mother dances wildly, out of control, until I fear she will have a heart attack. I don't want to kill my mother. I only want to tell her who I am and why I am angry with her. I want to let her blaze like a forest fire until she burns herself out. But I don't want to combust with her.

I back away from my mother, but she keeps dancing toward me.

"You wanted to dance," My mother cries, hair scorched, eyes wild. "Why don't you dance with me now?"

Every blaze, every storm, every war, every conflict, every life exhausts itself eventually. I tell my freshman students this in conflict resolution class.

Everything winds down eventually. It's a scientific principle. Yet Leah flappers on, defying entropy. I can contain the fire, but she won't burn out.

Leah needs her own story. Marcy will be out of the picture, living her own life, far away from Cleveland, in another midwestern state. Jack will be dead for four years, the dog for one, the cherry tree long ago disintegrated. David will live nearby with his wife, Rhoda, and their little boy and girl. A son leaves his mother when he takes a wife. Leah knows this on one level, doesn't understand it on another.

Leah likes Rhoda, though she thinks she's too skinny (Leah is plump in this version) and a little self-centered. But David loves her, that's the important thing, and she's a good mother, even though the daughter doesn't look like anyone. She doesn't look like David's side of the family and she doesn't look like Rhoda's. A pretty girl, twelve years old, just approaching the age where she's going to give her mother trouble.

Leah would like to know where the daughter came from, but doesn't ask. She doesn't visit David much, even though he invites her often, much more often than she would like. She lets him visit her. He usually brings the boy, who is ten and looks like David did at that age, but is a lot more rambunctious. The girl and her mother don't come. They're allergic to dogs and even though the dog has been dead one year, they claim the house holds traces of it.

"Fine, be that way," Leah mutters under her breath sometimes when she's all alone doing laundry or washing the kitchen floor on her hands and wobbly knees, or going out for a walk on the same round-the-block route she used to take with the dog. "See if I care, Rhoda."

But in her heart, she'd really like Rhoda and the girl to visit.

Otherwise Leah doesn't want much from life. She wants her house and her independence. She wants her children to be small again and living with her. But what can she do? They grew up. Maybe she did something right in that department, after all, though Marcy, the daughter who lives far away and seldom contacts her, doesn't seem to think so. Sometimes Leah wishes Jack were still alive, and that maybe this time around she would weather his moods more gracefully. But Jack is gone and she doesn't want anyone to think she can't get along without him. They'd take her house away if they thought that.

They'd lock her in a nursing home, throw away the key, if they knew that sometimes—well only occasionally, really, though it's been happening more and more—that sometimes she doesn't remember things. Doesn't remember, for instance, that Rhoda came with David when he visited last week, though David insisted in his most recent phone call that she did. She forgets to wear her glasses sometimes, maybe that's why she's not seeing right, Leah thinks, but doesn't suggest this to David because not wearing glasses may have caused other calamities she'd rather he not know about.

He'd regard her cross-eyed and open-mouthed if she told him she sometimes puts the laundry in the washer and forgets to turn it on; sometimes lets the tea kettle whistle on and on, her craving for tea obliterated into steamy vapors. They'd put her away. Her children could do that to her, her own children. And Rhoda, too. They could become her mortal enemies overnight. Leah needs everyone to know that she can survive in this house without Jack.

She puts an ad in the paper under rooms for rent. She takes in a boarder.

"A wife should go places with her husband, don't you think?" she presses Germaine January, who calls the very day the ad runs, and drives over immediately to see the room.

"That depends on where he's going," Germaine January offers noncommittally, smiling brightly at Leah.

She is tall and big-boned, an old-fashioned looking woman into her forties, with long, dusty brown hair pulled sharply off a soap-and-water face, a sturdy, smooth-complected face, honest and uncomplicated as a midwestern prairie.

Hippie, Leah thinks suspiciously, held over a little too long from the 1960s. Or a runaway from Amish country. Either way, she can almost hear Jack muttering: *get her out of here.*

"My son visits me every Sunday," Leah says, leading Germaine January upstairs, ignoring Jack's opinions. Jack is gone, after all. She can make her own decisions about who will live with her. But she wants to explain to Germaine about Rhoda and the girl and their refusal to visit her. She doesn't believe Rhoda came last week, despite what David tells her.

"Your family will be no problem for me," Germaine January observes as they enter Marcy's old room, the one at the top of the stairs next to Leah's room and formerly also Jack's. "I go visiting myself on Sundays," Germaine continues. "I won't mind if your son comes over here."

"He always brings my grandson and he's so rambunctious," Leah elaborates, staring past Germaine at the rose-flowered wallpaper and the beautiful rag rug on the floor that she bought years ago, on sale at Higbee's. Everything in this room has held up so well, Leah thinks proudly. Everything.

"I really think a mother should come along to help control her kids," she tells Germaine January, wanting this stranger to understand her. If she doesn't understand her, how can she let her move in?

"Oh, you just like for families to be together. I know your type." Germaine January smiles broadly and sits down on the bed, and in this moment with these words, wins Leah over. She wears Birkenstock sandals, a simple white blouse under a calf-length, full-skirted blue denim jumper; puts Leah in mind less of a hippie in this room than a little girl. She almost expects her to pull out a worn little book from the backpack on her shoulders and ask Leah to read to her. Instead, she bounces up and down on the bed a few times to check out the mattress.

"Well yes I do put family first," Leah observes proudly, when Germaine January stops bouncing. "And there's nothing wrong with that."

"Oh, nothing at all," Germaine agrees and Leah rejoices that she and Jack replaced that mattress when Marcy left for college. They'd both banked on her coming back to wear it out, but of course that never happened.

"I would have gone with Jack to visit his mother all the time," Leah admits, recalling a topic she hasn't thought about for years. "But Jack's mother didn't like me. None of them did." The sad truth of it still stings after all these years. "Jack had two skinny sisters and two skinny brothers and none of them cared a whit about me. They always accused me of trying to make Jack fat."

"Did you?" Germaine wonders neutrally, the bulk of her balanced agilely on Marcy's quilted bedspread in a pose that makes Leah think of storybooks again and the old Mother Hubbard rhymes she used to read to Marcy.

"It was nothing I did," Leah replies honestly. "Jack was meant to be fat. He didn't belong in that family."

"How sad," Germaine agrees, and Leah's chest puffs out with happiness that Germaine catches on so quickly.

"Jack had a study down the hall and you could have that room if you like. . ."

"Oh, no this room will be fine. It'll get the morning sun. It's exactly what I want."

"Well, then..." Leah sighs, very much relieved. Jack's room needs a lot of work. David has been after her for years to redo it. But she hates to go into it even, with its formerly bright walls and draperies yellowed from cigarette smoke. And the desk and file cabinets needing a good going through before she can get rid of them. Jack spent so much time alone in that room. Alone and sometimes with Marcy after she turned fifteen, the door closed, the two of them in there deep into the night. Leah hates that room.

"So how is everything working out with Germaine January?" David asks when he visits the following Sunday. Leah starts in her little round-backed living room chair. Her dark eyes widen, her chin juts forward in angled surprise. How does David know about the boarder? she wonders, but doesn't ask because maybe she told him already and she wouldn't want him to think she has forgotten such an important fact.

"Everything is working out just fine," Leah says. "She goes visiting on Sundays though, so you won't meet her today. Unless she returns early."

"I met her already, Mom," David says. "Don't you remember?"

No. No, of course she doesn't remember. What is he talking about? What can he possibly be thinking? But she doesn't ask. Certain things you don't ask a grown son, especially when she can't remember everything anyway.

"Well yes, I know you met her." Leah regards the handsome, lean-faced man who sits before her on the living room couch, one ankle resting above the opposite knee, arms folded lightly into his chest. She always wanted a son. A daughter yes, she loves her daughter. But a son. The world opens up so much more fully to men. And here this successful man sits, an executive, no less, whose corporate promotions she can't even keep track of. She scarcely recognizes him sometimes, a tall handsome man with a full head of dark hair, intelligent lips, a proud, fourteen-carat nose that could have been her father's nose or her paternal grandfather's nose, though she only knew that *zaede* from the worn photograph her father carried away from Russia and its deadly pogroms.

"I know you met her," Leah crosses her legs too and smiles approvingly at her son, who has soared so far beyond the dangers and penurious lives those other men faced. "But I thought maybe you wanted to meet her again."

"I'm sure I will," David says mysteriously. And adds nothing that might enlighten her. A man of few words, this steely, bright son of hers. Where he got brevity, she doesn't know. Jack talked a blue streak once he got started, and her own father…To tell the truth, she still misses the lengthy chats she had with her own father nearly every day until he died, even though they mostly discussed Jack and how hard he was to live with.

She offers David lunch, some chicken soup maybe, or a brisket sandwich from the leftover roast she cooked the other day for Germaine, who eats with her frequently.

"Germaine January loves my *luchen kugel*," she informs her son, in an attempt to whet his appetite and also, yes, to steer the conversation away from this boarder of hers about whom she hadn't planned to tell David anything yet. She really would prefer to keep Germaine January for herself. Then, too, there are things about the boarder she doesn't want David to know.

"I like your noodle kugel, too," David admits. Leah sighs mightily and rushes toward the kitchen with weighted joy before David can say he just ate or will be eating later at some fancy-shmancy restaurant with Rhoda and the kids.

The things Leah doesn't want David to know about her life with Germaine start at night, late at night when the house reverberates with a stillness that keeps Leah awake. Leah strains in her bed, one ear cocked vigilantly toward the wall, straining to hear Germaine January snore, snort or even snurkle under her breath, and when no sound comes, no sound at all that would indicate the boarder still breathes, Leah creeps stealthily from her bed and into the doorway of the bedroom next to hers and stands watching, watching, until she discerns, stained into the shadows of the room, the dark mound on the bed of Germaine January's blanketed body. Leah watches, until she assures herself that the mound moves up, down, up, down in the unmistakably rhythmic motions of breathing. She continues to watch, counting breaths, just in case, she tells herself, you never know. Germaine January is young—forty-three, forty-four—just about Marcy's age. But you never know. Death snatches young people as well as old.

By day Leah worries less about January's physical health, more about her mental state, looks forward to their talks over lunch, tea, maybe supper. Germaine January goes places on Sunday, but during the week seems to have little to do, makes herself useful to Leah, tells her things about herself that Leah would have recoiled from once. But now...now Leah is seventy-eight years old, not much time left for anything, let alone cringing. And yet, and yet there is so much so foreign about this boarder, so much that David, the high-minded son she so carefully raised, might not approve of.

First off there's the name, which Leah had questioned from the get-go.

"What sort of name *is* January?" she'd asked that first day, when they'd wandered downstairs from Marcy's room into the kitchen.

"It's ersatz, actually." Germaine had replied, absently poking her head into dark cupboard shelves that Leah had suggested could be hers.

"Ersarz?" Leah echoed dumbly. "Where is Ersarzia?" There were many new countries these days, what with the fall of Communism, the disintegration of the Soviet Union. But she'd never heard of this one and she watched the news every night, read the paper.

"Made-up, manufactured," Germaine January explained, color annotating her round face with rattled amusement. "I changed my name when I left my husband two years ago," Germaine January said. "I wanted a new life, a new beginning, and you can't get much newer than January."

"No, I suppose not," Leah agreed, astounded at the notion of altering one's life through a simple sleight of name.

"Germane, of course, means relevant, pertinent," the boarder had elaborated, "both concepts I'm trying to steer towards. And then, of course, there's Germaine Greer."

"Germaine Greer?" Leah drew a blank, as she did with so many names these days. Names she couldn't put faces on; faces lacking names. "I had a neighbor once named Germaine Greer," she blurted, not remembering if this were so or not.

"My Germaine Greer is a writer," this Germaine elaborated in a neutral, school teacherly voice. "A very staunch feminist, an advocate for women's rights. She wrote the *Female Eunuch*."

"Oh," Leah said. "Oh." She knew what a eunuch was and it was definitely not female. She began to feel woozy, as if she were on Oprah right in her own home. She began to wonder if this boarder thing was a good idea.

But as it turned out, Germaine January was not difficult to live with. She kept regular hours, rising at six a.m. every day to fill Marcy's room with a flurry of drawers opening, hangers rattling, slippered feet paddling across hardwood floors to the bathroom first, then down carpeted steps to the front door to bring in the *Plain Dealer*. Leah always waited until she heard the muted roar of whirling coffee beans in the electric grinder before tumbling forth herself into the new day, rejoicing as she washed her face, plugged in her teeth, at the activity resounding through this house after so many silent years. Such a young, energetic woman brewing coffee in her kitchen, pulverizing beans in the very grinder Marcy had given Leah for a birthday long ago. Leah seldom used that grinder anymore; it had gotten so much easier to just spoon up coffee from a trusty name-brand can, the way she had for years when the kids were small, before anyone had heard of electric grinders.

"How would you like your eggs this morning, Leah?" Germaine greeted her each day with the exuberance of a hash house chef firing up the grill.

"Now, now you make whatever you want for yourself and I'll fix my own," Leah would insist, circling the kitchen a bit to get her bearings, the way her dead dog, Ginger, used to circle before cozying down beside Leah's chair, strategically placed beside the heat register.

"I already ate." Germaine would look up from the Ann Landers column or horoscope she'd been studying and push her reading glasses up off her nose onto her spacious forehead. "I don't mind, you know, cooking for you too."

Leah inevitably gave in to the boarder and took her seat. Something in Germaine's cheery, fresh-faced, no strings attached offering persuaded Leah to loosen her grip on her culinary domain. Germaine cooked well and elaborately, amplifying each dish with tangy bouquets of spices and herbs she bought in bulk from the new co-op down the street. Leah cooked well too, but had never bothered much with seasonings. She still had half-full spice tins in her cupboard from the earliest, most experimental years of her marriage.

"But you really shouldn't be cooking for me like this day after day," she would remind Germaine as the woman blended eggs with a little milk, a little allspice and savory. "You should get a job, Germaine," Leah would quietly urge, believing age and motherhood awarded her the license to lecture so. "Don't get me wrong. I don't mind you staying here, that's no problem at all, though it does seem a little strange to have the two of us lolling around this house all day. Don't get me wrong, but you're an intelligent, capable woman. You should get a job, Germaine, and find another husband while you're still young."

Her daughter Marcy would have bristled at these words, but Germaine let them fall on her shoulders like rain onto a dry, expectant field.

"I like what I'm doing," she'd smile, handing Leah a platter of fragrant eggs garnished with tomato, a little bacon, and buttered wheat toast made from a fennel-kissed loaf Germaine had baked the day before. She was a great one for baking bread, filling the house with warm, brown, yeasty aromas that turned Leah inside out with longing for bygone years.

"You'll be old before you know it," Leah advised one day, savoring the bread and then the eggs whose amazing unegg|ike flavors tilted her heart upward, into a dusty attic full of unrealized intentions. "Where are you going to find a decent husband when you're old?"

"But I don't want another husband." Germaine smiled across the table, sipping coffee meditatively while Leah ate. "I went crazy with depression during my marriage to Hank. Besides," she said, "besides," regarding Leah long and steadily and with utmost care, as if eyeing a live grenade. "I *am* married again. It's where I go on Sundays. To see my wife."

Leah almost asked her boarder to pack her things and leave that morning, but took another bite of resplendent toast, another forkful of triumphant eggs and reconsidered. She recalled instead her honeymoon trip with Jack forty-seven years ago that month and the craggy, middle-aged mistress of a tiny Niagara Falls inn who had studied Leah approvingly as Jack signed them in.

"You have a lovely wife, young man, a lovely wife," the woman had declared with an unexpected fervor that made Leah blush and look downward at the elegantly curved outlines of her new soft wool suit. "I'd marry her myself if I could."

Jack had laughed heartily, lifted their one bag, and led Leah upstairs, refusing to speculate on what the woman really meant, covering Leah's questioning mouth with hungry lips as they fell upon their quilted, lush bed.

There were other types of people, Leah had long since deduced. And here was one of them, revolutionizing her kitchen with aggressive bread, strategic herbs, revitalizing Marcy's room with clanking hangers in the morning, silent breathing at night. There were other types of people and so long as they did what they did behind their own closed doors, what did she care, who was she to say, who should marry who.

But David, David mustn't know. She had raised him to believe that sort of thing was wrong and she had been a good mother, turning out a son who'd married Rhoda and had two fine kids; Leah forgot for the moment that the boy was so rambunctious and the girl resembled no one.

"Bring her over here, sometime," Leah prodded Germaine, curious hospitality outdistancing fear like an insurgent race horse. "Bring your wife over here sometime. I'd like to meet her."

And so Germaine brought Moondust to Leah's house for dinner one late winter day. Leah scrubbed the woodwork and washed the curtains to honor the occasion. Germaine prepared a celebratory soup that called for six whole bulbs of garlic, five enormous leeks, a swatch of kale, and untold turmeric and cumin, creating such a powerful thrust of aromas that Leah was sure—absolutely certain—that the house lifted off the ground that afternoon and floated around the block a few times before settling back ever so gently on its old foundation without so much as disturbing a china teacup.

"The view was magnificent," she exclaimed that night, spooning soup and gazing happily at Moondust. It was the most fortifying soup she'd ever tasted, robust and medicinal beyond even Leah's own immortal chicken soup, whose ethereal matzo balls alone, she believed, had kept her family solid and strong, even on its bad days.

"I was standing on a chair in Marcy's old room hanging curtains," Leah told the table at large, but particularly Moondust, whose beauty and quiet manner enthralled her. "I was standing on a chair and suddenly we flew over the neighborhood, listing to starboard a little, then to port. But I didn't get seasick." Leah had no idea where this nautical language came from. Her father had steamed around the Great Lakes years ago, stoking coal for the merchant marines in the bowels of a cranky freighter. Maybe that was it. Maybe not.

"How amazing!" Moondust agreed, glancing neutrally at Germaine who squinted back at Moondust, neither woman's face registering contradiction.

"Looking down onto the treetops I could see every season of the year," Leah continued. "Winter first, like today, but with fluffy snow frosting every naked branch, then a profusion of buds and blossoms, followed by leafy summer and finally the absolutely brilliant colors of fall." Leah finished, pleased to share her unexpected joy with her guests, especially with Moondust, a more spectacular-looking woman than Leah had seen in ages. Leah fixated on Moondust, not just on her mass of rich dark curls set against a composed, creamy face that seemed to glow as from an unseen light, but also on her eyes, her deep-set, deep-brown, gentle eyes. This woman's face contained the sunshine great artists tried to paint. Once again she recalled the innkeeper's words from so long ago.

I could marry her myself, Leah thought, knowing that these were her words now, not just the innkeeper's, and she nearly jumped out of her chair to realize all in the same moment that the lovely Moondust reminded her of Marcy.

"It sounds like cleaning the house turned into quite an adventure for you," Moondust tossed her perfect head unselfconsciously toward Leah, lips blooming into a generous smile.

"I wish *I* would have seen it." Germaine winked at Moondust and rose to clear away the soup bowls. "Cleaning house has never been so much fun for *me*," she said to Leah.

"Nor for me," Moondust agreed.

"Your friend could spend the night," Leah replied, startled at her own *non sequiter*, but her guests seem not at all to mind. "You and Germaine could have my room, if you like and I'll take Marcy's."

"Oh, no, oh no. We'd never put you out of your own bed like that," Germaine set the dishes she carried down onto the counter and came over to the table to take Leah's hand and then her girlfriend's hand, and one by one, and with great affection, kissed each woman on the lips.

"It's like a family again," Leah tells David two Sundays later, leaving out specifics about who sleeps where and with whom. Moondust has stayed over quite a few times, always in Germaine's room, and Leah assumes they crowd into the same bed—there's only one bed in Marcy's room, after all—but doesn't know for sure, because she doesn't get up at three a.m. anymore to check on the boarder's safety. But she hears noises coming from the room. Delicately muffled, contented sounds like kittens at play and she knows the women are safe and happy, so she sleeps soundly, less concerned about death seeping through the walls.

"We go places sometimes, too," she tells David, facing him across a wide expanse of living room, Leah on the narrow love seat she'd love to share with someone, David on the couch, eyeing his mother warily. "Germaine takes me to the co-op to help select garlic for the soup." (Every time she makes that soup, the house has levitated, though never as extravagantly as on that first occasion. But of course Leah doesn't tell David about how the house has moved, for fear he'd call in a repairman and put an end to it.)

"Sometimes I go places with both of them." Leah leans forward, trying to spark David's pleasure, because he perches so stiffly on the couch. "Moondust teaches English at the high school and sometimes all three of us walk there together in the morning."

"You don't go anywhere, Mom." David folds his hands in front of him, crosses, recrosses, uncrosses his long legs while from faraway in the attic Leah hears clomping sounds, then bird-like thrashing. Her grandson's up there, she knows. He always heads for the attic when he arrives with David, hunts for things up there, in the many boxes she's packed away, boxes brimming with toys, clothes, table linens, papers, everything old and veneered with memories. "Germaine *tries* to take you places, but you're never interested in more than a walk around the block," says David.

"But I do go places. Not too very many, you know. That poor Moondust..." She hesitates, then proceeds, confident he can handle it. "That Moondust had a bad time of it as a child, molested by her father, it seems, and I for one don't understand the sort of mother who could let that happen under her roof. But Moondust says it happened and I don't think she'd lie. So anyway," Leah looks at David, wanting him to understand. "Anyway she goes to work and comes home, but she's not a social butterfly, David, so we don't go many places yet. But my plan, of course, is to bring her out of herself a little more." David takes a generous breath, cocks his head upward toward the attic, from whence diverse sounds emanate—pounding sounds and galloping sounds, and thrush like, flapping sounds and David smiles to think of his son so happily at play among all the packed and wrapped treasures of his own childhood, frowns to think of what he must tell his mother.

"Mom," he begins, "This house is getting too much for you, even with Germaine January here. Don't you think....I mean wouldn't you consider...I mean there's a place near Rhoda and me....they'd take good care of you."

"I don't need such a place!" Leah sits upright in her chair, horrorstruck that the thing she has most tried to avoid now descends upon her like a wire net from the sky. "I have a boarder," Leah insists stonily. "I'm doing fine."

"You don't have a boarder, Mom," David eyes her from across the room and Leah squints back because she's forgotten her glasses again—or rather can't remember where she put them—and everything suddenly looks more blurry than usual, edges of one object bleeding into another.

"I have Germaine January," Leah asserts again, feeling like a chess queen dodging a belligerent rook. "I ran an ad in the paper. I found her myself."

"*We* ran an ad in the paper, Mom. Under 'Help Wanted.' Don't you remember?"

Looking at David now she can't quite tell where his solemn face ends and the tall lampshade rising up from the table beside him begins, and she's not certain if he's orchestrating this trick, or if it's her eyes, welling with unbidden tears that are refracting her son and every other object in this room into fragile bits.

"No," she says, "no," feeling like a little girl for the first time in seventy years, feeling more like a little girl than she had at age eight when somebody—she can't remember who—her father, an uncle, an older male cousin—sat her down in a room not unlike this one and announced that her mother was dead.

"No, I honestly don't remember," she tells David, and smiles hopefully, just in case what he tells her is true and the memory of it will rush back to her like a flock of geese headed north in the spring. It's almost spring anyway. Leah reminds herself of the blossoms she saw when the house circled the trees. The geese will be back soon; she can manage until then. "David," she begins, a beleaguered plaintiff defending her own case. "I still have Germaine January, whoever she is, and Germaine January has Moondust, her friend, and sometimes she stays over here, David, and it's like a family again, and one of these days very soon they're both going to help me clear out your father's old study. You know what an awful mess that is. So I have to stay here until I get that done. I can't leave this house without undoing your father's mess."

"Mom," David leans forward on the couch, places a hand under his chin, rests an elbow on his arm to steady himself because she looks like she will cry and he had hoped beyond hope that tears wouldn't be part of this. "Mom, we took care of that, don't you remember, the summer after Dad died? We went through the desk and the file cabinets, boxed up the things you wanted to keep, gave away the rest. Don't you remember the painters we hired, the new carpet you picked out, the workers who installed it? I was always surprised you didn't give Germaine January that room, instead of Marcy's, right up against your wall." He feels more sure of the situation, having spoken the truth, feels relaxed enough to let go of his face and lean back again, into the couch.

Leah shrinks into her chair, feeling smaller and smaller as the list of events she seems to have blanked from her mind grows longer and longer. No, she doesn't remember anything about emptying Jack's office or fixing it up, but does that make her incapable of living in this house, she doesn't see the correlation. She doesn't see much of anything right now, the water in her eyes having reduced the entire living room and David along with it to light-streaked diamonds and circles and odd, elongated shapes. She hears thrashing in the attic, where if what David says is true—and why should she doubt her tall, efficient son? If what David claims is true, the remains of Jack's office lie carefully packed into boxes and crates in the dense bulrushes of the attic from whence she hears thrashing and thrushing and flapping of wings. But it's not the geese up there, coming back with the memory she sorely needs. It's the grandson of course, releasing the loud, careless sounds that perpetually follow him through this house. The geese, she knows—watching David's strong, capable face crystallize into lovely geometric patterns—the geese took her memory to the tropics this winter and will not be flying north again soon.

"Mother," I say softly, "Mother," because I want to see her before the story ends. I must see her again. I tiptoe up to the table where she sits in the windowed day room at the nursing home near my brother's house in Chagrin Falls, Ohio. I don't want to startle her, though the doctors say her heart is strong, very strong, that the way her heart beats she could live another five, ten years, maybe more, so long as she remembers how to breathe. "Mother, it's me, Marcy."

"Marcy!" she exclaims, glancing up from the colorful magazine photos she is puzzling into a collage and smiles warmly. "How did you get here?"

"I drove," I say. "I drove from Wisconsin with a friend."

I have seen Leah at my father's funeral, Uncle Paul's funeral, Aunt Ida's funeral. Death has been bringing my mother and me together in recent years. This time I came on my own.

"What were you doing in Wisconsin?" Leah asks. There's a new sallowness to her skin, a basement dankness about her eyes. But you wouldn't know by looking at her. You wouldn't know by looking at her that Leah isn't home.

"I live there, Mom, remember. I teach at a university."

"I thought you lived in Chicago," Leah says pleasantly.

"I used to. I moved."

"Oh," she says, "that's nice. I moved too." The face tilting up at me with perennial concern, has always been a map I could read, though thick with roads I wouldn't want to travel. It hints of new highways now, devoid of regret and recriminations.

"How are you?" I ask my mother, a strange question considering her reduced mental circumstances, considering that when she relocated to this nursing home three months ago, it was only at my brother's insistence.

"I'm fine. How are *you*?" My mother returns question for question, but in a gentle, lamb-like way I am not used to. Her voice, her manner, her earnest face indicate that this is no pop quiz with tricky nooks and hidden crannies. She just wants to know how I am.

My brother has advised me that she's changed. My brother, whom fate selected as the family curator, sold our childhood house and installed our mother in this shiny corporatized home with neo Victorian facade and branches in many cities. It is a beautiful place with a grand piano in the lobby, a mahogany banister curving up the wide staircase to this locked ward.

I lived in a locked ward once, but for the opposite reason as my mother. My mother has forgotten things. I remembered. I remembered things that happened between my father and me long ago, and I spent days devising ways to kill myself. When I narrowly missed hitting a viaduct while driving seventy miles an hour on Chicago's Kennedy Expressway, I pulled myself together long enough to find the psych ward at Presbyterian St. Luke's. I haven't thought about suicide in years. I'm more pulled together than I've been in years, but the more I pulled myself together, the more I pulled away from Mom.

"I'm fine, too." I stoop down to get closer to this cheery no-fault version of my mother.

"I'm glad you're fine." She smiles up at me, purses her lips into a dull crimson wreath that she plants softly on my mouth.

"Sit down," Leah urges expansively, waving at an empty chair and I obey, but not just out of habit. "We're making pictures." My mother indicates the magazine photos splashed in front of her. She pushes some of them toward me—odd-sized cut-outs of fruits, vegetables, breads, baked beans, hot dogs, hamburgers—selections from all the food groups. "You can make one too," she says.

There are other old people in this room. Other peoples' age-varnished, barely-functioning parents, arranged at this and other tables like extras in a movie of Leah's life. Women mostly, a few men. Some mumble to themselves or stare into space, with blank, washed chalkboard faces. A dazed woman at my mother's table turns a photo of a fish around and around and around in her bony hand as if she mourns the fact that she will never ever again know which end is up. A man at the next table dozes shakily, chin affixed to chest, wisps of thin gray hair cha-cha-cha-ing in the invisible breeze of his breath.

"Is this an orange?" my mother asks brightly just when I've begun to think she's way above this crowd. "Is it a fruit?"

"Yes. Yes." I respond to both questions, nodding at the picture she dances in front of me. It's as plump and orange an orange as I've ever seen. She's got it right. It's just her certainty that's missing. Mom used to be sure of everything. Sure that my father knew best, and that I didn't. Sure that I shouldn't leave Cleveland for a job, shouldn't marry Gregory, shouldn't divorce him, shouldn't stay in Chicago after I'd divorced, shouldn't go to graduate school to get a Ph.D. Should return to Cleveland, should return to live with her, in her house, sleep once again in my old childhood bed.

"It's a beautiful orange," I tell my mother, who sets it down and lifts another photo.

"Is this an apple?" she asks.

"That's an apple," the woman with the fish picture agrees, continuing to turn the fish around and around, even as she studies the object in my mother's hand, which *is* a photo of an apple. These people may not know much else, but they know their apples and oranges.

"This is my daughter, Marcy," Leah says to the fish lady, who must have been beautiful once. There's still a clarity to her skin, under the translucence of age, a softness to her hair, which circles her addled head like a thick, heat-tempered meringue. She contemplates me open-mouthed for a few silent seconds, then turns again to her revolving fish.

"Marcy," Leah adds the apple and orange to her collage, which already contains a baked potato and box of Rice Krispies. "Marcy," Leah says softly, kindly, matter of factly. "I feel like I don't really know you," she says and I smile awkwardly, realizing that something has shifted for both of us in this relationship.

"But I know *her*," exclaims my mother, who used to be beautiful too, still is beautiful if you focus on her long, proud nose, wide smile, glistening eyes as she points a happy finger toward the back of the room. When I turn I see Jane, my good friend Jane, wandered up from the lobby where I'd stationed her.

"Mother, this is Jane," I begin tentatively, wondering if even in the dream-like world she occupies, the nature of our relationship will be obvious. It wasn't to David and Rhoda, though I suspect my niece and nephew are on to us.

"How do you do, Mrs. Rosen?" Jane makes her way to our table, proffers a long, friendly hand. She's tall, about five inches taller than I, and a little chunky-comfortable around the waist, wears her faded brown hair in a longish style, pulled off her face with a playful barrette.

"I know you," my mother insists, dredging up her shrill, self-assured voice from yesteryear.

"Jane and I went to school together, Mom, way back when." I smile. "But I don't think you ever met her."

"I know Jane," Leah insists again mightily. "I'd know her anywhere."

Jane and I exchange glances. I barely recognized Jane myself, when we ran into each other last summer at a women's music festival. *Jane? Jane Majeski?* I'd squinted at her name badge in the dim hall light of a midwestern university dorm. I squinted from her name badge to her face, her exquisitely handsome face come into its own in the years since the awkward miseries of Herbert Hoover Junior High flattened into harmless shadows for both of us.

"Marcy *Rosen*?" she had squinted back, a slim dormitory towel draped across one arm, outstretched hand clutching a flowered toiletry bag. "Marcy Rosen, you look great!"

"But how did you make that *soup*?" my senile mother bursts into my little memory trip before I can reach the part about Jane and I making lunch plans and dinner plans and concert plans and all the really juicy plans after that. I'm back in the Ohio nursing home, Jane come to stand comfortingly beside my chair, Leah puzzling over paper apples and oranges and a sudden, mysterious soup.

"Jane's a doctor, Mom," I offer energetically, trying to steer mom back into charted waters. "She's a pediatrician, treats little children."

"I know what a pediatrician does," says my stalwart mom, who maybe knows, maybe doesn't at this point in her cloudy life, but for a flash of an instant she's my omnipresent mother again, ready to take charge. "But I don't know how to make that soup, the one that lifted the whole house off the ground. So I'm glad you came to see me," she eyes Jane almost beseechingly. "I need the recipe for that soup."

"Maybe you can give us one of *your* recipes," counters Jane, graceful Jane, formerly square peg Jane in junior high. We were both square pegs back then, too busy trying to squeeze into a round crowd to have much use for each other.

"Marcy is always telling me what a wonderful cook you are."

"I don't cook much anymore," Leah lifts a paper cruller from the pile and stares at it vacantly. "But they have good food here. Stay for lunch." Leah addresses me now as much as Jane. "They have good food. Maybe they can give you recipes."

Jane and I managed to smooth our corners well enough as adults. But it took us each years to awaken to the life that really fit us. Jane married. I married. We could live with men, sleep with men, but we didn't connect with men, not in the way we connect with each other.

"Honey," Leah flags down a young aide in white pants, blue tee shirt. "Honey, this is my daughter and her friend. They want to know how I made the soup that lifted the house off the ground. I thought maybe you had the recipe."

"She talks about that soup all the time," the aide laughs, her smile big and white against ebony smooth skin. "It must have been *some* soup," she adds, only slightly condescendingly.

"It was a wonderful soup," agrees Leah focusing on me with feverish eyes. "It was a wonderful soup," she repeats almost sadly, her sadness more understandable than the soup. "The whole house lifted off the ground," she tells the addled tablemate with the peaked egg white hair.

"Things happen," the old doll replies, and actually offers my mother the fish, worn as her rice papery skin from incessant handling.

"Things happen," my mother agrees, ignoring the fish, looking at me again. "Things happen and then they end, Marcy. That's the whole secret of life."

This feels like an apology of some sort, even though Leah seasons it with reckless cheer, like Robin Williams broadcasting the war news in *Good Morning Vietnam.*

All your recipes are gone, I want to tell my mother. David threw them out with the bathwater and a ton of other trash, desperate to sell the house before bills starting piling up from this fancy place. The good things you cooked for us have been tossed out with the bad.

Now would also be a good time to tell my mother what my father did to me, under her roof, all those years, and how I cracked up with despair as a result. But I think she knows about my father anyway on some level—I think she's always known—and she's the one in the locked ward now, so what can I tell *her* about craziness.

Anyway, Jane is standing close beside me, as comforting as warm milk and the aide clears her throat and the fish lady concentrates on her fish, and the world hiccoughs on, oblivious to what happened to any of us in our childhoods.

"Are these your favorite foods?" the aide asks Leah, pointing to the Rice Krispies tableau my mother has arranged on manila art paper. "Can you tell me about your favorite foods?"

"Apples are delicious," Leah recites dutifully. "Oranges are good for you, too."

"My husband liked oranges," Leah continues, taking the assignment further than required. "I miss my husband," she adds. "I wish I had him with me now."

"You've still got the oranges," I quip, a lame excuse at humor, but Leah doesn't seem to mind. Her lips already bulge with a plump new question, as plump as her art therapy fruit.

"Are we married?" Leah blurts and at first I suppose she means all of us—her, me, Jane, the nursing home aide, who's moving on now to another table, the zonked out fish lady. Then I think she means just her and me. Or maybe she's still remembering Jack.

"Nobody's married." I smile, stroke the side of her, smoothly-weathered cheek. It gives slightly to my touch like a loaf of bread just out of the oven. "If anybody's getting married though," I tease, "it might be Jane and me."

"Who's Jane?" Leah stares vacantly at the woman who minutes ago meant so much to her.

"This is Jane." I wave an upward hand at lovely Jane, who looks at my mom like the gentle pediatrician she is, ready to spring a lollipop on a patient.

"I'm so happy, Marcy, that you have a good friend," Leah replies. "And where do you live now?" she wants to know. "What are you doing with yourself these days?"

"I live in Wisconsin," I reply patiently. "It's north of here, about five hundred miles. And I teach."

"Marcy's a good teacher," puts in Jane, my loyal cheerleader. "She's a good researcher too. NBC wants to use some of Marcy's work for a documentary they're doing on family communications."

"You could move in here," Leah asserts out of the oxygen-thin sky of her mind.

"Jane's going to move in with *me*, Mom," I say, "as soon as she finds a position in Wisconsin."

"This is a nice house," Leah says. "They make good meals. And I have plenty of room for both of you."

I don't know where she thinks she is. The house on Chelsea Way, perhaps, where she lived for nearly forty years. Or maybe the one before that, a cramped little apartment in which we all tumbled around like rats in a maze between my father's rages.

"Thanks," I say, kissing her on the mouth, this suddenly soft mouth of hers that burbles with so many strange questions and answers and statements in between. "Thanks, but we need to be going, and anyway, it would never work out," I add lightly, knowing that in a minute, maybe less, she will forget what I said, what she said, what I said, what she said, that I was even here at all.

"Goodbye, Leah. It was so nice to meet you." Jane leans over my mother's chair and kisses her too, and my mother suddenly rises, still within Jane's embrace, and squeezes her tightly.

"I'm happy my daughter has such a good friend," Leah says. "Please take good care of her."

"We look after each other," Jane assures mom. She disentangles herself from Leah's embrace, and dusts a wet speck of something off my cheek.

I kiss my mother one more time, her breath warm and oatmealy against my face. Then the aide positions herself in the center of the sunny room and starts soft-pitching questions about foods.

"I like apples," my mother shouts, immediately alert to new stimuli. She's a leader in this crowd, still has more vocabulary than most of them, more of a memory about how to use it.

"Are apples sweet or tart?" the aide presses.

"Apple are sweet *and* tart," Leah proclaims, not letting anyone pin her down, even in crumbling old age. I have to admit, it was a dumb question.

"What other favorite foods do people have?"

"Oranges!" Leah leads the pack again, as Jane and I wend our way out of the room.

"Are oranges sweet or tart?"

"Oranges are delicious," Leah sings, not looking back. I look back, catch one more glimpse of Leah's open, engaged face, washed with the happiness of remembered fruits.

"Goodbye, Mommy," I cry, wanting to be heard above the hubbub of favorite food time at the nursing home. "Goodbye, Mommy," using a word for her I haven't used in ages.

Leah turns finally, as do nurses and social workers and many of the aged heads in this room, their faces fuzzy as lint balls with incomprehension.

Leah turns toward me, and a bright smile spreads across her clouded face.

"Look at those beautiful young people!" she points, waves. "Isn't it nice that they're so happy?"

"Goodbye, Mom," I half whisper, wanting to rush back into her arms for one more hug, one more kiss, but I follow Jane instead, out of the room, into the deserted hall, remembering, between the two of us, the combination that unlocks the locked door. Down the luxurious, curved staircase, past the polished grand piano and into a graceful spring day that asks nothing about time, memory, or love.

"You drive." I hand Jane the keys to my car, not trusting my ability just yet to concentrate on the road.

"No problem." She grins, pecks my mouth lightly in full view of the world. And we're off, Jane's hand in mine, headed into our own future now.

But I know Leah's in the car in one form or another. I take comfort in that. It wouldn't be like Leah to desert me so soon.

[Photo by Mary Langenfeld]

Fran Zell grew up near Cleveland, Ohio, and lives in Madison, Wisconsin, where she writes fiction, poetry, plays, radio essays and other nonfiction. She is a former feature writer and restaurant critic for the *Chicago Tribune*. Her work has appeared in numerous publications, including *Other Voices, Playgirl Magazine, The Writers of Wisconsin, 1995, Lonesome Traveller Press, Key Log Press, Chicago Magazine, Chicago Reader,* and *Milwaukee Journal-Sentinel.* Her plays include the musical, "Lavender Rose," and "Meat Marketing." She has been a resident writer at Ragdale, Anderson Center for Interdisciplinary Studies, and the Dorset Colony, supported by an award from the Barbara Deming Memorial Fund/Money for Women. She has a masters degree from the creative writing program at the University of Illinois at Chicago.